WD

Cling To Me

ARmetRice

Thanks A lot

LOVE & PEACE

Gail

2004

Cling To Me

A novel

Gail Marie Mitchell

ZOMAY PRESS

Published by:
 Zomay Press
 Post Office Box 2282
 Baltimore, Maryland 21203-2282

Library of Congress Control Number: 2003097117

Mitchell, Gail Marie
    Cling To Me

l. Women — United States — Fiction. 2. Afro-American
Women — Fiction. I. Title

ISBN 0-9745638-0-3

Cover design by Lydell Jackson

Printed in the U.S.A.

This book is dedicated to my dear brother, Steven Mitchell; my uncle, Michael Woods; and my great grandparents, Florence and Milton Neville.

Knowing them has enriched my life.

ACKNOWLEDGMENTS

Writing a novel takes teamwork. First I give glory and honor to my awesome God. Thanks to my editors, Lucy Hoopes and Bob Lightman. I couldn't have done this without you, and to Tanai Sanders for her comments. Thanks to Robin Green-Cary of Sibanye Bookstore and the folks at the Pratt Library for putting together great writing events and helping a lot of aspiring writers. Also to Susan Monroe, Lisa Monroe, Kay Garrett, and Karen Lewis, who helped on a prior manuscript, I appreciate your input. To my family and friends, peace and love.

You've lost her, and I found her
You had her love and you make her weep
You broke her heart, and I fixed it
We fell in love, so we mixed it
You wanted her at first,
but now you treat her like dirt

You've lost her
Now I'm going to treat her good, just like I should
Better than you said you would
You hurt her, deserted her

She proved her love to me in so many ways
And I took away the pain you gave her
That lasted for days and days
Now try to take her from me
Let's see just how bad you can be

Because you've lost her
You're too late, my friend
Go away and never, never come back again
Yes, you've lost her

Willard James Woods

Out of the darkness exploded a new world
Unexplored by man or mind
We enter into the world of millions

Unknowing we search for a way
And direction toward the living
Propelled by atoms within

The journey will decide
Who will live and who will die
This the greatest of all desires
Made into the cycle of Yin and Yang

We endured to beat the odds
Our destiny started by divine intuition
A higher power
Man or woman will never endure
Greater odds in a lifetime

Edward D. Grayson III

I wanted to talk with Jesus
Had a problem on my mind
So I ran to the telephone
Only to quickly find
My daughter using the line

Suddenly I remembered
Modern technology — computers
I will send the Lord an e-mail
Yes, that's better than a call
www.Jesus.com, I typed rapidly
But only to crash against a wall

Distressed, I fell upon my knees
And opened my mouth to pray
Only to realize that God was right there
Waiting happily
To send His awesome power
Into my very troubled day

Praise God!

Florence Hurst

CLING
TO
ME

1

"What's wrong, Aaron?" Twenty-one-year-old Shawanda Matthews stroked her boyfriend's arm as they sat in the kitchen of the deteriorating Baltimore rowhouse. When he didn't look at her, she followed his stare across the kitchen table and to her four-year-old son, Donte.

"I'm sick of this child playing in his food," Aaron said.

Shawanda turned to Donte. "Don't like Mama's cooking, Sweetie?"

"I work hard," Aaron added. "I try to help out with the bills around here, even though I don't live here. I don't appreciate him playing with food and throwing it away afterwards."

"I gon' eat it, Ma."

"Are you full?" The visiting Lena, Donte's thirty-seven-year-old maternal grandmother, asked.

"Please, stay out of this!" Aaron leaned forward. "You don't buy food here."

"Reminder: you live with your parents. Just because you've dated my daughter for what? Almost a year? And paid a couple of bills, which is the decent thing to do, doesn't give you the right to go off on me or Precious Baby."

"It's good he works and helps out." Shawanda quickly squeezed in the words. A few other men had run when discovering she had a child.

"His name is Donte," Aaron said. "Why do you always call him Precious Baby?"

Shawanda, an only child, knew the answer. After Shawanda's birth Lena tried to have more children, but couldn't. Her heart's desire – to have a boy – had been fulfilled when her grandson was born. Now Shawanda waited for the reply.

"None of your business," Lena snapped.

"I feel sorry for your husband. He's got to live with you."

"He ain't complaining." Lena shifted her body. "You worry about who you live with. Get real comfortable being twenty-two and with your parents. Because as I heard it, you can't move in here without a marriage license."

Aaron's head jerked toward Shawanda. "You told her that?"

"She guessed." Shawanda lied to maintain peace.

Aaron's glance rolled from Shawanda to Donte. "Eat everything on that plate and drink every drop of milk."

Lena folded her arms. "If you've had enough, Precious Baby, you shouldn't eat any more."

"He better eat."

"I'm full," the thin child with brown hair and big brown eyes said in a high voice.

"See that!" Aaron flipped around to Lena. "You're teaching this boy to disrespect me. If I treated my Pops like this, you know what would have happened to me? My Pops don't play."

"You're not his father," Lena said in a low tone of voice.

"Closest thing he's got to one."

"He has a grandfather who cares about him," Lena mumbled.

Huh?

"And I don't?"

"He's another man's child. You don't have enough patience with him. Besides, you expect us all to bow and worship you every time you do anything for Precious. I've never cared for your attitude."

"What's wrong with some appreciation? I do for your daughter and your grandson. Only thing I ask for is respect."

Lena sucked her teeth. "You ain't even the baby's daddy. Shawanda could do better."

"Come on, you two."

"And you won't give a Black man a chance."

"Listen." Lena rose. "You want to be his father, you can start by marrying his mother."

"Won't help now. You're teaching him not to listen to me. How is he supposed to figure out that a marriage license means he should change that around?"

Lena rolled her eyes, mumbled something, turned her back to Aaron, and left the kitchen.

Shawanda couldn't decipher Lena's words, and thought that best. Rising, she said, "I wish you two could get along."

"She's the problem! Talk to her!"

Shawanda settled behind Aaron and massaged his shoulders. "Can we cut this out now, please?" When he didn't reply, she moved away and began to clear the table. Soon, at the sink, she turned on the faucet.

"You not my Paw Paw," Donte mumbled.

"I know I'm not your grandfather, Boy." Then to Shawanda, "Baby, tell him who paid the rent this month."

"What?" She turned briefly to Aaron. "He's four. He doesn't understand rent."

"Some things he oughta understand."

"Please leave him alone."

"Like I'm bothering him! Know what the problem is? You women baby him. And you're not gonna realize how bad that is until he gets older. By then it'll be too late. Nobody will be able to do anything with the boy."

Wishing he would shut up, she tried mentally blocking his voice. Failing, she hoped this mood of his would pass quickly, and while she was wishing, her mother would go home. She would send Donte to bed early. Then she and her man could be alone. Times spent with only Aaron were usually quiet and comforting. But as she washed a pot and heard Aaron tap the table, she knew he wasn't calming down soon.

"I won't tell you again! Eat!" Aaron shouted.

Shawanda threw the pot back into the sink. With the intent of evicting Donte from the room and ending the nonsense, she twirled around but was startled when she saw Donte pick up the glass of milk and toss it. Her eyes followed the glass as it tumbled through the air, slammed into the refrigerator, and exploded. Bits of glass and liquid showered the refrigerator and spattered the floor.

Aaron leaped from the chair. Removing his belt, he grabbed the fleeing child and began to beat him. Donte screamed.

Shawanda yelled. Her body shook.

Donte convulsed.

She rushed over and began to pound on Aaron's back. "Let him go!"

Lena appeared and began punching him in the arm.

Aaron dropped Donte.

Donte's body hit the floor and lay there as his screams dragged life from the air.

Shawanda knelt, scooped up her son, and began to rock him.

Lena pointed her finger in Aaron's face and yelled, "You're crazy!"

"This is between me and Shawanda."

"Get the hell out of this house!" Lena hollered.

"You don't live here. And I paid the rent this month. I can stay."

Lena dashed to the sink and picked up a Teflon frying pan. "I bet you won't stay here tonight."

"Don't hit me with that skillet!"

"Aaron, get out!" Shawanda said while clinging to her son. She wanted to erase the last hour and do things a new way.

"Aw, Baby."

Shawanda thought he was about to say more, but instead he just stomped out of the kitchen.

The short, petite Lena followed, the pan still in her hand, held high over her right shoulder, positioned for quick use if necessary.

Soon Shawanda heard them in the dining room arguing. When their voices faded a little, she knew they had moved to the living room.

"I'm getting my coat," Shawanda heard Aaron say.

Blocking out the noise, she sat down, laying the sobbing child on her lap. Noticing his pants were wet, she thought it was milk and checked. It was urine.

The door slammed, and the front of the house went silent.

Shortly her mother came in and said, "That fool's gone." Then "Let me take Precious."

Shawanda tightened her hold. "He wet himself," she blurted.

Lena reached down and stroked the child's face. "Precious is probably in shock. He's never been treated like this before!" She ran her hands across his forehead. "I bet you're getting rid of that idiot now!"

Lena's words stomped through Shawanda's brain.

* * *

Next morning, a Wednesday, Shawanda was awakened at six-thirty by the ring of the telephone. "Hey, Mama."

"Did Aaron come back last night?" Lena asked.

"Naw. Didn't call, either."

"Not dropping him anytime soon, are you?"

"I love him. Besides, something only happened one time."

"One is a lot."

"It won't happen again."

"How's Precious Baby?"

"Sleeping. He has marks on his body. Can you keep him while I go to work?"

"Don't you usually leave him with the neighbor?"

"Kim? Yeah, but I don't want her to see him like this."

"Sure, I'll keep him," Lena said.

"Thanks."

"Your Aaron has a bad temper."

"Does not. He treats me special."

"Except when he's beating on Precious. When I remember last night, I'm glad I did what I did."

"What did you do?"

"Well . . . when I got home . . . when your father told me to calm down, I kept thinking Aaron will come back. Tonight. Tomorrow. And poor Precious Baby! The danger he's in. And you. You love Precious. And you love Aaron. Maybe you can't love both of them."

"What are you talking about?"

"Something has to be done about Aaron. I keep thinking good thing I was there because you wouldn't have thrown him out."

"I'm gonna talk to him."

"Your father said you might get hurt in the process."

"What process?"

"He said to wait and see how I felt in the morning. But I couldn't think straight."

"What's up?"

"I'm sorry. If I could undo it, I would. I wished I had listened to your father."

"Did you call the police on Aaron?"

"Social Services."

Shawanda dropped the phone. It hit the floor. Social Services? Really? Nah.

* * *

Three hours later on a cold Wednesday in February, Margaret Holmes parked in front of Shawanda's deteriorating Baltimore rowhouse. Margaret glanced around at the littered sidewalks and occasional boarded-up house. The area was typical of those she often visited in her work for the Department of Social Services. Spotting a teenager five houses down hand a small item to a middle-aged man, who then gave the teenager money, Margaret knew a drug transaction was in progress. She awaited its end before getting out of the car, hurrying through the snow, and knocking on the front door.

Because the cold air bothered her, Margaret shifted her weight from one foot to the other to keep warm. "Come on, Ms. Matthews," Margaret mumbled to herself, hoping this potential client wouldn't give her any trouble, would let her in and talk to her. Hoping, even, that the report she had gotten from the abuse hotline soon after arrival at the office this morning would prove false, although she knew the odds of a totally groundless report were small.

When the door opened, Margaret saw a tall, very thin, honey-colored woman with dyed blonde — actually yellow — hair, an oval face, and large brown eyes. She was dressed in tight jeans and a thin peach-colored v-neck sweater. "Hi," the woman said.

Margaret was grateful for the woman's politeness. "Good morning. I'm looking for Shawanda Matthews."

"That's me."

Margaret thought Shawanda looked younger than her reported twenty-one years. "I'm Margaret Holmes. I'm a social worker. Social Services received a report from a source I can't disclose."

"Mama called you. She told me."

"It's our job to check out every report. May I come in and talk to you?" When Shawanda opened the door wide and walked away, Margaret hurried from the cold. Inside, closing the door behind her, she felt the warmth of the nicely heated home.

Margaret surveyed the room. It was her job to note the child's living environment. The house looked small and narrow. The walls of the living room were paneled, the floor covered in dark carpet. The furniture looked old but well kept. There was a sofa that was upholstered with loud multi-colored flowers, a pale blue chair, and a coffee table covered with framed family photographs. The room was neat and clean.

Margaret laid her handbag and notebook on the coffee table and while taking off her coat wandered to the doorway leading to the dining room. No furniture or anything else there. Behind it was the kitchen, which looked fine as far as Margaret could see. Walking to the chair, she looked toward the stairs. She figured that upstairs there were probably two small bedrooms and a bathroom. Also, the house had a basement; she had noticed from the outside. "Nice place."

"I used to stay with my parents. Been here eight months. I've been trying to make the house look good. But I don't have enough money. All I can get is second-hand furniture."

Margaret wondered if nervousness made Shawanda talkative. "You've done well with limited resources." Margaret sat in the chair.

"I guess." Shawanda sat on the end of the sofa farthest from the chair.

"Is your boyfriend here?" the social worker inquired.

"No. He doesn't live here."

"If you don't mind the intrusion, may I ask what happened last night?"

Shawanda told her.

"So he lost his temper?" Margaret asked after hearing the full account.

"Mother helped set him off."

"She didn't mention that when making the report." Margaret smiled.

"You going to have Aaron arrested?"

"My concern is with Donte." She took a pen from her handbag. "If you don't mind, could I have the name and address of Donte's biological father?"

"Gary Austin. Don't know his address. We met at a party when I was sixteen. We fell in love. We were together for six months. Things were good until I got pregnant. When I called and told him, he only had one thing to say, 'Go get an abortion.' He asked me if I needed money for it. 'Where would *you* get money from?' That's what I asked him. 'You can't keep a job, or a woman.' Then I hung up. After that, I never saw or heard from him again. I was glad about it, too."

"You kept your baby and raised him alone." Margaret sympathized.

"I'm sorry Donte's never got to see his father. But I showed him pictures of Gary. And told him that we loved each other, but his father had to go away. He's disappointed, but so far he doesn't ask a lot of questions about it."

Margaret found Shawanda likable. "Where is Donte now?"

"Asleep in my room."

"Can I see him, please?"

The women went upstairs. There Margaret thought the child adorable. "He snores." Pulling back the blanket and pajamas, seeing the marks on his back and neck, Margaret swallowed hard. Gently covering him again, she left the room and hurried downstairs. There she quickly subdued anger.

"It's the only thing that's ever happened." Shawanda followed her.

"Or will ever happen again! It's my job to see to that!"

"You won't take him, will you?"

"You saw the bruises!"

"Please, I can't lose my son."

Margaret felt sorry for her, but considered the child first. "This boyfriend is an abuser."

"He's not like that. Donte threw the milk. Aaron lost his temper."

"Inappropriate response, don't you think?"

"When it happened, Mama and me stopped Aaron."

Margaret sank into the chair, thought, the child threw milk, got beaten. If she removed him from his home and mother, would he understand it wasn't further punishment? She considered the fact that there was a watchful grandmother and that Shawanda had done nothing to Donte. Margaret closed her eyes. Hard decision. The safest and easiest thing to do was to remove Donte from the house at once. Yet Margaret didn't mind taking risks to keep a family together. While she didn't care to leave Donte in a home where he had been bruised, she felt separating the child from his mother would scar him more. Opening her eyes, she said, "Maybe, if you can keep Aaron out of the house and away from Donte until further notice, maybe . . ."

"I'll try."

"Not good enough!"

"I will."

"Here, write it down." Margaret passed a notepad and pen to Shawanda and waited for her to immortalize her intentions. When Shawanda finished, Margaret took the pad and read: *I promise to keep Aaron away from the house and Donte.* Returning the paper to Shawanda, Margaret said, "Please sign and date it." That done, Margaret reached into her handbag. "Here's my card. I'm the supervisor. The social worker assigned to your case is Vanessa Graves."

"I have a case?"

"Understand if anything else happens, you'll lose your son. Of course, I'll have to explain to *my* supervisor why I allowed him to stay with you in the first place."

"I understand. Thanks."

"Please cooperate. Vanessa's with another client now, which is why I came instead. I'm giving you an appointment with her. It's on Tuesday at ten. I'll write it down for you." Margaret gathered her things. "Remember our agreement."

"Keep Aaron away," Shawanda recited.

"Or lose Donte."

2

That same evening, after leaving her clothing store job at Mondawmin Mall, Shawanda got into her old black Cavalier and drove to Baltimore's west side. Arriving at Aaron's home, she found his parents, Gladys and Peter, at the dinner table. "Did Aaron tell you what he did last night?" Not waiting for their reply, she said, "He was beating on Donte."

"We heard Donte was throwing milk," the gray-haired Gladys said.

"The boy needs discipline. My son is trying to help you with him." Peter adjusted his eyeglasses on his nose. "But Donte is spoiled."

"Is not," Shawanda countered. "Besides, Aaron's not the one that's suppose to punish him, especially the way he did it."

"Somebody needs to be a father to him." Gladys put down the fork. "And teach the boy how to act."

"Aaron was wrong," Shawanda persisted.

"Really, it's not our business." Peter looked away. "I'm staying out of it."

"That's right. You two work it out on your own," Gladys added.

Shawanda wanted to say, now that you've got your opinion out, you're going to pretend to stay out of it. She started to leave the room. But then she decided she could speak her mind while still being respectful to her elders. If Peter and Gladys didn't want to hear the truth, so be it. "You're always taking his side even when he's wrong. You know Aaron had no business beating on Donte. On top of that, Mama called Social Services."

"She shouldn't have done that!" Gladys snapped.

"That social worker wanted to take my son," Shawanda continued. "Now Aaron has to stay away from the house and —."

"Stay away?" Peter interrupted. "I hope you don't expect him to pay the rent on a house he can't come to."

"Bad enough he never lived there and was paying the bills." Gladys pushed away her plate. "And buying clothes for a child that ain't his."

"He doesn't pay that many bills. I work."

"Aaron's upstairs," Peter said.

Shawanda decided that talking to them any longer would be a waste. They had their viewpoint. She had a different one. She twirled around and marched out. Upstairs, she found Aaron in his room lying across the bed. "When were you going to call me?" Shawanda asked when walking in.

"Thought you were mad at me." He sat up.

"I am."

"I screwed up. I didn't mean to hurt Donte or you."

"Donte hasn't talked much since last night."

Aaron fell back on the bed. "I'll make it up to him."

She sat beside Aaron, who was shorter, five-eight to her five-ten. He had cinnamon-tinted skin, cottony brown hair, and small hazel eyes. His build was muscular, due in part to his construction job.

"Why did you have to act like that?" she asked.

"I don't know."

"You can't lose it like that anymore."

She touched his arm, believing she understood him. He was the youngest of seven children. When he was born, his parents were in their forties. Shawanda thought Aaron's views tended to be old-fashioned because he was reared by older parents. But she loved the family-oriented aspect of his personality, which she felt had developed from seeing his parents married for over forty years, living in the same west Baltimore rowhouse for almost thirty, and from seeing his father get up and go to work every day until retirement, bringing home the paycheck and paying the bills.

Shawanda found within Aaron great character. He had the courage to stay out of what his peers fell into: arrests, drug dealing, and dropping out of school. He graduated, got a job, and kept it. Aaron was always there for her. She liked his lighter side. Aaron liked rap music, action movies, and basketball. Had an attraction to nice jewelry: gold chains, rings, and watches. And fancy tennis shoes. And while he displayed a hard exterior to the world, she had discovered his gentler side.

"Gotta tell you something about Mama," she said. "She was mad, not thinking, and called Social Services."

"What?" He jumped up. "Why would she bring all that trouble on us?"

"She says she's sorry."

"I didn't mean for all this to happen." His head fell into his cupped hands.

"The social worker came this morning. I have to go see another worker on Tuesday."

"What are they gonna do?" He looked at her.

"Take Donte, unless you stay away from him and the house."

"Stay away? Who's gonna pay the rent next month?"

"I wouldn't ask you to pay rent on a house you couldn't come to." She found it interesting he, like his father, so quickly thought of that. Now Shawanda considered the question. With her minimum-wage job at the clothing store in the mall, she would barely have March's rent. "Maybe Daddy will help."

"Yeah, sure, he wants to support a twenty-one-year-old daughter."

"I don't want to ask him." In fact, she was ashamed to ask. Eight months before, she had moved out of her parents' home because Lena complained about Aaron's frequent visits and wouldn't allow him to stay overnight. His parents wouldn't allow her to sleep with Aaron at their home. After moving, she had an immediate struggle to pay bills. First she got help from her father, then from Aaron. Aaron wanted to move in, but she held out for marriage.

Now, the twenty-two-year-old Aaron leaned forward. "How are we gonna see each other?"

"Here, malls, bars. Maybe Denise's new apartment." She spoke of her cousin and friend.

"Ah, Baby! That ain't gonna work."

"It's got to. I won't let the state take Donte. Just keep away from the house until everything's straightened out."

Aaron said nothing.

"Do you love me?" she inquired.

"What do you think?"

"What do you think?" she asked back.

"Yeah." He pulled her close. "If I stay away, a good looking woman like you might stick another Negro in my place quick."

"Don't want another man. Want you."

He stared at her.

"I want you," she repeated.

He touched her hair.

"I want you," she whispered. "Promise you won't come to the house."

"I don't know. Coming over might be the only way to find out if you got some other man in my place."

"Please promise." She waited for his response. The silence was loud.

* * *

Midnight Saturday, Shawanda and her cousin Denise Jones hopped out of Denise's car and strutted down North Avenue and around the corner to their favorite club.

Shawanda was too depress to party but didn't want Denise going out alone.

"That Negro won't stay away," the twenty-seven-year-old hair stylist said. The two women had grown up in the same neighborhood.

"Aaron wouldn't hurt me. He cares about me."

"He wouldn't promise to stay away." The dyed redhead chewed gum. "The man pays a couple of bills and thinks he owns you."

"You introduced us," Shawanda said.

"Yeah, and I can introduce you to someone else!" Denise stopped in front of the club.

The two women waited in a short line. At the door, two husky men checked their identification in order to verify their ages. They paid the admission price, and walked inside to find the club dimly lit and crowded.

Shawanda wondered what the room looked like in the daytime, when lit and sparsely populated. With Denise behind her, Shawanda pushed past well dressed, perfumed, and sweaty patrons, while swaying to the screaming rap music. At the bar she signaled to the bartender, and the two woman ordered beers. Turning to the dance floor, she was astonished at the high number of dancers that night.

Denise tapped her on the shoulder. "People leaving over there. Grab that table!"

They rushed over and jumped onto the chairs. Settling down, Shawanda talked over the music. "Without Aaron's help, I've got money problems."

Just then a man dressed in a baggy jogging suit with several gold chains around his neck approached and asked Denise to dance. She consented, left the table, pushed in between gyrating couples, and began dancing with the stranger.

Shawanda watched the two. The stranger moved close to Denise, so close their bodies touched. He began to grind against her. Shawanda knew Denise wouldn't put up with that. She watched Denise turn and walk away from the man.

Returning to the table and settling in next to Shawanda, Denise said, "That idiot was rubbing all over me. I told him I would dance, not have foreplay. Now what were you saying? Money problems? You need yourself a new man."

Before Shawanda could respond, a tall male, who was maybe in his thirty's, sat at their table.

"Hey. What's your name?" he asked Shawanda.

"I've got a man," she quickly replied.

He turned to Denise. "What's yours?"

"Gabriella."

What? Shawanda thought. First time her cousin used that one. Last outing, she tried to convince a man she was part French and her name was De La Nise. Shawanda smiled at the recollection.

"Can I buy you two a drink?" the man asked.

"Already got one." Denise grinned.

"Oh, you can buy your own drinks."

"I guess I have been independent since Daddy died and left me a trust fund." Denise crossed her legs, waved the top leg in front of the tall man.

Shawanda looked away. She had never before heard Denise kill off her father, who was Lena's only brother. Usually Denise's pretend money came from being a shrewd businesswoman, winning the lotto, collecting from an accident case, or being lucky.

"Trust fund," the man was saying. "Yeah?"

Shawanda bet he wasn't listening.

"Give me your number. I'll call you and we can talk about it," he said.

"Sorry. A woman in my position has to be careful."

"Women tell me I'm amazing in bed." He grinned.

Denise smirked. "Men tell me the same thing."

Denise enjoyed games with men, Shawanda knew. And the object of any game was to have fun while playing and to win in the end. Shawanda turned to the man with the intent of putting an end to the game. "Sorry, but we were talking."

After he left, Denise asked, "Why did you do that? I was just starting to have fun."

"We're talking about my problems, remember? Help me. What can I do to get money? And what about Aaron and Donte not being able to go around each other?"

Just then a couple of particularly loud songs played. Denise couldn't answer the question until they were outside and headed to the car.

"If Aaron beat my child, I would get rid of him." Denise's body swayed as she walked.

"You don't take nothing off a man."

"Right," Denise said coldly. "If you want, I can introduce you to Claude. He works at the post office."

"Claude? What kind of help is that?"

"Okay. You want Aaron? Go ahead — keep him. Learn the hard way!"

"You don't understand!" Getting into the car, Shawanda meditated on the fact that Social Services could take Donte if

Aaron didn't stay away. Turning to Denise, Shawanda tried to convince herself otherwise. "Stuff can't get worse."

"Think so?" Denise started the car and pulled into traffic. "If I were you, I would get rid of Aaron before he gets Donte taken away." Stopping at a red light, Denise added, "Would you like to meet Claude?"

3

On Monday morning, Margaret Holmes sat in her Biddle Street office, which was a few miles from downtown. She prepared to eat lunch at her well-organized desk.

Her friend and coworker of five years, April Peters, settled in front of the desk with lunch and began to tell Margaret about her bachelor cousin. April added, "You're both single people who haven't dated in a long time; you two should get together."

"Do we have anything in common?"

"Find something in common. After all, you're thirty-two, never married, and haven't had a date since when?"

Margaret heard: Are you desperate enough for this? "I've never been on a blind date."

"So what?"

"I don't know." Margaret bit into the dry tuna and crackers.

"You have nothing to lose."

"Is he kind and gentle?" Margaret asked.

"He has rough edges . . . like, stubbornness. But he's available."

"Besides being available, what are his positive qualities?"

April shifted positions in the chair. "How would you like to be single and childless at forty-two or fifty-two or sixty-two?"

No! No! No! Margaret mentally replied. "Of course that wouldn't happen."

"Last weekend, did you take work home?"

"Only two folders."

"Did you spend the rest of the day cleaning your apartment?"

"What's wrong with a clean apartment?" Margaret enjoyed cleaning and decorating. She'd been in the apartment only ten months, having moved from her mother's home at her mother's suggestion. Kathleen's exact words were: 'You need a life.'

"Is there even a dirty breakfast dish in the sink right now?" The short, heavyset April tossed back a braid.

"Definitely not!"

April bit into her sandwich and with a full mouth continued. "Saturday night, did you go out with your mother?"

Margaret hated it when April put it that way. But now she recalled picking up Kathleen at five o'clock, and seeing a movie early to avoid the couples. Afterwards, the two ate at a Chinese restaurant. Watching her weight, Margaret had chicken and steamed vegetables while her mother ordered fried rice.

"When you ate out, did your mother complain about the food?" April asked.

"She could have cooked it better!"

"Were you home by eight?"

"Eight-thirty."

"And when *was* the last time you were out with a man?"

Margaret remembered Thomas. She had known him for ten years, dated for nine, engaged for six. He was thin with maple-colored skin. Some called him nerdy-looking. At Johns Hopkins University he was an honor student. Tommy did well in medical school, too. But his growing devotion to career and self eventually killed their relationship. "It's been two years since Tommy."

"Two years!"

"I'm not over him yet."

"Let go already!"

"Easy for you to say. You've never been in this position. You have a husband of ten years and sons."

"Which is why I'm trying to help you," the twenty-eight-year-old April said. "Come on, what would meeting my cousin hurt?"

"But a blind date?"

"What did you do last Sunday after mass?"

She recalled the day. She and Kathleen parted at the Basilica. Kathleen went off with friends, while Margaret returned home. There was really no reason for her to go home. There, alone, the silence annoyed her. "I had a relaxing afternoon."

"You can relax *with* someone. I can have my cousin call you."

With someone, the words repeated in Margaret's head as she envisioned meeting April's cousin and spending Saturday nights with a man again. Maybe the two of them would fall in love, get married, and have children, two girls, and two boys.

Her sister had three boys. Brittany was two years older than Margaret. The two women were very different people. Brittany was extroverted and easily attracted males, while Margaret was awkward, especially around desirable men. Sometimes, Margaret envied Brittany. She recalled one particular day. Kathleen happened to mention Brittany's productive life — married to a doctor, living in Los Angeles.

Then, looking at Margaret as if to console her, Kathleen said, "Don't worry, Dear. You'll have a good life soon."

Now Margaret asked her friend, "Do you think this will work?"

She felt responsible for April's nagging. Fifteen months after breaking up with Tommy, Margaret tired of telling April about her lonely, dull weekends. It was embarrassing. One Monday morning, Margaret bounced into work and described her new lover, Pierre Champagne. He was Black, French, and handsome, an extraordinary gentlemen in every way. It was all a lie. She had snatched Pierre from a romance novel read in high school and colored him brown. After a few weeks, exhausted by the pretense, Margaret admitted the fantasy. April felt sorry for her. Margaret could tell. A month later, April made the first offer to set Margaret up on a date. Margaret declined then, and every man afterwards.

Yet, now, the loneliness becoming more and more painful, Margaret pushed away the tuna. Looking at her friend, she said, "Okay, one blind date."

* * *

Tuesday Shawanda drove toward Biddle Street and Social Services. It took her a little while to find the building. Pulling into the parking lot, she surveyed the long, unimpressive old structure. Inside she found a few receptionists and guards behind a long gray screen and a crowded waiting area with dingy green walls and hard brown chairs.

"I have to see Vanessa Graves," she told the woman behind the screen.

The woman looked at the appointment book, then the clock. Shawanda glanced toward the clock also. Fifteen after ten.

"Your appointment was for ten. Next time get here early."

There would be a next time? Shawanda pondered.

"Have a seat," the woman said.

Shawanda obeyed. Looking around the waiting area, she wondered what business each person there had. Fifteen minutes later she noticed a tall, husky, black-haired woman with dreadlocks who was maybe thirty-one or two get off the elevator and come toward the waiting area. The woman had a serious, even mean, facial expression. Shawanda hoped this wasn't Vanessa. The woman called her name. Shawanda went over. Without a hello the woman introduced herself as Ms. Graves.

"Follow me," Vanessa said, heading back to the elevator.

The social worker walked as if in a hurry, Shawanda thought. She followed her into a tiny, windowless third floor office. The room was filled with manuals, files, and boxes.

"I'm behind schedule already," Vanessa sat behind a small, paper cluttered desk. "Don't stand there. Take a seat."

Shawanda followed instructions. She felt out of place.

"Here's the deal." Vanessa spoke fast. "I'll set up counseling and parenting classes for you and your boyfriend."

"Classes? I don't need those."

"Listen, I have other people to see. Are you going to the classes or not?"

Vanessa's stern tone shook Shawanda. "Yeah."

"You'll have to excuse me," Vanessa quickly explained. "I've been on the job five years. I lost my patience awhile ago."

Then get another job, Shawanda thought. But to Vanessa she said, "Sure."

"Now, I have a contract for you to sign." Vanessa shuffled papers and pulled out a form.

Would she have to sign something every time she saw a social worker? Shawanda wondered before saying, "Okay."

"The contract says that you agree to go to parenting classes and counseling until successfully completed. Of course, we won't force the boyfriend to go. But he can't come near the child until he completes the classes and counseling."

Shawanda tried to imagine Aaron in counseling with someone like Vanessa. Aaron didn't appreciate *any* woman telling him what to do, Shawanda had long ago concluded. "Why do you call him the boyfriend? His name is Aaron. And the child's name is Donte."

"I will make unannounced visits to your home and the child's school."

Shawanda resented Vanessa's ignoring her and so coldly explaining the rules. "He's four. He doesn't go to school."

"Where does he stay while you work?"

"With Kim, my neighbor."

Vanessa wrote it down before continuing. "I will personally call the police and have boyfriend jailed if he touches this child again."

"He won't." How many times would Shawanda have to say that to herself and others, she pondered.

"Don't cooperate and you will be a childless mother."

Shawanda shifted positions. Instead of disliking Vanessa, she tried to explain. "Me and Aaron might get married someday." It was her heart's desire.

"What?" Vanessa lowered her voice. "Couldn't find any terrorists to marry?"

Shawanda took a deep breath. Using all of her might, she managed to hold back her response.

Vanessa handed her the contract. Taking it, telling herself to calm down, Shawanda read it. She let the sheet of paper fall into her lap. "Can I write things on here?"

"Of course you cannot."

Next question, can I choose not to sign? But she didn't bother asking that one. Shawanda had fallen into the system and felt she had to surrender in order to keep her son. Maybe the system would be merciful. She signed the paper.

Vanessa made copies and gave her one. "This concludes our meeting."

Shawanda felt dismissed. She got up and walked out. Standing at the elevator, Shawanda felt misunderstood and pessimistic about the future.

* * *

On the first day of March, Shawanda sat at the kitchen table and made a list of her bills, assigning a number to each one. Those with the highest numbers were paid first. Money could run out before she got to the bottom of the list. List done, the cable company had the lowest number. She relaxed. Living without cable was possible. Second to last was the department store at which Donte's clothes were purchased. She had to pay them. Third was her friend and neighbor, Kim, who kept Donte while Shawanda worked. Knowing she couldn't mistreat a friend, she took Kim's name from the bottom of the list and rewrote it at the top. She added up the amount of each bill. Coming up short, she quickly concluded there was no money for the last three creditors. Disgusted, she grabbed the list, crushed it into her right hand, and tossed it across the room. Her head dropped — one, two seconds. Inside she screamed.

She couldn't ask Aaron to support a home he wasn't allowed into. Left was only her father. She owed him more money than she could pay back. But had few choices. A loan from him would get her through March. But what would she do in the future? Maybe she could get a second job? That idea jumped and tumbled in her head, ran to her tongue and left a foul taste.

* * *

The next Sunday afternoon, Shawanda and Donte went to her parents' home. She found her father, Ernest, watching a basketball game. While Donte immediately hopped onto his lap, Shawanda yelled toward the kitchen, the direction from which clanging pot noises and the aroma of fried chicken emerged. "Hey, Mama."

Sitting on the sofa, she placed her arm on Ernest's shoulder as she had done many times before, and looked toward the television, although it didn't interest her. "How you been, Daddy?" She knew how he would answer before he spoke. Troublesome problems were not discussed with the women; his way of protecting them, Shawanda surmised.

"Okay." He was usually a man of few words.

"How's work?" she asked her insurance salesman father.

"Busy," said the tall, muscular man.

Shawanda had awesome childhood recollections of him taking her to class, attending school plays, buying a box of candy, taking a couple of pieces out for himself and giving her the box. Often they watched television together. He was never critical, judgmental, or condemning of her, Shawanda felt, but always on her side. Relatives said he spoiled Shawanda. She disagreed.

"Miss Shawanda."

She turned to see Lena standing in the doorway with her hands on her hips. Donte ran to his grandmother.

"How's my Precious Baby?" Then to Shawanda: "How long have you been in this house and I haven't seen your face?"

"I said 'hey.'"

"Hello, Miss Shawanda. Now get into the kitchen and peel some potatoes."

Shawanda got up and followed Lena through the large, immaculate, beautifully decorated home. Lena was an excellent homemaker. She loved to shop, although she couldn't afford to do a lot of it. But Lena had managed to collect wonderful knickknacks and fill the house with them.

The short Lena entered the kitchen. She had short, neatly cut dark brown hair, and was always nicely dressed and color coordinated. Lena gave Shawanda a knife from the drawer and pointed to the potatoes.

Lena and Ernest, who were the same age, had met during high school. When Lena became pregnant, they got married.

"Ever wanted an outside job, Mama?"

"Never." Lena removed the last pieces of chicken from the skillet.

"I'm thinking about a second job."

"Who'll raise Donte while you're working two jobs?"

"I can do it." Shawanda finished peeling a potato.

"Bad enough he doesn't have a father. With you working two jobs, it'll be like he won't have a mother, either."

Shawanda shook her head. Lena almost never understood her, Shawanda felt.

Within the hour, the family had dinner and pleasant conversation around the dining room table. Afterwards, in the living room, they all watched a movie on DVD. During the movie, Donte fell asleep.

"Shawanda's thinking about taking a second job," Lena told Ernest.

"Why?" he reclined in a chair.

"I need the money, Daddy. With no help," she swallowed, "I can't pay all the bills this month."

"How much are you short?" he asked.

"At least wait until she asks to borrow money," Lena said to her husband.

"This will be the last time." Shawanda wrung her hands. "Promise."

Lena chuckled. "How many times have we heard that?"

"I'll pay you back."

"Maybe we might live long enough to see it," Lena said.

"How much?" Ernest repeated.

Shawanda told him.

"We can manage that, can't we Lena?"

"Thank God we only had one child!" was Lena's response.

Shawanda disbelieved Lena was grateful for that fact. Besides, she was convinced her parents gladly wanted to help.

"Instead of taking two jobs," Ernest began, "you can move back here."

Shawanda looked at Lena.

"Good idea." Lena looked toward the television. "At least then I wouldn't have to worry about Aaron's coming near Precious Baby. He definitely won't get inside this house."

Shawanda knew moving back would feel like failure. Turning to Ernest, she said, "I'll see." Then, "Disappointed in me, Daddy?"

"Never."

* * *

The next day, on Baltimore's east side, Margaret woke alone in her double bed. To force herself out of bed and to work, she gave herself a pep talk. It's a sunny new day. There are important things to do, work, people to help, appointments to keep.

Rising, quickly dressing, she surveyed her image in the full-length mirror in the bedroom. Her skin was clear and pecan-colored. She was average height and size, with a thick build common to women of her race. And plain, she decided, with a square face and small dark eyes. Her best feature was her full lips. Yet she wished God had shared with her the beauty he'd given her sister. Immediately ashamed of the thought, she mentally snatched it back. One final look in the mirror, her eyes roamed to the hem of the conservative gray suit that fell just past her knees. She looked like a retired spinster, Margaret concluded, and hurried away from the mirror.

Walking through her clean, one bedroom apartment, which was decorated with pretty, color coordinated furniture, cute knickknacks, and lots of plants, she passed through the living room. It had several bookcases filled with biographies, art, history, and political books. They were all of her favorite things to read.

Reaching the kitchen, she prepared breakfast, eight ounces of skim milk, eight ounces of dry cereal, and one piece of fruit. Washing the bowl, she tidied the apartment, made the bed, and put the dirty towels in the hamper. Everything in its place, she grabbed the folder worked on the night before and headed toward the door.

Emerging from her Charles Village apartment, which was a few blocks from Johns Hopkins University and a few miles from downtown, she crossed the street to a block lined with businesses: a bank, a bagel shop, grocery store, bar, two restaurants. Around the corner, Margaret got into her car, turned onto busy Saint Paul Street and stop-and-go traffic, which never bothered her, and headed to her office.

Early for work, finding no one in her division, Margaret went immediately to her medium sized office, which had one large window overlooking the parking lot, and began work. At ten, Vanessa came in to discuss the hardest cases. A mother killed one child. She wanted Social Services to bring the others to prison for visits. A father wanted visitation with the son he had sodomized. A drug addict resurfaced after five years and wanted the immediate return of her children.

Margaret decided none of them should have visits now. Vanessa nodded. Discussion over, Vanessa got up and sighed. "Too, too many awful cases! I need a long break." Margaret sympathized. She had been told that once Vanessa, who grew up on welfare and worked her way through school, had been eager to help the community she came from. But after a few years on the job, she hardened, blaming the clients for what she came to view as their weaknesses. Vanessa lost patience with them. Her distress with the job and the clients had caused her to lose a supervisor slot.

Vanessa left.

Margaret listened to the silence. One, two minutes passed. But it seemed a long time. Returning to work, she always welcomed it to fill her day.

At the end of the afternoon, Margaret left work and drove home. In the empty apartment, she wandered aimlessly about before focusing on dinner. Alone at the kitchen table, Margaret admitted to herself that which she seldom acknowledged. She felt like the only person in a theater watching a play, a comedy about the joys of life. Everyone in the play laughed and had a pleasant time while Margaret felt odd, different, left out. Now, in her unbearable painful loneliness, Margaret prayed April's cousin would call.

4

On a Saturday in mid-March Shawanda met Aaron near Lexington Market. "I've got money problems," she told him. "I might have to look for a second job."

"What about Donte?" Aaron asked.

"If I get night work, maybe Kim will keep him until I get home."

"When will you see him?"

"I don't know." They passed hair supply and dollar stores.

"You don't need a second job."

"If I get something right away, I can have money for all of next month's bills." She walked close to him.

"No second jobs!" he said.

"What do you mean?"

"You know what *no* means!"

Since they were on the street, and she didn't want to get into an argument in public with him, she tossed the subject. Passing a store, Shawanda halted in front of it. "Let's go in here, please." He consented. Inside she browsed. She noticed the Asian owner's stare follow them around the room. She called to Aaron and they left. Outside, she almost said to him — the storeowner wasn't friendly. But she didn't want to get Aaron started on the subject of Asians in the Black community.

The next stop was Lexington Market. Inside the market, they passed numerous food stalls, fruit stands, and meat counters before stopping at one and purchasing lemonade and crab cakes. She followed him upstairs to the huge dining area, where they found a table and sat on wooden stools.

"I've got to do something." Shawanda wrapped an arm around his.

"I'll pay the rent next month, even if I can't come near the place," he said.

She was touched by his offer. "I don't want you to do that. It's not fair to you."

"You don't need to wear yourself out with two jobs. Plus you should be with Donte at night, you know, have dinner with him."

"You care about him." It's what Lena and Denise didn't understand, Shawanda felt.

"I don't know what I am to him." He lifted an eyebrow. "Or how to act around him, but I want to figure it out."

"That social worker is gonna set up some counseling and some classes. Want to go with me?"

"I'll do anything to get us all back together. I'm sorry about what happened. I want to be with you."

She knew that. Changing the subject, "Mama and Daddy said if I don't have enough money to stay on my own, I can move back with them."

"Wouldn't do that, would ya?"

"Wouldn't need two jobs if I did."

"I told you. I'll help you out."

She kissed his cheek and laid her head on his shoulder. She thought him strong enough to lean on.

Images spiraled in her head — pieces of her childhood — like Lena forcing her to church every Sunday. A sermon, the preacher teaching: love nothing and no one more than God. Shawanda understood, but had trouble worshipping what she couldn't see, touch, or have the usual conversation with. Instead, she depended on Aaron. He permeated her thoughts and heart. He was her peace and what made her content with life. Let others adore the unseen. Shawanda had Aaron. He was her religion.

* * *

The following week, because she cared about Aaron and couldn't ask him to pay bills for a house he couldn't visit, Shawanda searched the newspaper daily for part-time jobs. She found nothing appropriate. At the store, she asked the manager for additional hours. The reply: business was slow. In the mall, her inquires were fruitless. On North Avenue, the large, commercial street nearest her home, she applied to a few fast food stores, but found success in the least expected place.

Arriving home from work, she first went to Kim's.

"Come on in," the neighbor greeted.

Inside, Donte ran to her.

"Hey little man." Shawanda hugged him.

"He ate all of his snack." Kim sat on the sofa. Two of Kim's four children gathered around. "Sit for a while," the neighbor said.

Shawanda sat. Just then the oldest child ran into the room. When he called the others to the back, the living room quickly cleared of all young people.

"I have to take a second job," Shawanda told her friend.

"That's going to be hard with a child." Kim was older than Shawanda, thirty-five, and had been married for twelve years. Fourteen months before, her husband, Otis, was shot to death during a robbery attempt. He had no money or valuables on him. His death left Kim on welfare, and with a one-hundred-pound weight gain. She didn't want to overeat,

Kim told Shawanda. Although for now, eating sometimes temporarily relieved her depression. Now looking at Shawanda, Kim said, "But if you *have* to work nights, I can keep Donte."

"Thanks, friend."

"Do you have a job in mind?" After the negative reply, Kim said, "A couple of years ago, I worked for a company that cleaned offices after hours. They might have openings. Do you want the name and number of the owner?"

Nodding, and after taking the information, Shawanda said goodnight and took Donte home. She was excited about the job lead.

The next morning, she dialed the number, and got a woman who transferred her to the company's president, a Mr. Carter. "I have one opening. Come on in and we can talk about it." He gave her an appointment.

The conversation ended and she hung up. Smiling, she hoped for success.

The following day, arriving downtown for the interview, Shawanda filled out an application and handed it back to the secretary. Returning to the chair, she tapped her feet and pulled on her fingers. She was perspiring, she noticed. Fanning her upper body with her hands, Shawanda quickly acknowledged that wouldn't help her nervousness.

Soon a man came out of the adjoining office. "I'm Herbert Carter." The short, rounded, gray haired man extended his hand.

After they shook, Shawanda followed him to his office. There she sat near his desk.

Mr. Carter told her about the company he started twenty years ago. "I was a janitor in a federal government office for twenty-two years. One day, I counted the years I had before retirement and got sick. I had almost no money saved, but I decided to start my own business. When I told my coworkers, they stopped, laughed at me, and went back to work. My wife said, 'Ah, Herbert, you can't throw away something solid for a dream.' But I wouldn't let anything stop me."

Shawanda saw pride reclined across his face.

"Look where I am now. Up to thirty folks work for me."

"Thirty!"

"My business is well-organized," Herbert Carter continued. "My employees work hard. I don't tolerate nonsense — you know, people who call in sick or can't get here for whatever reasons." He leaned back. "Tell me about you."

Shawanda told him about graduating from public school. She left out that it was with C's and D's because by high school she was too busy partying with the in-crowd to pay attention to her studies. Shawanda mentioned Donte and assured him there were adequate night care arrangements. She ended with her less-than-full-time work at the store.

"Why do you want to work for me?" he asked.

"I need the job, and I can do it. Please give me a chance."

"What we do here is start everybody off on a six-month probation. Do a good job and you can stay. But if you can't keep up, you're out of here. Okay?"

"I've got the job?" Shawanda clapped with excitement. She was grateful for the opportunity.

* * *

In early April, Margaret got the call she had been waiting for. She hurried out to tell her mother. Driving to a middle class section of Baltimore known as Ashburton, Margaret floated up the walk of the two story, old wood frame house and knocked on the door.

Kathleen opened the door. "Wipe your feet, Dear."

"I have wonderful news," Margaret announced.

"So do I."

"What news do you have?" Margaret wiped her feet, took off her blazer, and hung it up. Maneuvering through the antique-filled and overly cluttered room — Kathleen never threw anything away — Margaret cleared newspapers and magazines from a corner of the sofa and sat.

"Tell me your news first, dear." Kathleen sat in a nearby chair after pushing aside a stack of mail.

"April fixed me up with Joe Norris, one of her cousins. It took him long enough to call, but finally. . . ." Margaret grabbed the excitement in her voice and forced it to calm down. "He's forty-nine, conservative, and a cab driver."

"Too old for you. Besides, you need a liberal-minded professional. And as for this blind date business, what are the odds of success?" the short, stocky, dyed black-haired woman of sixty-two asked. Originally she was from rural Louisiana. She met her husband there when he was an intern at the local hospital. They married and soon she returned to Baltimore with him. He was a doctor, Kathleen a high school counselor until retirement. Now the widow worked part-time on a suicide hotline.

"We talked for about ten minutes. He seemed nice."

"So would a serial killer — for ten minutes."

"Please, Mother, don't make me nervous about this. He wants to meet at a pizza place downtown in Mount Vernon on Wednesday."

"Wednesday? Why? Seeing his girlfriend on weekends?"

Margaret hadn't thought of that. "Maybe weekends are busy for cab drivers. April wouldn't have fix us up if —."

"If she knew he had a girlfriend. People don't always tell their cousins everything. Besides, you swore off junk food — like pizza."

"I'll have a salad."

"Why didn't you suggest another place?"

"Because no man has looked my way in two years." She twisted her face. "And the last one stopped looking long before we broke up." Margaret waited for Kathleen to respond. Since Margaret's father died three years before, the two women had grown even closer. They were best friends.

"Okay, go on your blind date," Kathleen said. "Just don't expect a lot. After all, he probably isn't Mr. Right. Look at how long it took him to call."

Margaret slumped in the chair, wishing Kathleen wrong. But, "After we confirmed a time, I told him where I lived. I wanted him to volunteer to pick me up. He didn't."

"I wouldn't make anything of that." Kathleen waved a hand. "He doesn't know you."

"I want a man to come to my apartment and bring flowers. Doesn't have to be roses. He sits down and talks to me for a while and enjoys it. We get into his car. I don't care what his car looks like, although it should be clean. We go to a nice restaurant, where he gladly offers to pay because he sincerely likes me. You know, I'm hoping for what you had with father all those years."

"Listen, this blind date doesn't have to be the man you'll spend the rest of your life with. Go out, have a salad, enjoy the conversation."

"But I'm getting old! Forget the biological clock. If I don't meet the right man soon, my whole body will explode."

"Please, nothing's exploding!"

Then Margaret remembered. "What's your news?"

"Let's not talk about it now," Kathleen said.

"Sorry, didn't mean to be selfish. I want to hear it."

"It's about Milton. You know, Milton from the senior citizen's center."

"I remember you telling me about him."

"He's taking me to Julio's."

"Julio's!" Margaret considered the expensive Spanish restaurant.

"He doesn't drive anymore," Kathleen continued. "So he's renting a limousine."

"A limousine! How fantastic!"

"I like him a lot," Kathleen added.

"I'm happy for you," Margaret sincerely said.

"I know, Dear."

Margaret leaned back. Amazing, every woman in the entire world had a man — except her.

* * *

Wednesday afternoon, Margaret left work promptly. She drove home and changed. Rushing from the apartment, she sped downtown and looked for parking — for twenty minutes. Ten minutes late, she was usually never late for anything; Margaret hurried across the street and into the pizza place.

"Margaret?" A man stood by the door. "I'm Joe Norris." He extended his hand.

He was short, balding, and had a big belly. He looked older than his age, she thought. But as usual, she did not judge others by their looks. Although, she wondered about the old jeans and sweater he wore. Was he not into clothes? Or the date?

The first thing he said after they settled was: "I want you to know I'm not desperate. I can pretty much date any woman I want."

She didn't believe him. Soon they ordered.

"I only decided to call you as a favor to my cousin."

Thanks for pointing that out, Margaret thought.

"She told me you hadn't dated in a while," he continued. "I decided to help you out."

All the excitement Margaret had mustered for the date was pumped into a balloon and tied up. Now she released the string, and watched the balloon float away.

They ordered.

"April tells me you're a church-going woman."

"Mass, regularly." She managed a polite smile.

"You're Catholic? April didn't mention that. I'm a Christian."

"Catholics are Christians."

"You know what I mean."

She didn't. The waiter arrived with their orders. Margaret welcomed the interruption.

"So you work with April. What are you, a clerk?" He bit into a slice of pizza.

"Social worker."

"Oh, you're one of those educated women."

It sounded negative when he said it. Margaret pressed on. "Hopkins undergrad and the University of Maryland School of Social Work. I'm a supervisor, like April."

"Oh, you like to supervise. But you aren't one of those, ah, woman libbers, are you?"

"Of course I believe in women's rights."

"Yeah? But you aren't one of those people who believes homosexuals should have rights, are you?"

"I believe everyone should be treated equally. No group is better than another."

He threw the pizza down on the plate. "You must know where all homosexuals are going, don't you?"

"Where?"

"I wouldn't live next door to one."

She pulled out polite words. "If you did, I'm sure they wouldn't bother you."

"Bet you believe criminals should come out of jail and be able to vote, too?"

She had never before considered it. "Yes, they should. Why punish them indefinitely?"

He grabbed the slice of pizza. "At least, you're Catholic and don't believe in divorce, birth control, or abortion."

Margaret's back straightened. "God would know when two people have abandoned a relationship. There's no point in their physically staying together after that. And as for birth control, that's an individual decision." She had seen too many unwanted children taken into custody by Social Services. "With abortion, I wouldn't have one. But I wouldn't condemn a woman who, for whatever reason, decided to have one." She generally wasn't into condemning others for their life choices.

"You must know what the Bible says about these things. And about women," he continued. "They should be seen and not heard!"

What did he say? She stared, having forgotten there were people who thought that way. But before she got to ask him about it, he reached into his back pants pocket, pulled out a small notebook, and flipped through the pages. "I wrote down what the Bible says about women." He began to read.

She listened. After hearing what he had to say, she found it hard to believe any of it came from the Bible. And Margaret thought him rude.

Finishing, he shut the notebook and laid it on the table.

Margaret signaled to the waiter. When he came over, she asked, "Can I get a glass of wine, please?" She rarely drank, but was in need of any type of assistance.

"Sorry, we don't sell alcohol."

Her eyes traveled from the waiter to Joe. "Should we get the check now?"

"You like to run things, don't you?"

No one had ever accused Margaret of that before.

Soon the waiter brought the bill. Joe looked at it, then her. He told her what she owed. When he didn't leave a tip, she left a big one.

Outside he said, "Maybe I'll call you."

She shivered. "We don't have anything in common. It's best you don't."

"What? Too educated for me?"

Margaret shook her head no. She mumbled good night before running across the street. She didn't know if she could date again anytime soon, so disappointing was the night.

* * *

The next morning Margaret avoided April.

But before lunch, April cornered her in the bathroom. "I'm sorry, Margaret. I thought he would like you."

"He didn't?" Margaret blurted.

"He said you were dull."

Dull? Unbelievable, Margaret thought. But she decided to keep unkind things about Joe to herself.

"He thought you were uninteresting, boring, and unattractive."

Yeah? Her father often told her she looked like an African princess. But Margaret understood he was biased.

"Of course, I know you're not any of those things," April assured her. "You two weren't a good match." Suddenly April's face lit up. "I know. I'll introduce you to Chadwick. He's a friend of my husband and a librarian. He's kinda geeky —."

"No more blind dates!" Margaret darted around April, out of the door, and down the hall.

"Everybody likes Chadwick." April chased her.

"Stop matchmaking! You're no good at it!" Margaret fled to her office, but didn't find safety there.

"I know who you would like." April stood near. "But he's younger, about twenty-three."

"Twenty-three!"

"He must have turned twenty-three by now," April mumbled.

"Please, get out!" Margaret pointed to the door.

"Come on, I'm trying to help. I've gotten my other best friend married. You're a hard case! You take more work."

"One more word and I'm jumping out of that window."

April frowned. She shifted her weight from one foot to the other, turned around, and left.

Margaret fell into the chair and took a deep breath; glad April was gone. She hoped April would never mention matchmaking again. But what were the odds? Calming herself, Margaret returned to work.

5

On a Saturday evening in mid-April, Shawanda hid a secret from Aaron. She sat in the front passenger seat of Aaron's car and mentally rehearsed ways to reveal it.

Aaron stopped the car.

"I know you're not gonna try to get into that little space," she said.

"Watch me." He reversed the car and eased into the space.

"Look at you," Shawanda said. He loved driving, she knew.

He smiled and turned off the engine.

They were parked a few feet from the Jewel Box, Aaron's favorite bar. It was only four blocks from his parents' home and was frequented by lots of his acquaintances from the neighborhood. Shawanda didn't like the place. She still felt like an outsider, yet went there because of Aaron.

"I'm glad we're together tonight." He unfastened his seat belt. "I hardly see you anymore."

"That's because you can't come to the house." She held on to the other reason.

"I don't like this." He removed the keys from the ignition.

"Did I tell you to hit Donte or Mama to call the state?" Maybe she should try to explain to him the price of sticking with him: appointments with Vanessa, criticism from her mother and Denise, the loneliness of loving someone who couldn't now come over and keep her company or spend the night.

After a minute he said. "Come on, let's go in. I've gotta have a beer."

"I need to tell you something." When he paused and turned, her eyes caught his. She quickly rolled her glance toward the windshield and watched the rain drizzle the cars and the street. She didn't want to tell Aaron about the second job and start an argument. Instead, she desired to get out of the car, walk into the bar, sit at their usual table, unless it was occupied, and have a drink too, maybe one of those sugar and alcohol concoctions she often ordered. She wanted to have pleasant conversation with Aaron, or even listen to him as he talked to friends. She desired to have good times with him all of the time. But life kept tossing them trouble. "Wasn't anything else for me to do." She kept looking at the rain.

"What are you talking about?"

"I don't want to move back with Mama and Daddy. I don't want you to pay for a place you can't even step inside of." She wanted the rain to wash away her distress. "I'm twenty-one. I'm gonna try to stand on my own two feet."

"You gonna try to do without me?"

"No! That's not what I'm saying."

"What you got to tell me? You've got another man?"

"Don't ask me stupid questions! I need money."

"There are men out there that will give it to you."

"Cut it out! Why do you have to say things like that? I've got two jobs."

"I told you, no second job."

"Kim told me about this cleaning company she used to work for." Shawanda took a deep breath and struggled on. The man who owns it is named Herbert Carter. He gave me a chance and put me on probation. I started a week ago. I clean offices from six to ten at night, during the week. It's hard work. The whole time I'm on my feet, sweeping and mopping. Mopping is the hardest. It bothers my back. One of the ladies there told me after I get used to it, it won't be so bad. The last thing I do at night is the bathrooms. Never thought I would have to clean toilets for a living."

"You don't have to, Baby."

"Whatever it takes to make it, that's what I gotta do," she said.

"You're being selfish! I'll never get to see you now."

"On weekends," she said. "Know what I really want? It's not two jobs. It's to get married and live in a pretty house in a place where there are no drug dealers. Maybe something in the county. And another child, a girl. I want to stay at home with my children."

"Okay Baby, let's get married."

She was suddenly disgusted by the proposal. "We can't! You can't even be around Donte. We've got nothing right now but problems with Social Services." She shoved opened the door and jumped out of the car. The air chilled her. She folded her arms, as if doing so would shield her from the moisture and the cold. Running down the sidewalk, she paused in front of the bar and waited for Aaron to join her. When he reached her, Shawanda waited for him to open the door. He did, and held it for her. They went inside.

Aaron spoke to the bartender. "Hey, man." He greeted a few of the male customers with a slap of raised hands. The couple went to their usual table. Aaron always sat facing the door.

She looked at him. "The two jobs are only until I get my money straight."

"Since you started listening to Social Services, you don't pay me no attention." He got up. "What do you want from the bar?"

She told him and watched him walk to the bar. He talked to a friend while waiting for the bartender. She knew he was angry with her. Maybe he felt she was slipping away from him? Shawanda asked herself. When he returned with the drinks, a beer for him, a tequila sunrise for her, she attempted to address any fears he may have. "I'm not looking for anybody else. I've got you. I'm staying with you."

"So you say." He lifted the bottle of beer to his mouth while keeping his eyes on her. "You could do better than me."

"What are you talking about? Do you really believe that?" She hoped he didn't.

"Hanging with me, only thing it's gotten you is cleaning toilets."

"Make sense. I care about you. It doesn't have anything to do with the kind of work I do."

"I hear you," he said.

"Believe it." She watched him stare at her and drink the beer. "Say something," she told him.

"Nothing for me to say. You got yourself two jobs." He turned toward the door. "Look, one of my boys just walked in. I'm going holler at him." Aaron got up and left the table.

Shawanda fell back in the chair.

* * *

On Monday, Shawanda got up at seven-thirty and dressed. She then woke Donte and dressed him. Next she made breakfast, threw the dirty dishes into the sink, and took Donte to Kim's. At the mall, she clocked in on the first job. Immediately starting work, she unpacked boxes, tagged clothes, hung them on racks, politely helped customers, and assisted at the cash register. At quitting time she headed downtown. No time for dinner, Shawanda paused at a drive-thru window for a hamburger and soda. Continuing while eating, she hoped she wouldn't get indigestion. At the office building she quickly changed into a uniform and began to empty the wastebaskets. Sweeping and mopping the floors followed that. Shawanda finished the night with the bathrooms. She thought she did it all well.

At ten she headed home, thankful it was only a fifteen-minute drive. She first went to Kim's. Kim talked to Shawanda about her day. Too tired to listen, Shawanda wished she could go straight home and to bed. But she couldn't be impolite to her friend. So she sat and talked. After twenty minutes Kim said goodnight. Shawanda got the sleeping Donte and carried him home. On the way she admitted to herself that this schedule was crazy.

At home she put Donte to bed, went into her room, and fell across her bed. Shawanda promised herself she would only lie there for five minutes, then get up and put on her nightgown, and wrap a scarf around her head. Before the five minutes were up, she had fallen to sleep.

The phone rang. Shawanda was startled out of sleep. Two, three, four rings. "Shut up," she moaned before rolling over and grabbing it.

"Went to work last night?" The voice didn't bother to say hello.

"Aaron, hey."

"Called you at ten-fifteen and ten-thirty last night."

"I was over at Kim's. Please let me go back to sleep."

"It's six o'clock. Don't you have to get up and go to work? I'm headed out myself."

"I don't have to go to work now," she yawned.

"This stuff is making me mad," he said.

She let exhaustion speak for her. "Get over it."

"Don't talk to me like that!" He hung up.

She didn't speak to him for a couple of days after that. Then he started calling again. On the last Friday in April, Aaron phoned just before midnight. Shawanda agreed to meet him the next day at the new movie theater in the county, that is, the extensive suburban area surrounding Baltimore. Her preference was to spend the day in bed. Knowing that with an active child in the house, a day in bed was unobtainable, she quickly gave up on the idea. The next day, she left Donte with Lena and headed to the theater.

"You look tired." It was the first thing Aaron said when seeing her.

"After the movie, I'm going home and take a nap, and after that, get some cleaning done," she told him.

"Well, let's hurry up and see the movie since *you've got other things to do.*"

She had a response for his attitude, but was too tired to sling it at him. Inside the lobby they waited in line. "What movie are we gonna see?" When he told her, she sighed. It was nothing she was interested in.

"What? You don't want to see the movie?" he asked.

"Yeah, yeah, I want to." It was easier to consent than to argue about it. Besides, she would gladly sit through any movie he really wanted to see.

He purchased the tickets. "Want popcorn?"

She shook her head no, too tired to eat. Shawanda waited while Aaron stood in line and got a soda and a small popcorn.

Inside the theater, they searched for two adjacent empty seats. Finding them high up, they mounted the steps and climbed over other patrons. Once they were settled, she wrapped her arms around his right arm, laid her head on his shoulder, and listened to him smack on popcorn. When the previews showed, she watched with interest and promised herself she would see one of the movies. By the time the credits rolled, her eyelids had started feeling heavy. The first scene, with its images of firing guns and exploding cars, as loud as it was, Shawanda managed to close her eyes and block it out. By the third scene, she was snoring.

"Wake up." Aaron shook her.

Shawanda lifted her head and opened her eyes. She saw people standing, moving to the aisles and leaving. "What? They didn't like the movie?"

"It's over. You slept through it."

"How was it?" She rubbed her eyes.

"Okay. If you weren't working two jobs, you might have liked it."

"Let's not go through that again." She stood. She heard Aaron grunt.

Yet, the following day, the first of May, it all seemed worthwhile. Shawanda settled at the kitchen table with her bills and the worn notebook. She assigned a number to each bill, calculated their total, and yelled with delight. For the first time since getting her own home, she was able to pay all of her bills. There was even a little money left over. Shawanda lifted her chest and smiled.

Later that week Aaron called. "Got your bills paid this month?" he asked.

"Why is it you only like me when I'm begging you for something?"

"You never had to beg."

He sounded hurt, she acknowledged.

"Answer the question," he said.

"What question?"

"Did . . . you . . . get . . . your . . . bills . . . paid?"

"Yeah. What about it?"

"Used to be, first of the month all you had to say to me was thank you."

"I'm tired, Aaron."

"You're always tired. Really, now that I'm thinking about it, you don't seem like the kind of woman who would have two jobs."

"What do you mean?"

"How do I know you've got two jobs? How do I know you're not seeing some other Negro and just telling me anything?"

"You think I'm lying to you?" She didn't believe he was serious.

"Cheating, lying, they go together. You haven't heard?"

She felt insulted.

He continued. "You seem more like a woman who needs to have a man around to pay her bills."

She was, Shawanda mentally agreed.

"Did you get yourself another man? I wondered because I know you don't have time for me, anymore."

"Don't talk crazy."

"Oh, now I'm crazy?"

"I didn't say that."

"Did you get money from your father this month?"

"Nope," she said proudly.

"Oh, you paid your own bills?"

"I paid all of them." Realizing he could misinterpret the joy in her voice, she added, "I need you. Don't have nothing to do with bills."

"You don't act like you need me."

"I like being with you." She tried to reassure him.

"You fall asleep when you're with me! I'm about sick of you playing games. And probably lying to me. I think when Social Services told you to keep me away, you starting looking for another Negro. And when you said you had a second job, what you really had was a new man. And the reason you gotta run home right after the movie is because you've got somebody else to run home to. And you can't stay awake in the middle of the day, most likely, because you spent the night fu —."

"Don't say that!"

"Tell me the truth!"

"I'm not hiding anything. What's wrong with you?"

"Oh, now I've got something wrong with me."

"Why don't you get a hold of yourself?"

"Why don't I get a hold of you? And teach you that I ain't nothing to play with?"

She opened her mouth. Calmly explaining her situation to him was proving useless. Her next urge was to lose it and go off on him. But she didn't have the energy. "Call me when you've got all your senses back."

"You better not hung up on me, Woman."

"What do you want me to do when you talk crazy?"

"Don't call me crazy again."

Okay, she mentally consented. She wouldn't call him anything, any time soon. Shawanda slammed the receiver down.

For the next eight days, Shawanda didn't talk to him. On the ninth day, she left the evening job, got Donte from Kim's, came home, put Donte to bed, heard a knock, went downstairs, saw it was Aaron, opened the door, told him she was exhausted. "Go away. You aren't suppose to be here anyway." She started to close the door, but he blocked it with his body and forced his way in. "Get out before Donte sees you."

"He's asleep. He was sleeping when you walked over from Kim's with him."

"You've been sitting outside watching me?"

"Yeah."

That scared her. "Get out."

"You're always tired. You can't call anymore, and you're never at home. Tell me the bastard's name."

"Whose name?"

"The name of the Negro that paid the rent this month."

"What?"

He looked around the room. He walked to the small dining area and flicked on the lights before roaming into the kitchen.

Shawanda stood at the front door, folded her arms, and tapped her feet. When he returned from the kitchen, she said sarcastically, "Hungry?"

He stomped past her and up the stairs.

"Donte's up there," she announced as if it was something he wouldn't already know. He continued up the stairs. She moved to the foot of the staircase and looked up, her eyes following him until he neared the top and disappeared. When Aaron reappeared, she rolled her eyes at him. Coming down the stairs, reaching Shawanda, he brushed against her and didn't apologize.

She spoke under her breath. "What do you think you're doing?"

"I think I'm letting a woman screw me around. And trick me into thinking she's got two jobs when what she's really got is another man."

"Do you think I went to see a man dressed like this?" She pulled at the blouse of her uniform. "You're a jealous fool!"

"I feel like an fool listening to you and Social Services."

"And not too sure about yourself," she added.

He stared a minute. "You just listen to this; if I find out you're laying with another Negro, guess what I'm gonna do to you?"

"Yeah? You listen to this: next time you come to my house, you come to keep me company, not to see if some other man has been here, and not to keep track of me. Got that?"

He took a step toward her. And raised his fist.

She didn't move. "You're acting like you want to hit me." She kept her eyes on him, listened to his heavy breathing. "It better be an act!"

He lowered his hand before turning to the door. He looked back at her and rolled his eyes before leaving and slamming the door behind him.

She cursed him in her head. Suddenly there was a noise behind her. Shawanda swung around.

Donte was at the top of the stairs.

* * *

In the succeeding days, Shawanda didn't speak to Aaron. She loved him. But for Shawanda, who was already overwhelmed, he was one more stressor. Worse, after Donte saw Aaron, Shawanda became convinced Social Services would somehow find out. One afternoon at the mall, she thought she heard Vanessa behind her. Twirling around, it was two women she had never seen before.

But her paranoia mocked her by running and changing into reality the night Kim told her some things.

"Donte was playing in the backyard with my boys," Kim began. "I kept going to the door and looking out when I saw this woman talking to him. I went right out and asked her who she was. She said, 'A social worker on Donte's case.' She was making a routine visit. How did she know he was here?"

"I had to tell them where I left Donte when I worked."

"Anyway, I told her she couldn't talk to him and she had to go. She did."

"Did Donte tell her anything?"

"I don't know."

"Did the social worker say anything else?"

Kim shook her head no.

Shawanda said good night to Kim and her four boys and grabbed Donte. She rushed home as if doing so would somehow protect her from Social Services.

Early the next morning Shawanda answered a knock at the front door. Opening it, she found Vanessa standing on the steps. Shawanda wasn't surprised, only sad and scared.

"Are you going to let me in, or should I stand out here and discuss your business?"

In the living room Shawanda didn't offer the woman a seat. Nor did Vanessa take one, but instead she stood in the middle of the floor. "I spoke to your son yesterday. He says Aaron was here. It sounded to me like the child was asleep when he was awakened in the middle of the night by yelling. You and the boyfriend were either arguing or physically fighting. I came over here to get your explanation."

"He didn't go near Donte."

"He wasn't supposed to be here at all!"

"He pushed his way in. I couldn't stop him. It's hard to make a grown man do what he don't want to."

"That's the point. And when he gets ready, he'll do it again," Vanessa told her.

"No, he won't." Shawanda realized she had said that before.

"You're so wrapped up in this boyfriend, you can't see what's best for your son."

"Are you going to take Donte?"

"I didn't come here to take him, only to get information that I will pass on to the supervisor. You remember her, don't you? Margaret Holmes? She let you keep your son after he was beaten. That's something I would never had done."

"What is she going to do?"

"What do you think she should do after you broke your promise to keep the boyfriend away?"

Leave her in peace, was Shawanda's honest answer. "I don't know!" she said.

"Ms. Holmes is a nice person. Maybe she'll let you keep your son again."

Maybe she would. But Shawanda didn't believe Vanessa sincerely thought so. "You got anything else to ask me?" Shawanda inquired, not caring about the answer. The question had been her polite way of suggesting it was time for Vanessa to leave.

Vanessa smirked. "You women are all alike — weak."

"What women?" Shawanda asked.

Vanessa rolled her eyes, turned, walked to the door and opened it. "I'll let you know what my supervisor says."

After Vanessa went out, Shawanda kicked the door shut. Her body trembled. Maybe Margaret Holmes would take her side again? Or maybe Social Services would come after Donte, and no number of explanations would stop them? Fearing the last possibility more likely, Shawanda felt like she was being chased. Maybe she should run and hide — with Donte. Looking around the room, she concluded the house was unsafe and considered places to take her son. Coming up with none, she made a decision. A decision to fight. Vanessa wasn't taking Donte. She would see to that.

The next day, out of necessity, she took Donte to Kim's and told her about Vanessa's visit. "Keep Donte in the house, please."

"I will," Kim promised.

"If that social worker comes for him, tell her I didn't bring him here."

"I will." Kim placed her hand on Shawanda's shoulder.

"I wish Social Services would leave me alone," Shawanda cried.

Before leaving Kim's home for work, Shawanda hugged her son. That day there was no peace for her.

6

Margaret was on the phone with a therapist on one of the cases when Vanessa knocked. Margaret waved her in. Soon ending the conversation, she turned to Vanessa, who approached the desk with a file.

"There's a problem. I went out to see the Matthews mother today." Vanessa passed the file.

Margaret took and opened it. Looking at her own notes, she remembered a snowy February morning and a young woman named Shawanda Matthews.

"I don't know why, but you let her keep the child with the promise to keep the boyfriend away," Vanessa said.

Flipping through the pages, Margaret saw Shawanda's handwritten note and read: *I promise to keep Aaron away.* Margaret's eyes dropped. She imagined the boyfriend had returned to the house and this time seriously injured the child. "Is Donte okay?"

"Yes. I saw him at the neighbor's. It's how I know the boyfriend was in the house and there was a fight of some sort."

"What happened?"

"I'm not totally certain. I spoke to Ms. Matthews. She admits the boyfriend was there. Apparently he forced his way in, wasn't there long, and didn't go near the child."

"Do you have any reason to disbelieve what Ms. Matthews told you?"

"No. But he shouldn't have been there at all."

Margaret again glanced at Shawanda's signed promise and was disappointed.

"Lucky he didn't hurt the child." Vanessa stood near the desk.

Margaret didn't appreciate Vanessa's rubbing it in. "Exactly, nothing else happened."

"That's not the point!" Vanessa said.

"But if he was there a few minutes and told to get out —."

"We can't trust her!"

"Is Donte better off separated from his mother?" Margaret wondered aloud.

"We can't wait until something else happens."

Margaret leaned back, swirled to her left, and looked toward the window. Outside the day was sunny. She had a decision to make and couldn't be timid about it. When Donte was left in the home, the only safeguard put in place had been the promise to keep the boyfriend away. Now, with that violated, Margaret didn't know if Donte was in danger.

"You told her to keep the boyfriend away; she didn't." Vanessa persisted. "There's nothing else to discuss."

Margaret kept her glance toward the window, knowing Vanessa was right.

"I believe we should place him in foster care immediately." Vanessa folded her arms.

"Are there any relative resources?"

"The grandmother made the original report."

"Will she take Donte?"

"I can check. If not, there's a foster home available."

Margaret took a deep breath and turned from the window. She picked up the file, closed and handed it back to

Vanessa. Sometimes performing the harder parts of her job bothered Margaret. Yet she had to do them. "Take custody. If possible, first place him with the grandmother. If not, foster care."

* * *

Shawanda was at the store clearing out the dressing rooms and replacing clothes on the racks when Joyce, the young manager, rushed up to her and said, "You have a call. It's an emergency."

Shawanda hurried to the phone. Her first thought was that something had happened to Donte. Picking up the receiver, she heard Kim's voice.

"Don't be mad at me, Shawanda. I couldn't help it."

"What happened?" Shawanda felt she already knew and was only requesting the details.

"That social worker came to the house. I told her exactly what you told me to say. But she acted like she didn't believe me. 'Why are you asking me about Donte?' I said. 'Find his mother and ask her.' She just looked at me funny and went away. After she was gone, I was thinking she might come back. I got real scared. I figured I should hide Donte just in case. I thought about Georgia, you know, who lives around the corner. She's eight months pregnant and just stopped working. I thought about taking Donte over there. I got my youngest and Donte and went out the house. It was about fifteen minutes after the social worker had left. I didn't think she might still be out there. I didn't look around before I went out. I got a couple of houses down when she came up behind me. I told her, 'You can't take Shawanda's child. She only has one!' That social worker said, 'I'm not taking him. They are.' She pointed at something. I looked around and saw a police car coming down the street. She must have called them on the cell phone and sat in her car waiting. She showed the police her I.D. and told them she needed to take Donte. They asked me what was going on. I told them I was in charge of Donte and they would have to take him from you. The police said the social worker didn't have to wait for you. She took Donte and put him in the car. He didn't cry or anything. I'm sorry, Shawanda."

"No, I'm sorry. I shouldn't have got you caught up in this. Thanks for trying to help."

"What are you gonna do?"

"I'm gonna get my son." She said goodbye to Kim, and hung up the phone.

"Do you have to leave?" the manger asked.

"I'm gonna get my son." Shawanda repeated. Her mind was starting to disconnect from her physical surroundings. She stiffly went to her locker, got her handbag, and walked toward the door.

"Clock out first," Joyce said.

Shawanda retraced her steps and clocked out. The walk through the mall and the parking lot seemed endless, the interior of the car too hot, the traffic too burdensome, the drive to Vanessa's office too hard a thing for anyone to have to do. Finally she stood in front of the receptionist. "I have to see Miss Graves."

"Do you have an appointment?"

"Do I have an appointment?" Shawanda repeated, trying to listen to the words this time. "I had one before, but not today."

"I'll see if she's in." The woman picked up the phone, and pushed buttons.

"She must be in. She has my son. She's gotta give him back."

After talking and hanging up the receiver, the woman said, "Ms. Graves will come down shortly."

Shawanda moved away from the desk and began to pace. She soon returned. "Where's Miss Graves?"

"The elevators are slow, Ma'am."

"Tell her to use the stairs." Shawanda noticed the woman's smirk, but kicked the image from her head; too cluttered was her mind.

Vanessa arrived and simply said, "Follow me."

Shawanda submitted. On the elevator, silence ran about and was generally annoying. In the small, congested office, Vanessa sat behind a file-covered desk, and motioned to a nearby chair. But Shawanda was distracted, didn't register the motion, and continued standing.

"We placed your son with your mother."

"He should be with me."

"You're not to remove him. If you try to do so, we'll immediately take the child and place him in foster care."

"But Donte won't like foster care."

"You're entitled to an emergency hearing before a judge within two working days. Your hearing will be on Friday afternoon at the Clarence Mitchell Courthouse, room 695. Three things are done at this hearing. First, if you have an attorney, he or she will enter an appearance. You're entitled to a lawyer. You can apply at the Public Defender's Office. Secondly, the judge will decide where Donte will go between Friday and the next hearing. If he decides you can't protect him from the boyfriend, he will give temporary custody to Social Services. We can do anything with that custody. If —."

"Maybe the judge won't give you custody."

Vanessa grinned. "As I was saying, if we decide the grandmother is inappropriate, we can place him in foster care without further court review. Thirdly, another court date will be set. It'll be anywhere from eight to twelve weeks away, depending on how crowded the court dockets are. That hearing is essentially a trial. Social Services proves you're unfit to raise your son, and we'll get custody indefinitely."

"Unfit? Who do you people think you are? I took good care of Donte. You give him back!"

"Would you like me to call security?" Vanessa picked up the telephone.

"How can you do this to us?" Tasting her own tears, Shawanda realized she was crying. She considered explaining her strong ties to Donte, ties formed when he was life moving and kicking inside of her. She had wondered then what he would look like and what sort of an adult he would become. Maybe he would make a difference in the world. "I'm getting my son back."

"Leave my office." Vanessa held the phone.

Shawanda looked at Vanessa, and rolled her eyes. She didn't know what else to do, so she did what she was told. She left. In the hallway the wait for the elevator seemed unbearable. The ride on it annoying. In the parking lot Shawanda couldn't find her keys and ended up emptying the handbag's contents onto the hood. No keys. Checking her pockets, she found them there. Inside the car, starting it, she tried to concentrate on driving. Twice missing her turn, Shawanda drove blocks out of the way.

Finally reaching home, she first called Lena, who assured her Donte was well. Next, she dialed Aaron and told him what had happened.

"I'm sorry, Baby," he said.

"I'm sick of you being sorry."

"He's only at Lena's." Aaron reminded. "If she keeps him, we can be together."

"Why would she keep him? She's not his mother!"

"I love you, Baby," he said.

"My son's not with me."

"As long as Donte's in the house, I'm out. The state putting him with Lena is the best thing for us. Forget about the court date. Let him stay with Lena."

"You keep talking like that and you'll be the only one I'll forget about. I'm getting my son back." She said it aloud to convince herself as well as Aaron of Donte's return.

"Want me to take off and come to court with you?" he offered.

"No." She didn't want to see him right now.

"I know one thing," he began, "you're my woman, and we *will* be together."

She tried to listen to his words but couldn't concentrate long enough to appreciate their various layers of meaning. She wanted to promise him that although things were bad now, she wouldn't give up on their relationship. But when Shawanda spoke, all that sprang out was, "I'll talk to you again."

Shortly, she went to Kim's house.

"When I had a problem with the landlord," Kim said after Shawanda told her about the visit to Vanessa's office, "I went to the Lawyer's Referral Service. They had a list of lawyers who take one or two cases a year for free. They do it as a service to the community. I was happy with my lawyer. Want the address and number of the Service? Maybe you can get the same lawyer."

"Sure." Shawanda nodded, thinking that getting a lawyer would be a good idea. She waited while Kim got the information. Kim returned and handed her the card.

"Don't listen to Social Services," Kim continued. "You're a good mother."

Shawanda appreciated her friend, thanked her, and went home. There she tossed water on her face and ran out to the evening job. Pushing to get the work done, she calculated the hours until quitting time. Eventually, back home, quickly dressing for bed, Shawanda remembered she had eaten only a sandwich all day. But she was too mentally preoccupied to pay attention to her hunger. Setting the alarm clock, she looked forward to the morning.

She woke before the alarm went off. She jumped immediately out of bed and rushed to the bathroom and into the shower. Minutes later, she dressed in a short jeans skirt and a clinging orange blouse. Rushing out of the house, she stopped first at the gas station. Shawanda easily found the Lawyer's Referral Service's office. But it was closed. The sign on the door said the office didn't open until eight-thirty. Glancing at her watch, she saw it was only seven forty-five. Shawanda paced in front of the office, then decided to walk around the block. As she passed people headed to work, she felt anxious and disturbed. Promptly at eight-thirty she returned to the office.

A short, brown haired woman greeted her with a cheery smile. "I'm Patsy O'Brien."

"Hey. I need a lawyer for tomorrow," Shawanda said. "I'll take the one my friend Kim had."

"Your friend Kim? Oh, sorry, it doesn't work that way. We have a list of available attorneys. I have to start at the top of that list. But tomorrow? That's nearly impossible."

Shawanda's legs suddenly felt weak. *Nearly impossible.* Her mind repeated the words. But within seconds her determination was back. She lifted her eyes, looked at Patsy, and said, "They took my son. Please help me."

"Okay, okay. Let's see. First, here, fill out the forms. When you're finished, I'll look them over and see what I can do."

It was hard, but Shawanda tried to calm herself. She sat down and filled out the forms, supplying information on her income and legal problem.

Afterwards Patsy made a telephone call. "I know it's short notice," she told the person on the other end. "Just thought I would try." She hung up, and looked at Shawanda. "I'll make five or six more calls. That's all I can do."

Shawanda nodded and thanked her for the effort. She remembered Miss Graves had mentioned the Public Defender's Office. If Patsy couldn't help, she would go there. Maybe Patsy knew the address.

Next call, Patsy had no success. The following two, Patsy got the same negative response. On the fifth try she greeted the person on the other end. "Hi, Nina. Let me tell you about the situation I have here." After explaining, Patsy looked at Shawanda and said, "I'm on hold. Nina's checking with her boss. Apparently, he's not scheduled in court tomorrow, has no appointments in the afternoon, but has a big meeting in the morning. She doesn't know how long it will last."

Shawanda moved to the edge of the chair and almost crossed her fingers.

"Thanks, Nina." Patsy hung up. "Good news! Mr. Cooke has agreed to talk to you at four o'clock this afternoon. He's such a nice guy. Have you heard of Charles Cooke?"

Shawanda shook her head no.

"He's a great trial lawyer! Won a complex murder case last year. It was in the papers. Did you read about it?"

"Don't read the papers."

"Anyway, his uncle was a very prominent judge. His father — he's deceased now — was also known for his trial skills. Now the son has the practice. He takes only one referral from us a year. This year, you're it." She wrote something down. "Here's his address and telephone number."

Shawanda took the paper and looked at it. Hopeful, she smiled. "Thank you."

"Good luck."

Leaving, Shawanda hurried to the first job. She left it early to rush to the lawyer's office. Arriving at the downtown Franklin Street office, she promptly found the two-story brick building, which clearly had been originally built as a home. The scent of garlic and onions emerged from the restaurant next door. Ringing the bell, she heard a woman's voice over the intercom. Shawanda stated her business and was buzzed in.

Inside she stood in the foyer. In front of her was a winding staircase. She looked up at the impressive chandelier, then down at the polished hardwood floor. What a beautiful hallway, she thought.

"Good afternoon. I'm Nina Rossini, Mr. Cooke's secretary." The tall, slender, dark-haired woman, who wore a pretty floral dress, appeared in the doorway and extended her hand. After they shook, she said, "Please come in."

Shawanda followed her into the front office.

"I have forms for you to fill out and sign." Nina handed them to her attached to a clipboard, and included a pen.

Shawanda sat on the soft, comfortable black leather sofa, completed the paperwork, and returned it to Nina. Nina placed the papers in a folder and disappeared into an adjacent office. Shawanda surveyed her surroundings. The ceilings were high, the windows elongated. Oil paintings decorated the walls, and tall plants stood near the windows. The furnishings were black and tan. The room was pretty, she concluded.

Shawanda recalled Patsy's words. Last year, Mr. Cooke was in the newspaper. His uncle was a judge, his father a big-time lawyer. Mr. Cooke was obviously successful and rich. She asked herself, why would he care about the state hassling a poor woman?

Suddenly, she began to cry. She wept for her son, even though he was not far away. Shawanda felt she had lost something greater than the legal custody of him. She had lost the right to look after Donte the way a mother would. And then there was the label, which was as real to her as if it had been carved across her forehead, 'You are a bad mother.' It was unfair. While it was hard being abandoned by the child's father, hard raising a son and she couldn't have done it without help, yet everyday Shawanda had persistent.

"Good afternoon, Ms. Matthews." The voice was deep and gentle.

Wiping her eyes with the back of her hand, Shawanda looked up and saw a tall, bald, husky man with a pale complexion and small gray eyes. He was dressed in a tan tailored suit.

"I'm Charles Cooke."

"The state took my son."

"Please come into my office."

Shawanda walked into the next room. The first things she noticed were the slender black desk and soft gray leather chairs. On a side wall were two framed newspaper clippings.

Charles didn't sit behind the paper-cluttered desk, but instead sat in the chair stationed next to Shawanda.

She began to tell him about Aaron, the milk, Lena, Margaret's coming to the house, and what ensued. Finishing, she awaited his response.

"Sorry, I've never done that type of case before. Primarily I represent medium-sized businesses. Occasionally I'll take on a criminal case. The few referrals I've gotten from the Lawyer's Service have been minor, routine matters."

"Oh." Her head dropped. "I need someone to go into court."

"Court! I definitely do that. And I do it well. Your case is at the Clarence Mitchell Courthouse. Ever been inside it?"

"Nope."

"The building's over a hundred years old. It lacks windows, is poorly lit and gloomy. People from all walks of life pack its hallways. Shackled prisoners escorted by guards are a usual sight. But I pay it all little attention. It's just the courthouse! And the courtrooms. Some are distinguished looking, some dismal. I could freeze in one and sweat in the one next door. But when the cases get going! Some I should lose — the client has no legal wings to fly with. Some I should win, the opposing side should never have started the case. But the ones in between! Those get my adrenaline going. If I do a good job, I'll win. If not —."

"You don't win all your cases?"

"Lawyers do that on television! Besides, that's no fun. Know what's really exciting? It's when the other side has put on their case, leans back, and starts to chew on victory. I put on my case — and pull victory right out of their startled mouths!"

With refreshed hope, Shawanda tried to keep up with him. "Will you help me?"

"Sure." He grabbed a notebook and pen from the desk. "Tell me about Aaron, you, your mother, and Social Services. Tell me everything. I need to know what the other side will use against you."

She complied. Afterwards she asked, "Do you think Social Services can keep Donte away from me?"

"I won't lie to you. Almost anything can happen inside of a courtroom."

7

The following day, because parking near the courthouse was hard to find and expensive, Margaret and Vanessa took the transportation van from their office. Hopping out of the van into the whispering rain, they entered the courthouse through the side entrance reserved for employees. They flashed identification cards to the sheriff. Walking down the hall, they saw and greeted a fellow social worker before taking the elevator to the sixth floor. There, in the conference room with its small desks, clicking computers, ringing phones, humming copier, buzzing fax machine, and chatting people, Margaret found a vacant space.

"How many cases today?" Margaret asked Vanessa.

Pulling folders from a bag, Vanessa answered, "Thirteen."

"Any particularly nasty ones?"

"Only the usual," Vanessa sighed.

"I have cases with you two today." Iris Harper, a lawyer for Social Services for six years, approached. The short blonde woman, who was dressed in a gray business suit, pulled out a chair and sat down. "Which ones do you want to discuss first?"

"Shawanda Matthews." Vanessa gave her all of the details.

"All she had to do was keep the boyfriend away?" Iris repeated.

"That's all," Vanessa confirmed.

"And sweet-hearted Margaret gave her a chance to keep the boy. Great, now I can use that against her."

"Can you?" Vanessa asked.

"Sure, we did everything to help her. She won't cooperate."

"Donte's with his maternal grandmother," Margaret told Iris.

"Even better. He's not in foster care. Why would any judge object to a child visiting his grandmother? This one's an easy win. It should take about ten minutes of the court's time. What's next?"

They had progressed to case number nine when Margaret happened to spot a tall, well-built man in a tailored light green suit entering the room. She thought him rugged, and striking in appearance. Because his eyes scanned the room as if he were looking for something or someone, she asked, "May I help you?"

"I have the Matthews case."

"Who are you?" Iris inquired.

"Charles Cooke. I represent Ms. Matthews."

"We're on the Matthews case." Margaret introduced the three of them.

"Shawanda works in a mall," Vanessa said. "How can she afford private counsel?"

"It's a referral through the lawyer's service."

"I'm certain you have paying clients who need you." Iris smiled. "If we have an agreement, I can call your case first and get you out of here quickly."

"Certainly. I can agree to the immediate return of Donte to his mother."

"We just took custody of him," Vanessa said. "Why would we return him now?"

Before Charles could reply, Iris interrupted. "Here's the child's Legal Aid attorney, Princess Williams. Let's see what her position is."

The tall woman with straightened hair neared and greeted them with a smile. After Vanessa filled her in, Princess faced Charles. "Donte should have been removed after the grandmother first reported the abuse." Then to Margaret, "Sorry to disagree with you."

"Margaret's not afraid to make hard decisions," Iris said. "It's one of the reasons she's such a good supervisor." Then to Charles, "Ever been before Judge Marco?"

"Once, years ago, in a criminal case, I recall he yelled throughout the proceeding. And at sentencing he used very descriptive nouns to tell the client what he thought of him."

"He hasn't changed." Iris glanced at her watch. "Please excuse us. We were in the middle of discussing other cases."

"In a minute," Charles responded. "What are Social Services' plans in the Matthews case?"

"Let's see," Iris began. "We've got custody of Donte right now. You want to get him back. But how can you with an unsympathetic judge and all sides in opposition? Get my point? All your client has is the graciousness of Social Services. Be nice, and maybe we'll throw your client a few good things."

"Nothing happened to Donte when Aaron came to the house. Can we resolve this matter in favor of Ms. Matthews? Maybe make it part of a court order to keep Aaron away?"

Iris looked at Vanessa.

"Absolutely not," Vanessa said.

"Look," Iris told Charles, "I've done maybe fifteen hundred of these cases. The reality is always the same. If something happens to the child and it reaches the paper —."

"I know, Social Services looks negligent."

"And someone loses their job," Iris explained. "Bottom line, no way we're agreeing to the child's return. Best I can do for you is to send the mother and boyfriend to counseling. Maybe in a year or so, she'll get the child back."

"A year!" Charles responded. "Not good enough."

"Don't toss our mercy so quickly," Iris warned. "Your client may need it."

"Maybe you should agree with us," Princess said. "We'll let the judge know she's cooperating."

Charles clutched his black leather briefcase. "I'll leave you to your other cases now." He turned and started toward the door.

Margaret watched Charles walk away.

After he was out of sight, Vanessa faced Iris and asked, "Think he'll talk to Shawanda and they'll agree?"

"I remember reading about him last year. I'm certain he'll put up a fight. I'll put his case last so I can give it my full attention."

"He's never seen you inside a courtroom," Vanessa said. "Doesn't know what he's in for."

Vanessa and Iris laughed. Margaret didn't join them. In fact, she looked forward to seeing Charles in action for reasons she didn't bother to examine. Big fight or not, by the end of the day Social Services would win. They usually did.

* * *

Outside, the weather worsening, the rain kicked hard as Shawanda approached the front door of the courthouse, her clothes damp, and her body icy despite the umbrella. Inside she waited in line and had her handbag checked. She passed through the scanner. The procedure made her uncomfortable. Mincing down the hall, she thought the building looked cave-like. She searched the distressed faces of the people she passed.

Shawanda stopped a man and got directions to the elevators. On one of the elevators, Shawanda squeezed through the group of people to a corner. On the sixth floor she couldn't find the courtroom and wandered for a seemingly long time. She saw Charles standing in a crowded hallway. Somewhere an infant cried.

"I spoke to the other lawyers," he said soon after she reached him. "Social Services won't voluntarily return Donte. They suggest you give him up now, cooperate, and maybe in a year or so, you'll get him back. Also, the judge who'll hear the case isn't known for his patience."

Shawanda's head dropped. "I've already lost."

"Perk up. Winners and losers aren't declared until the end."

"Should I just agree?" Shawanda looked at him.

"Want to give up already?"

"I don't like it here. It's scary."

"My guess is, if you lose the case today, you'll have a chance of getting Donte back in a year."

"If I lose, at least he's with my mother."

"Listen, we aren't losing, or agreeing, or giving up," Charles said. "Instead, let's made it a bloody fight."

"I couldn't take that right now."

"All you have to do is just sit there. I'll do all the work."

The words echoed in her brain. *Just sit there.* Charles went into the courtroom. Shawanda followed. She sat on a bench in the back of the cold, crowded, ugly room, finding the mere sitting unpleasant. She watched as the black haired Judge Anthony Marco walked out. Cases were called, completed, and the room's population gradually decreased. At four-thirty she considered her second job. At five, her case was the only one left. Charles signaled for her to join him at the trial table.

After her case was called, Iris spoke to the judge first. She started with the bruises and ended with "Social Services must protect this child because his mother won't."

Princess rose and agreed with Iris.

Charles spoke last. Standing, he said, "After Social Services investigated the original report, Donte was left with his mother. Nothing has happened to him since. Sure, Aaron forced his way in. He was asked to leave and complied."

The judge leaned back. "Thank you, Mr. Cooke. Anything to add Ms. Harper?"

"Yes, your Honor." Iris again stood. "I disagree with Mr. Cooke. A lot has happened. On that night, there was shouting, maybe even violence. A child was awakened and frightened —."

"Ms. Matthews and Donte are victims." Charles had remained standing. "Let's not punish them."

"She is not a victim," Iris hissed. "She chose to date an abuser."

"She chose to protect her son."

"Why don't you tell the court, Mr. Cooke," Iris taunted, "if your client is still dating this man who beat and bruised her son?"

Judge Marco turned to Charles. "Is she, Mr. Cooke?"

Charles looked straight at the judge. "She and Aaron are dating."

"As long as they're dating, he's a threat to Donte," Iris said.

"This isn't totally about Ms. Matthews or whom she dates," Charles continued. "It's also about a child who has never seen his biological father, but is bonded to his mother. Separation will be traumatic for him."

"Miss Williams, anything to add?" the judge asked.

"As long as Ms. Matthews dates child abusers, Donte's in danger."

Shawanda jumped up. "Aaron's not a child abuser. He lost it once. And I'm not the bad person they're calling me." Suddenly, she dropped back into the chair, feeling no one would ever understand.

"Counsel, tell your client to control herself," Judge Marco instructed Charles.

Charles didn't tell her anything, Shawanda noticed.

Judge Marco continued. "Should I wait until he loses his temper again, Mr. Cooke?"

"Donte's mother has never harmed —."

"What's your point, counsel? She was there when her boyfriend abused the child. Besides, Social Services tells me the child is with the maternal grandmother. Is she unfit for custody?"

"Not at all."

"Then what's the problem? The child's visiting his grandmother."

"He belongs with his mother, and in his own home."

"Why should I send the child back there, Mr. Cooke?" the judge asked.

"Ms. Matthew is a loving and caring mother. Only one thing has happened in Donte's entire four years. She and the grandmother stopped it. Aaron was asked to leave, and he did. Ms. Matthews can and will protect Donte."

The judge sighed. "You think there's something here worth salvaging?"

"Yes."

"Should we try again, Ms. Harper?"

"Until he seriously injures the child?" Iris replied.

The judge leaned forward, rested his elbows on the bench, and appeared to ponder the situation. "The child is four and bonded to his mother. She has never done anything to him. Is that correct, Ms. Harper?"

"Yes, as far as we know, Your Honor."

Marco continued. "If the boyfriend somehow manages to stay away, there isn't a problem."

"That's correct, Your Honor," Charles said.

Rolling his glance toward Charles, Judge Marco continued. "Your client really wants her son back?"

"Yes."

"If I return him, she won't like the conditions."

"Ms. Matthews will abide by any condition set by the court."

"She'll have to attend counseling and parenting classes and make face-to-face contact with the social worker once every week. If the boyfriend returns, instead of opening the door she will call the police and as soon as possible inform Social Services. If anything else happens, even something small, Social Services shall take immediate custody of the child and urgently return this case to court. Then Ms. Matthews can wave farewell to custody of her son. Got that so far, Mr. Cooke?"

"Yes, Your Honor."

"Does your client still want her son back?"

"Yes, Your Honor."

"I'm issuing an order controlling her conduct. If any boyfriend so much as spanks this child, I will have your client dragged into court faster than it takes to say 'Please Judge, don't,' and I will find her in contempt. And we know where she's going then."

Controlling orders? Contempt? Shawanda didn't understand. She tugged at Charles's sleeve. "Where would I go then?"

"Madam Clerk," Judge Marco was saying, "give them the next court date."

"July tenth."

Charles wrote in his calendar before leaning toward Shawanda and answering, "Jail."

8

The following Thursday, Margaret was working at her desk when the phone rang. Picking it up, she said, "Services to Family and Children Division."

"Ms. Holmes?"

"Speaking."

"I'm Charles Cooke."

"The infamous Mr. Cooke. Still reveling in victory?"

"Actually, I've moved on to the next case."

"Iris was very surprised by her loss." So was Margaret.

"She tried."

"Iris thought you won because when you were shot down, you quickly recovered."

"It's my job."

"You did it well." Margaret relaxed in the chair.

"Thanks. But I didn't call to rub it in. Minutes ago I spoke to Vanessa Graves. I understand your agency's files are available by law."

"By court order."

"I could get a court order, but —."

"You thought you would call first and ask, maybe saving yourself the trouble of —."

"I lose nothing by asking."

"The Matthews case is only a few months old. There's very little in the file. No harm can come from your reviewing it." She meditated on the subject aloud. "Please make an appointment with Vanessa. I'll let her know I okayed it."

"I tried to make an appointment. Ms. Graves declined, and in a very interesting way."

"Did she tell you in so many words to go to hell?"

"How did you know?"

"Vanessa hates losing. When would you like to see the file?"

"Wednesday at ten."

Margaret flipped the pages of her desk calendar and wrote him in. "I'll be here then. I can show you the file."

"Two other things. My client doesn't have an appointment for counseling or parenting classes."

"I realized yesterday that Vanessa has been too busy to set them up. I will personally complete those arrangements today."

"Judge Marco ordered weekly face-to-face contacts. Shouldn't Ms. Matthews have weekly appointments?" Charles asked.

"His rather creative order didn't specify."

"Can she get an appointment for today at four-thirty?"

"Vanessa has home visits this afternoon. But I can see Ms. Matthews."

"In the future I can have my secretary call weekly for appointments."

"Don't trust your client to keep up with them?"

"She's young and overly stressed. The first time I saw her, she was in tears. Thanks for the help."

After the conversation ended, Margaret called Iris.

* * *

At four-thirty Margaret greeted a disheveled looking Shawanda. "You look tired," Margaret noted. "Have you been sleeping?"

Shawanda shook her head.

"Have you lost weight since last week?"

"Don't know."

"What did you eat today?" Margaret asked out of concern for the young woman.

"I had half a hamburger at lunch. I couldn't get it all down. I hope the Judge doesn't send me to jail."

"You have to take better care of yourself. Here, I wrote down the time and place for the counseling and the classes." Margaret handed her the piece of paper. "Have you seen Aaron?"

"No. I've talked to him on the telephone."

"Phone contact is okay. You only have to keep him away from Donte. It'll be great for Aaron to come with you to the classes."

"I think he will. He loves me."

"I'm sure. Would you like to come back this time next week? You can see me. I'm available."

"Yeah. Thanks. I don't think Miss Graves likes me."

"She's a little burnt out on all of her cases. Can you go home and rest now?"

"I have to go to my second job, cleaning offices."

"That's a lot of physical activity on an empty stomach."

"Last week I was an hour late because of court. I'm slowing down at work. But I can't get fired because I need the money."

Margaret imagined being in Shawanda's position. Filled with sympathy, Margaret desired a happy ending for the young mother. She extended her hand. "See you next Thursday."

* * *

The next day Margaret was gathering files to take home for the weekend when April dropped in.

"I'm dragging my husband to this new restaurant in D.C. We may hit a few museums first." April stood in the doorway. "Would you like to come?"

"Mother wants to see a movie. I promised."

"Another Saturday night with your mother?"

"Looking forward to it."

"Bet you're taking work home, too."

"Only three files."

"Please, Margaret, let me give it one last try? I want to help."

"Enjoy D.C."

"You're too nice a person to end up a lonely old maid."

"I didn't know anyone still used that term."

April sighed. "Have a good weekend."

Margaret waved, packed up her things and went home. As she unlocked her apartment door, the telephone rang. Margaret rushed to get it.

"Hi, Mother."

"Hello, Dear. I have a favor to ask of you."

"Sure. Anything."

"When I told Milton I wanted to see that movie, he insisted on taking me. I couldn't tell him no. Do you mind if he joins us tomorrow?"

"Of course not. But you two should go without me. I have work to do. Besides, I would feel awkward."

"I can call him back and arrange something for Sunday."

"No, go, have fun."

"Are you sure?"

"See you Sunday at mass."

After the conversation ended, Margaret slumped into the nearest chair. There were only three files to work on. She decided to spend the rest of Saturday cleaning the apartment, although it didn't need it. Margaret could clean out the closets. She hadn't done that in two months. Taking a deep breath, Margaret decided she had to do something about her life.

* * *

At ten o'clock on Wednesday when the receptionist buzzed Margaret, she responded, "Yes?"

"Charles Cooke is here to see you."

"Please send him up." Margaret neatly put away the papers she had been working on and grabbed the Matthews file from the corner of the desk.

There was a knock on the door.

Margaret glanced toward the door. "Please come in." She walked around the desk with the file.

"I inadvertently walked into the room with all of the state secrets."

"There are no secrets here, Mr. Cooke." She smiled.

He looked toward the wall at her framed diplomas. "You graduated from Hopkins. So did I." He looked closer. "Although I graduated several years earlier. And the University of Maryland."

"Did you go there?"

"No. After Hopkins I went to Georgetown Law."

"Nice. Please follow me. You can sit in the conference room."

Reaching the large room whose only contents were a gray oblong table and eight brown chairs, she gave him the file. Margaret watched the gray-suited gentleman place his briefcase on the table, sit down, open it, and take out a pad and fancy pen.

Turning to Margaret, he asked, "Are you going to stand there and watch me?"

"Actually, I think I'll sit awhile." She sat two chairs down. "Don't trust me?"

"The file is state property . . . and, well, you *are* a lawyer. What are you looking for anyway?"

"Anything that will help win the next round."

"I'm sure. But how bold of you to come right out and say it."

"You asked. Should I have lied?"

"What are you writing?"

"About Aaron. No criminal record. No prior abuse complaints. You sent him a letter and he signed and returned it, agreeing to go to counseling. He's cooperative."

"Of course he's cooperative. He's trying to hold on to his girlfriend. And if he doesn't go to counseling, Iris will use it against him." She watched Charles examine each page in the folder.

"There's a new social worker assigned to the case?" he asked, looking at notes in the file.

"Danielle Wallace. She's a recent graduate who was hired three weeks ago. Friday Vanessa didn't come in or call. I had to contact her. Vanessa said she was fed up. She doesn't think she'll ever come back to work here."

"You're firing her?"

"I've never fired anyone."

"I would have gotten rid of her the hour she didn't show up or call."

Margaret shyly shook her head. "I told her to think about it. If she really wants to quit, I would accept her resignation."

Charles closed the file and returned it.

"Found anything helpful?" Margaret inquired.

"All pieces of information have the potential of becoming useful." Then, "What would Social Services do if Shawanda managed to do everything right?"

"She'll do well just to stay out of jail. But if somehow . . . . I guess we would eventually close the case."

"Thanks for showing me the file."

"Helping the enemy. Iris won't appreciate that. Although when I told her there wasn't much in the file, she said there was no harm in showing it."

"Iris has this problem —."

"She does?"

"Underestimating her opponent." He stood, briefcase in hand. "I'll contact Ms. Wallace to get a sense of her direction on the case." He walked to the door, turned, and asked in a deep, gentle voice, "Do you think Donte will be okay?"

Margaret stood and faced him. "Wondering if you won a case you shouldn't have?"

"It has happened."

"As far I can tell, it was an isolated incident."

"I'm hoping." He smiled briefly and extended his hand. They shook, and he left.

Returning to her office, Margaret admitted to herself, although seldom noticing White males in the past, she was attracted to Charles. But he was the enemy. He was an advocate for the opposing side who had even gotten victory in the first round. Returning to work, she quickly forgot him.

* * *

The succeeding week, when Herbert Carter called Shawanda aside, she was so tired that following him took effort. They stood at the end of the hall.

"You're taking a long time to half clean," the brown skinned man began. "Last night I had someone else do the bathrooms because you never would have gotten to them. What's the problem?"

"I have two jobs. I have to see a social worker every week. My best friend and my mother are telling me to leave Aaron. Really, I can do the work. All I need is one good night's sleep."

"Why can't you sleep?"

"The judge might put me in jail. I have to keep my boyfriend away from Donte. But Aaron never promised to stay away. When I can't see him at night because I'm working here, he thinks I'm with another man. I told Aaron if he comes back to the house, I'll go to jail. He just says, 'Ah, Baby, nobody's putting you in jail.' I'm always tired, but at least the bills are paid. I don't have to get money from Aaron or Daddy."

"I'm sorry you're having all these problems. But I have a business here. I have to get the work done."

"I'll do better." Shawanda wrung her hands. "Promise."

"Listen, Miss Matthews, I would like to keep you on. But your work is starting to drag. I'm not doing you or me a favor by letting you stay."

"Please don't fire me!"

"I'm sorry. I have to let you go." He turned and quickly walked away.

Shawanda stood in the middle of the hallway. She felt like a failure. With great effort, she managed to organized her thoughts long enough to gather her things and get to the car. At home, after putting Donte to bed, she went to bed. While angry about the firing, something in her knew, but had trouble acknowledging, she had started doing poorly on both jobs. With the loss of the second job, Shawanda had to admit she would now get a chance to rest in the evenings and take better care of Donte.

The first night after the firing, Shawanda came home from work at the mall. She made dinner and forced herself to eat. By nine o'clock, Shawanda was in bed and asleep. Yet, it was a week before she felt rested.

* * *

At the end of May, Shawanda paced in front the Social Services office. Her watch read two minutes before seven. Aaron was late for parenting classes. She cursed under her breath. Just as she decided to give up, Shawanda noticed his car pulled into the parking lot. She watched him get out and saunter toward her as if he had nothing to do and no place to get to. She cursed again. When he reached her, she rolled her eyes at him.

"Come on, Baby. You know what dirty work mixing cement is. I had to go home and change."

She sucked her teeth. Knowing there wasn't any time to argue, she turned and hurried inside. She walked up to the receptionist. "Where are the parenting classes?"

"Sign in."

Shawanda signed her name, and Aaron's.

"Go to the end of this hall and make a left. The room is three doors down on your right."

Shawanda and Aaron wandered down the hall and soon found the room. It had bright yellow walls. It's only furnishings were a table stacked with booklets and fourteen chairs that were placed in a circle in the center of the room. Approaching the circle, Shawanda sat next to Aaron.

Within minutes, a woman stood in the middle of the circle. "My name is Ellen Polanski," she announced to the group of fourteen people. Listen carefully. I will explain the rules only once. You must attend all ten classes on time and remain until the end. You must participate, meaning listen and contribute. Before you speak, raise your hand and wait to be acknowledged. There will be no arguing, no disruptions, no gum chewing, eating, reading or earphones during class. Any noncompliance will be reported to the court. Remember, I am the teacher. I lead the discussion. Any questions?"

Shawanda squeezed Aaron's hand.

"If none," Ellen continued, "let's have everyone introduce themselves." After the introductions, Ellen moved on to the substance of the class. "It's important to teach a child proper behavior. If that fails, what are acceptable ways of discipline?" She acknowledged the first woman to raise her hand.

"Take away his privileges," the woman responded.

"Correct. An example of the wrong answer is beating the child. Beating a child degrades him or her. It is never the proper thing to do."

"My father used to beat me," Aaron blurted.

"Your father was wrong!"

Shawanda saw Aaron move about in his chair. She hoped he wouldn't tell Ellen where to go.

"I came out all right," Aaron told Ellen.

Ellen moved on to the next point. Shawanda was happy and relieved nothing got started between the two of them.

After an hour and a half, the class ended. Aaron and Shawanda quickly left the room and then the building. Once outside, Shawanda exhaled. "That was rough! Can you do this nine more times?" Shawanda knew she didn't want to.

Aaron looked at her. "I'll do anything to keep us together, Baby."

* * *

During the month of June, Shawanda was busy with counseling and parenting classes. In July she prepared for the approaching court date. A few days before the hearing, she went to Charles's office. There she found herself becoming more comfortable with him and his elegant surroundings.

"What will happen in court?" she asked Charles.

"It's essentially a trial. Because Social Services has the burden of proof, they'll call witnesses first. They have two, the new social worker who'll rehash the entire case, and your mother. She'll detail the initial incident. I'll call you. After closing arguments, the judge, Peter Norton, who's new to the bench, will decide if Social Services has proven its case. If you lose, you may have to deal with them for years to come. If you win, case dismissed, it's over."

"Do I have a chance of winning?"

"Well, the fact that you won the first hearing should have taken the wind out of the state's case. You and Aaron have attended counseling and completed parenting classes. That helps. Hopefully, you'll do well."

"Hopefully? Can't you guarantee I'll win?"

"Sorry. In court, nothing's guaranteed."

* * *

July tenth came too soon, it seemed to Shawanda. Inside the courtroom, looking around, she noticed Margaret Holmes wasn't there. The new social worker was. Shawanda was glad Vanessa had quit and there was a new worker. She liked Ms. Wallace, who was always pleasant and helpful.

Danielle Wallace approached Shawanda and Lena. "Good morning." The woman with brown cottony hair smiled and said, "I have the certificate showing you completed parenting classes."

The three women talked briefly before Danielle walked away.

Charles approached.

"I'm nervous," Shawanda said to him.

"It's natural under the circumstances" was his response.

Within minutes, Iris called the case. Charles and Shawanda gathered at the trial table. Iris first called Lena and questioned her about the evening in February.

"Aaron is an idiot." Lena sat in the witness chair. "That night I tried talking sense into him. He wouldn't listen. He kept yelling at all of us. When poor Precious Baby couldn't eat anymore, Aaron tried to force food down Precious' throat. When that didn't work, he got madder and started punching my poor grandson. I screamed and grabbed Aaron by the neck, forcing him to let go of my Baby."

Shawanda knew this was Lena's view of the incident, but considered this version somewhat embellished.

Iris finished her inquiry. Princess didn't ask any questions.

On Charles's turn he queried, "Mrs. Matthews, would you say your daughter is a very good mother?"

"Yes, definitely, except for, well, you know, this thing with Aaron."

"That evening in February, your daughter also went to her son's rescue?"

"She punched Aaron until he let go."

"When you told Aaron to leave your daughter's house, your daughter didn't protest?"

"Not at all."

"She wanted him out as much as you did?"

"Objection." Iris stood. "She can't testify to what someone else wanted."

"Sustained," the tall, young, blonde Judge Norton said.

"Nothing further." Charles stood when addressing the court.

Iris called Danielle, who constantly rummaged through the file looking for the exact date or place before answering Iris's questions. But she had no problem responding to Charles's inquiries.

"Ms. Matthews and Aaron have completed parenting classes?" Charles asked Danielle.

"Yes."

"And attended counseling as scheduled?"

"Yes."

"Ms. Matthews has kept every appointment with Social Services, hasn't she?"

"Yes."

"Nothing further."

The last witness was Shawanda. Her nervousness subsided gradually as she talked about everything, caring for Donte, the night Aaron returned, cooperating with Social Services.

When Charles ended his direct examination of Shawanda, Iris had only one question. "Are you still dating Aaron?"

Shawanda nodded.

"Did you hear the response?" Iris turned to the judge.

"Please speak up, Ms. Matthews," Judge Norton instructed.

"I still love him."

"Mmm," Iris looked at Shawanda. "How very interesting."

"Is the state still conducting a cross examination?" Charles stood and addressed the judge. "Or has it move into commentary and innuendo?"

"Any more questions, Mrs. Harper?" Judge Norton asked.

"No, Your Honor."

"Any more witnesses, Mr. Cooke?"

"None."

"I'll hear closing arguments," the judge said.

Iris stood. "Ms. Matthews' short term cooperation is meaningless. She will never let this child abuser go; therefore, Donte remains in as much danger now as he was in February. Social Services is his only hope of safety."

Princess Williams agreed.

Charles disagreed. "Social Services has nothing. Donte has been home since February and has been completely safe. There have been no further incidents of inappropriate discipline. Not only has Ms. Matthews cooperated with Social Services, Aaron Washington has also." Charles paused. "Here the state has the burden of proof. They can't possibly meet that burden on the testimony of their two witnesses. The first witness, Lena Matthews, told us that Ms. Shawanda Matthews is a good mother who immediately went to her son's aid on this night in February. Shawanda wasn't divided between protecting her child and supporting the boyfriend. The second witness, Danielle Wallace, testified regarding the total cooperation of both Ms. Matthews and Mr. Washington. Your Honor, there simply isn't enough here to warrant separating a child from his family." Charles sat down.

"I thank all attorneys in this case," Judge Norton said. "I find Social Services has not met its burden; therefore, the case is dismissed."

Shawanda covered her mouth to mask the sounds of relief and joy that threatened to escape her throat and fill the room with their presence. She embraced Charles and said, "Thank you."

"You're welcome."

9

Hours later at the West Baltimore rowhouse, Shawanda visited Aaron. Finding his parents away, she announced to him, "The judge threw the case out!" She almost jumped up and down. "I don't have to see no more social workers!" She grabbed him and kissed his forehead. "It's over."

"You still got Donte?" They stood in the middle of the living room.

"Don't you want me to still have him?"

"Like you said, he's your son. We'll raise him together."

"You can't hit him anymore."

"Okay, okay."

"If he's bad, we'll take away his privileges or send him to his room," Shawanda said.

"Sure, send him to his room."

She pinched his stomach hard.

"Stop, Woman."

"Promise you'll never hit Donte again."

He grabbed her around the waist and pulled her close. "You think I want you mad at me or to have to deal with Social Services again?" He looked her in the eye. "Now that all the mess is over, let's get married."

"Married?" She mentally shifted to the new subject.

"We can have a wedding at my parents' church and a reception in the dining hall."

"Then what?" she asked.

"We'll buy a rowhouse in a nice neighborhood. I've already saved up a down payment. You'll decorate it and keep it clean. In the mornings I'll get dressed for work while you fix breakfast. It has to be a big one, eggs, sausage, and pancakes. You know I'll need it to do all that heavy work. Then, before I leave, I'll give you a big kiss."

"And tell me you love me?"

"You already know that. But I'll tell you sometimes. I'll tell Donte goodbye. I'm raising him like he was my own. He won't have to go to Kim's after school 'cause you'll be at home. No more of this two-job stuff, not even one job."

"Yeah?"

"We'll have more kids," he went on.

"Two more, another boy and a girl."

"At *least* two more," he said. "What do you think? Want to get married?"

"Yeah." She hugged him.

The front door opened. Shawanda turned to see Peter and Gladys walk in. "We're getting married," she told Aaron's parents.

"With all the problems you two have had lately?" Gladys responded.

But Peter said, "It's about time our son moved out and got his own place."

Shawanda nodded agreement with Peter. Suddenly she considered Lena and Ernest, and their possible reactions to the good news. And her excitement dissipated.

* * *

On the following week, in the courthouse Margaret finished her cases and took the elevator downstairs. She headed toward the side door. Outside, she awaited the transportation van to take her back to the office. Having the van was convenient because downtown parking was problematic.

"Ms. Holmes."

She turned. "Mr. Cooke. I heard about your big win in the Matthews case."

"Just doing my job."

"And you're back in court already?"

"On a civil case. I represent a small insurance company."

"I don't know if I should wish you luck or save it for the other side. They may need it more." She smiled.

"It's only a pretrial conference. No one's hurting anyone — yet."

"Must be interesting to be a lawyer."

"Very. You have an interesting job. Your devotion to helping others is admirable," he said. "Maybe we could have dinner sometime and talk about our respective careers."

"Have dinner with the opposing side?"

"The case is over. There are no longer sides to take and no rules of ethics for either one of us to violate."

"Is this what you do after you've beat someone in court — ask them to dinner?"

"We weren't fighting any personal battles. We had a case. We did our jobs."

"You want to discuss Social Services and its procedures?" She saw the transportation van, which was a block away.

"Not at all. We can discuss art and music."

"I don't know very much about music, except what I like, which is jazz and r & b. With art —."

"It's called a date."

A date? She wished he would repeat that word about fifteen times. She hadn't had one of those since the nightmare at the pizza place. Searching for an appropriate response, she asked, "Do you think I should?" She immediately acknowledged that wasn't it.

"What's your home address?" he asked.

She gave it to him as the van neared.

"And your home phone number?"

"I've never dated a White —." She held onto the blunt words and supplied the number. "Maybe this isn't a good idea. We should both meditate on it."

"I'll pick you up Saturday night at seven. Okay?"

She thought of her plans for Saturday night — cleaning the refrigerator. It had been two months since last doing that. Meanwhile Kathleen had a date with Milton. Margaret's attitude reversed. A date with Charles couldn't be worse than the disastrous one with Joe. Besides, Margaret liked Charles. "Okay, see you then." The van pulled up. Margaret said goodbye and got on it.

* * *

That evening at Margaret's apartment, she stared into the full-length mirror. Unhappy with her looks, she concluded no man would be happy with them, either. It was time for a makeover. The next day at lunch, she made a hair appointment. At home she searched magazines for a new hair style. Saturday morning she appeared early at a beauty salon. She had her hair cut into a new style. Then she got a manicure and a pedicure, ending with a eyebrow and leg wax. None of it was for Charles, but for her. She wanted to feel attractive.

Afterwards she drove to the upscale Towson Town Mall in the suburb. She searched large department stores and small boutiques, not for her usual don't-look-at-me type of clothes, but for something sexy. She found a dark pink low-cut dress that was shorter than she was accustomed to and matching black accessories. In case she didn't have the nerve to wear the pink dress, Margaret got a plain black one, too. Glancing at her watch, she mentally kicked herself for having spent too much time shopping. There were no minutes left to grab something to eat. Now she would have to go hungry to dine with a man.

After rushing home, she showered. In the bedroom Margaret laid the two dresses on the bed. She stared at them. Putting on makeup and combing her hair, she returned to the bed. Taking a deep breath, she chose the pink dress.

Promptly at seven, there was a knock on the door. Prepared as she would ever be, Margaret calmly answered it. And there he stood. He stood relaxed with both hands in the pockets of his tailored blue suit. He looked good to her.

"Good evening," he said.

She disconnected his voice from the rest of him and admired the deepness and warmth of it. "Please come in." After he entered, she closed the door and stayed near it. "Please have a seat. Can I get you something to drink?" Margaret realized how out of practice she was at this.

"No, thank you." He sat on the sofa.

She wanted to know what he thought of her new hairdo and dress. But she would feel ridiculous asking. "Like my dress?"

"Is it your dress? It doesn't look like anything you would wear."

"I bought it today."

"You look uncomfortable in it."

"Decided to get rid of my conservative look."

"I liked the way you looked."

She rewound the words in her head and played them again. Only her father and Tommy had ever given her a similar compliment.

"It was one of the reasons I asked you out," he continued. "Of course, you look great in the new dress, too."

"Thank you." Margaret grabbed her purse from the coffee table. "Do you really like me?"

He stood. "I admire the confident social worker who went out on a limb to let a bruised child stay with a mother who never harmed him. While I have to work at unselfishness, compassion for others comes more naturally to you. Ready?" After she nodded, he opened the door. "On the other hand, this insecure, I-think-I-don't-look-good enough side of you is boring. My suggestion: get rid of it."

Margaret rejected the idea that she had an insecure side.

He held the door for her. She went out. Once she was in the hall, he clicked off the lights, went out, closed the door, and twisted the knob to ensure it was locked. Outside of the building he directed her to his car. It was a shiny new silver Mercedes.

While Margaret wasn't into cars, she was impressed by the looks of this one. "Business must be good."

"I'm not complaining." He opened the door.

Margaret saw a bundle of roses lying on the seat and picked them up. "For me?"

"Of course."

She smelled them, the scent dancing up her nostrils. There were probably a dozen of them, she calculated. She wanted to say, I don't know what your game is, Mr. Cooke. Clearly you have the income to play it. But I'll credit you with this: in and out of the courtroom, you're smooth. Instead she said the proper and polite things. "Thanks. They're beautiful. You're considerate." She got into the car, laid the roses in her lap, and put on the seat beat.

After Charles glided into the driver's seat, he asked, "Where would you like to eat?"

"I don't know."

"My favorite restaurant is in Little Italy. Of course, there's also Julio's. I haven't been there in a while."

Julio's? Milton took her mother there. Of all the restaurants in Baltimore, it was the one she most wanted to go to. "We don't have to go any place expensive."

"Little Italy?" He put the key into the ignition.

"Pasta's okay. I don't mind it."

"Julio's?" He started the car.

"We could have pizza." What nonsense she was talking. She almost hated pizza. Yet Margaret had a hard time simply telling him she wanted to go to the most expensive restaurant in Baltimore on a first date. She would agree such a request was unreasonable.

"Pick a restaurant." He relaxed in the leather seat.

"Wherever you take me, I'll be happy." Why was she lying? Margaret pondered.

"Julio's," he sternly said.

"It's too expensive, and you've already gotten roses."

"Enough! We're going to Julio's." Charles checked the mirrors, pulled into traffic, and headed downtown.

Margaret relaxed and hugged the roses. Inside, she skipped like a little girl. *I'm on a date. I have roses. I'm going to Julio's.* Wait until April and her mother hear about it. And Kathleen would probably tell Margaret's sister, Brittany. Cruising toward downtown, Margaret glanced at Charles. She thought he looked good behind the wheel of the Mercedes. Mentally punching herself for what seemed to her like shallowness, she forced her eyes from Charles and to the window and watched the sights. "I love the city."

"You can have it. I live in White Marsh. I built a house there. I come into the city mostly to work."

"White Marsh! You live way out there?"

"With traffic it's only a forty-minute drive from downtown."

"Don't you see wild animals out there?"

"Of course I'll seen an occasional fox, raccoon, possum."

"Possum! What did it look like?"

"Like its parents, I'm sure."

Margaret laughed.

Soon they pulled in front of Julio's. Charles handed the car keys to the valet. Inside they waited at the bar for a table.

"Would you like anything to drink?" he asked.

"No, thanks." She didn't want or need alcohol tonight.

He ordered a martini.

Forty-five minutes later they were escorted through the crowded, noisy restaurant to a white-clothed table. Once settled in, Charles ordered a second martini from the dark-haired, tan-skinned waiter who spoke English with a heavy Spanish accent.

The waiter gone, Margaret asked, "Do you need lots of alcohol to be with me?"

"I thought you were getting rid of the insecurity. And to answer your question, no, I don't. Dating you is my pleasure."

Relaxing, she felt comfortable with him. Opening the menu, looking at the price of the entrees, she slammed it closed. Kathleen said it was expensive, but Margaret hadn't imagined how expensive. If Charles took the attitude Joe had taken with her, she could end up paying for her own meal. And Margaret, who didn't plan on Julio's, had only forty dollars on her. Her only credit card was tucked away at home for emergencies.

"Decided on what you're having?" He looked up from the menu.

All she had had to eat that day was the usual breakfast. While happy she had lost eight pounds, she was now tempted by the aroma of fish and steak coming from the next table, tempted to gobble every tasty thing on the menu that interested her. "I think I'll have the house salad and the black bean soup."

"Are your kidding?" he asked. "You tormented me in the car for this? We could have gone to pizza joint for soup and salad."

He was right, she admitted. Taking another look at the entrees, not knowing exactly what to do, she simply told him the truth. "I only have forty dollars." The chicken entree alone was twenty.

The waiter approached.

Charles ordered an appetizer, shrimp in garlic sauce, and steak and lobster. Turning to Margaret, he asked, "Would you like the same?" When no response came immediately, he said to the waiter, "Two, please."

The waiter took the menus.

As the waiter departed, Margaret thought, steak and lobster. If Charles wanted only sex, he should have simply asked up front. Of course, Margaret would never have sex with anyone who bluntly asked at the beginning of a date, but at least it would have saved them both time. Shoving those thoughts to the back of her brain, she found new things to worry about. "My father was a doctor. My grandfather a janitor. And your family?"

"Lawyers, judges, engineers, businessmen, mostly, for several generations."

Margaret had figured as much. "As a child, you went to private schools?"

"Yes."

"Nannies?" she asked.

"Yes."

"Are you married, single or divorced?" she inquired.

"Never married. No children."

"I was engaged for several years. We broke up. Have you dated women of other races before?"

"I generally date educated, professional women of all races."

Women of all races? Sounded to Margaret like he dated a lot.

"It makes life interesting," he continued. "The last woman was Japanese and a model. She loved herself so much that it was pointless for anyone else to join in."

"What are your goals when dating?" she asked.

"Goals? I've never thought about it. When out I have a good time and enjoy myself."

"I'm a planner. I always have to have goals. I hate the unexpected. We're different people."

"Try relaxing and enjoying yourself." He leaned back. "Or is that too hedonistic a goal for you?"

"I can try it." Actually, she was having a good time.

After the shrimp arrived, he happened to mention, "I don't consider myself husband or father material." He looked her straight in the eye.

"I want marriage and children as soon as possible," she said. "You see, different goals in life."

"We'll search for common ground," he suggested.

Their orders arrived. Margaret savored the shrimp. As for the entree that followed, she had forgotten how full of flavor a juicy steak could be. "This is so good." Next she rolled a piece of lobster around in her mouth. Later, after the waiter took the empty plates away, Margaret said, "It's been a long time since I've enjoyed a meal so much."

"It's an excellent restaurant."

The waiter arrived with a tray of cakes.

"Would you like dessert?" Charles asked Margaret.

"Yes." It was a special night, she thought. She would celebrate it with a rich, delicious, ridiculously high-calorie dessert. When she got it, every bite felt worth the calories.

Dinner over, Charles paid. She thanked him and they left. In the car he suggested a movie.

"It's too late for a movie, isn't it?"

"It's only a little after ten," he said.

She was usually in bed by ten. Not mentioning that fact, she replied, "Yes, a movie would be great."

At a nearby theater, they selected the late showing of a movie that Margaret had mentally placed on a list to see with her mother. Margaret was happy to see it with Charles instead. During the movie, the room cold, she folded and stroked her arms to keep warm. Charles took off his jacket and put it around her. She appreciated that.

After the show they headed back toward downtown to one of Baltimore's landmark hotels. They took the elevator to the thirteenth floor and a club with an extensive view of the city. There they sat at a table near the window and admired the view.

"Did you enjoy the movie?" he asked.

"Very much."

They talked about it. Then about other things. She learned he was forty-four. He liked the opera and very creative modern art. She liked him. At some point Margaret became comfortable enough with Charles to stop talking and simply enjoy the companionship. Later, she leaned over and quietly asked while pointing, "What's that building?"

"I don't know," he replied. "It's your city."

Yes, tonight it felt that way, she mentally agreed.

At two, the bar closing, they left. Walking to the car, he took her hand and held it. She heard music as it dispersed a bewitching dust into the air. Or was the music only in her head? Passing a parked car, she realized a man sat inside of it, probably waiting for someone to come out of the hotel. The man sat with the windows down and the radio on.

Returning to the Mercedes, heading the two miles to her apartment, she laid her head on Charles' shoulder. If Margaret had been a light-headed, float-on-a-cloud, romantic, feel-the-chemistry, let-the-magic-lift you kind of a woman, if she had been, love would have been a soft, golden-laced pit that she could have easily fallen into tonight. But she was a practical woman.

At home he walked her to the door. There, not wanting to give the wrong impression, she debated on whether to invite him in. "Want to come in for a few minutes?"

"I shouldn't. It's late."

"You're certainly in the habit of going all out to impress a woman," she noted aloud.

"Let's say I'm capable of pursuing the woman I want."

"I had a terrific time."

"So did I." He came closer, leaned over, and kissed her lips. "I'll call you tomorrow."

"I go to mass at nine."

He smiled.

"You didn't mean at nine, did you?"

"Nine on a Sunday is early. I'll call later. If you're not here, I'll try again." He embraced her. "Good night."

She watched him walk down the hall. At the door, which led to the outside, he stopped and looked back at her. She smiled. He smiled. She went inside.

In her bedroom she changed into pajamas. Margaret regretted being a woman her age who had time only for dating marriage material. Charles definitely wasn't that. He was about impressing women and having a good time.

When a client like Charles' former client, Shawanda Matthews, came into Margaret's office, one who couldn't leave an abusive boyfriend, Margaret really didn't understand her. An individual should control one's emotions and consider the long term. That was Margaret's philosophy.

Now Margaret's mind told her heart not to fall in love. She explained to it that he bought roses, an expensive dinner, movie tickets, and drinks. He opened doors, was polite, humorous, and a great conversationalist. Almost any woman would have fallen for him under those circumstances. It was somewhat unfair to her that this was their first extensive contact. She didn't have a chance. Her heart snapped back, he wanted her — plain Margaret, who didn't feel plain at all when with him.

She fell onto the bed. Charles wasn't her type. She couldn't continue to date him, assuming he asked. Her head made a decision. She would find someone interested in marriage, marry quickly and start a family before it was too late. Crawling under the top sheet, her heart made an announcement. It said it was in love and intended to never date anyone other than Charles.

10

At mass the following day Margaret was sleepy. Afterwards she and Kathleen went to Sunday brunch at a nearby café.

"I spoke to your sister this morning," Kathleen said. "She plans to visit in September."

Margaret played with the scrambled eggs. She loved Brittany, although she often felt inferior when in her presence. "Will she bring the children?"

"No, nor her husband. He has to work."

"How long will she stay?"

"Friday through Monday."

Not too bad, Margaret decided. "It'll be grand to see her." At least for the first couple of hours.

"For four days, I'll have both of my darling daughters with me."

"How's Milton?"

"We had a long talk last night. How would you feel if I remarried?"

"Remarried?" Margaret's face lit up. "That would be wonderful."

"Brittany approves. Of course, Milton hasn't asked yet. But I think he will soon."

Margaret pushed aside the plate. "I had a date last night."

"Decided to give Joe a second chance?"

"A nice date. His name is Charles. He's a lawyer. I met him in the courthouse."

"I don't know any lawyers. I suppose they make a good living."

"He's in private practice, drives a Mercedes, and lives in White Marsh. He took me to Julio's and I ordered steak and lobster. He's White."

Kathleen put down the fork. "He doesn't sound like your type, Dear."

"What about him seems inappropriate?"

"Sometimes people do things, meet someone of another race, and for fun . . . . Your father struggled to become a doctor."

"Struggled against racism. I know, Mother. I respect that. But my having a few dates won't set civil rights back."

"Exactly, a few dates. That's all you'll ever have with this man. Some women are into casual dating and sex. Not you. You go to mass every Sunday. You've worked in soup kitchens and at Christmas put together parties for children in foster care. I'm proud to be your mother. I couldn't say that if you slept around."

"I don't."

"Why this Charles approached you is a mystery to me, unless he's mistaken you for some other kind of woman —."

"He likes me. I'm sure of it."

"Yes, yes, for the moment. This man is probably a playboy and you're the woman for this week, or two weeks, before he moves on to the next exotic . . . different woman. Before you get involved with him, realize he's probably just having a little fun. He won't be around long."

"But I like him."

"I expected more from you."

"You don't know him."

"Neither do you. Why did you have to break up with Tommy? So what if the fire was gone? Look at the many years I was married to your father. If I had ended it when we hit stormy times, the marriage would have lasted less than a year."

"Tommy's long gone."

"Is it possible you're getting a little . . . desperate? A smooth talking lawyer comes along in a fancy car, and of course you think you're falling in love. Don't. Hold on. Mr. Right will come shortly with something stable like marriage and children."

"I don't believe you feel this way." Margaret looked away. She was devastated.

* * *

On Monday at lunch time, Margaret sat at her desk. April came in with a brown paper bag, pulled up a chair, and began talking about her weekend.

"I found the perfect color paint for the bedroom walls." April pulled a sandwich from the bag. "This Saturday my husband and I will paint our bedroom. If all goes well, next month, we'll do another room."

Margaret sliced the steamed chicken breast. She itched to talk about Charles. Yet hesitated after the conversation with Kathleen.

"How's your mother?" April inquired.

"Thinking about remarrying."

"Good for her! What did the two of you do this weekend?"

"Saturday night mother had a date with Milton." Margaret stabbed a steamed carrot.

"Oh, poor Margaret, can't even get a date with your mother. Don't worry, things will get better."

Margaret hated having her friends feel sorry for her. "I had a date Saturday night."

"No, seriously, what did you do this weekend? Clean closets?" April bit into the roast beef on Italian bread.

"Seriously, I did."

"Okay, Margaret." April's mouth was full. "Who did *you* have a date with?"

"He's a lawyer, a very successful one, I gather."

"A lawyer?" April chewed and stared while holding the sandwich.

"He's built like a football player. Charles is very attractive. He has a rugged, macho look." Margaret watched April slowly take another bite of the sandwich. "And the most engaging voice. And the way he smiles, and walks. He has a serious walk. And he's bald. I've never dated a bald guy before. He's only forty-four. I guess he shaves his head, or maybe his hair fell out when he was young. That happened to a cousin of mine. Anyway, Charles is so polite. He opened doors, pulled out chairs, and waited until I was seated before he sat down. And he brought me a dozen roses! Doesn't he sound fantastic?" Margaret waited for April to get excited for her.

"A dozen roses? If you actually meet someone like this, we'll clone him and pass around the duplicates."

"I have met him." She tried telling April more. "He drives a Mercedes, a new one. He looks so good driving it, cool and all."

"A Mercedes?" April calmly repeated.

"Lives in White Marsh. Built a house there."

"Built a house? Well, that's expensive." April put down the sandwich.

"We went to Julio's."

"Julio's!"

"I had steak and lobster."

"Lobster? On a first date?"

"We went to the movies and then to this club."

"You? At a club?"

Margaret watched April twist her neck right and left as if to relieve tension. "I didn't get home until after two," Margaret continued.

"Did you have sex with him?"

"No. He called last night about six and told me again he had a great time. We talked for half an hour. I took his home phone number, although I haven't known him long enough to feel comfortable calling him. He wants to go out this Saturday."

April moved toward the edge of the chair. "This man sounds like something out of a romance novel. Have you been reading any romance novels lately?"

Margaret shook her head no. "Charles is White."

"Is he related to Pierre Champagne?"

"I made Pierre up. You know that."

"Yes." April nodded. "Mr. Champagne was rich, too. Remember? And part French."

"I'm not making up Charles. I think I'm in love."

"Are you confusing your life with something you saw in a movie?"

"I'm not psychotic." Margaret pressed on. "I don't know where's he's taking me this Saturday."

"Joke's over!" April jumped up. "You're not a party girl." She wrapped the reminder of the sandwich and stuck it into the bag while speaking. "You don't run around with wealthy White men who bring you roses and take you to the most expensive restaurant on a first date." Snatching up the bag, she said, "You're nice, dull, plain Margaret. We all like you just the way you are. You don't have to make up stories to impress your coworkers."

"I'm not. Honest. He —."

"Please, Margaret, stop! I hate to see you like this. Spend Saturday nights with your mother. There's no shame in that. But these lies!" April turned and stomped toward the door. "I fell for this once before. I won't do it again! And if you're going to make up lovers, make up one that others can imagine you with."

Margaret froze. Okay, she lied before, but this time she was telling the truth. Watching April disappear from the room, Margaret couldn't believe her friend's reaction.

* * *

Charles called her at home Tuesday evening, at work Thursday, and late evening on Friday. Friday when the telephone rang, Margaret quickly rolled over in bed and grabbed the receiver.

"How was your day?" Charles greeted her.

Margaret described it. "And yours?"

"I got a lot of paperwork done. I'm very tired, have decided to take the weekend off."

"You don't generally?"

"I often work them. Usually all day Saturdays. Sometimes half days Sundays. Would you like to go to Atlantic City tomorrow? We can leave early. I'll drive the entire three hours. When we get there, we can decide what to do."

"Can we see a show?"

"Probably, although that would put us there late. I guess I can stay awake long enough to drive back. If not, we can always get a hotel room."

"No hotel room."

"Separate rooms?" he said.

"No hotels."

"Separate hotels?" He laughed.

"You're very funny."

"Certainly you're safe from me if I'm in a totally different building."

"I'm going to hang up." She wasn't, despite hating his teasing.

"I'll stop. Will you go?"

"Yes."

"What time would you like to leave?"

"You're driving. What do you think?"

"Eleven?"

"Eleven's good."

"We can have a light lunch before getting on the highway," he suggested.

Margaret considered the possibility of lunch and dinner out. So many calories. Her thoughts quickly returned to Charles. "Looking forward to seeing you in the morning."

"Sleep well," he whispered.

"You too." She held the receiver after Charles hung up. She was excited about their plans.

The hours passed. Margaret slept later than usual, resisting her habit of getting up early and starting the household chores. When completely rested, she rose and dressed in the conservative black outfit which was purchased a week before. Ready early, she soon greeted Charles with a hug and "Good morning."

"Morning," he responded.

They walked outside into the sun-tossed day. In the car Margaret quickly got comfortable. Before leaving the city, they stopped at a coffee shop and got sandwiches and cold drinks. Shortly, on the highway, Charles told her about his latest big case, which was scheduled for court next month. She told him about her family and Brittany's upcoming visit. When they reached Atlantic City, Margaret couldn't believe three hours had passed so quickly.

They walked along the crowded Boardwalk first and stared at the ocean. Souvenir shopping followed, then a visit to the casinos. Margaret had forgotten what they were like, the gaudiness of the decor, the noise, the desperation of the lever-pulling customers. Yet it felt good to be there. For dinner they found a restaurant with a view of the ocean. Afterwards, at a nightclub, they saw a comedian perform.

By midnight, they were back on the highway. "Can you make the drive?" Margaret asked.

"Sure. I'm not particularly tired."

"I'll stay awake and talk to you."

"You don't have to.

"I want to." Turned out, while she was accustomed to an early bedtime, staying awake and talking to Charles was easy.

11

Life wasn't easy on Baltimore's east side as Shawanda paced her parents' kitchen. She glanced at Lena and Ernest, who sat at the kitchen table. "I . . . have to tell you . . . about . . . something."

"Is Precious Baby okay?"

"Yeah. He's with Kim, playing with her children."

"Social Services hassling you again?" Ernest asked.

Shawanda shook her head. "It's good news."

"The way you're stuttering, it doesn't sound like it," Lena said.

"Aaron and I have been talking." Shawanda hoped letting it out slowly would help.

"Perfect!" Lena jerked in the chair. "Of all the people you need to talk to, he is probably the last."

"We've decided to stick with each other."

"Wasn't that always your decision?" Ernest asked.

"You could have gone to jail because of him!" Lena added in a loud tone.

"We're getting married."

"Oh, no!" Lena fell back in the chair.

"Are you kidding?" Ernest asked calmly.

Shawanda expected the worst from Lena, the best from her father. With him, she could handle only support.

"Marriage won't stop him from beating up Precious Baby." Lena looked at her daughter.

"I'm quitting my job," Shawanda told them. "We're buying a house and having more kids."

"More kids!" Lena's head moved from side to side. "You don't know what to do with the one you have. And that goes double for Aaron."

"I don't want a wedding. We're going to Aaron's parents' minister. We're getting married in his office."

"You're moving too fast." Ernest placed an arm around his wife's shoulder.

"You two need a long engagement." Lena threw the words into the discussion. "Take time to talk about what you expect of each other."

"You don't need to quit a job right away," Ernest said.

"That's right," Lena added. "You're bringing an extra mouth into this relationship."

"We're getting married real soon." Shawanda stood against the counter.

"What's the hurry?" Ernest asked the question.

Shawanda felt both parents had joined against her. Out numbered, she fought harder. "No, I won't wait. There's nothing to wait on. I want what everybody else has, what you two have, and I'm getting it."

"What about Precious Baby?" Lena stood.

"Aaron will be his daddy."

"Aaron will never forget Precious isn't his. He needs to marry a woman who doesn't have kids."

"Enough goes on in relationships when there's no stepkids." Ernest leaned forward.

"And you saw how Aaron reacted when he was stressed out," Lena added. "What if he loses his temper again?"

"We had those classes and six weeks of counseling."

Lena folded her arms. "Let us take Precious Baby."

"That might be the best thing." Ernest nodded. "At least until the two of you are settled."

"Give him to you? Do you know what I went through to keep him? Sometimes my stomach was so upset I couldn't eat or sleep. I don't even know how I got through all that." She slowly shook her head. "He's my son. I'm not giving him to nobody. Aaron and Donte just gotta learn to live together."

"Why? Because you say so?" Lena moved from the kitchen table, farther away from Shawanda.

"If you won't let him stay with us," Ernest leaned back, "at least never leave him alone with Aaron."

"Call me and I'll come get Precious." Lena stood across the room.

"What are you worrying about? No one's doing anything to Donte." Shawanda shifted her weight. "I know you don't like Aaron, but try to be happy for us."

"What if something else happens?" Lena's voice cracked.

"It's not all about not liking Aaron," Ernest said.

"Daddy, please be on my side." She waited.

Ernest took a deep breath. "Aaron has a temper. Know what the Bible says about people with tempers?"

She couldn't believe her father was asking her such a question. He must know she knew nothing about the Bible. "Please, just understand."

Ernest stood. "You have a lot going for you. Don't waste your time on the likes of Aaron."

"I don't care if you don't like him!" She lied. "He's my man! I'm not letting him go!" Shawanda ran from the kitchen. She kept going, through the dining room, into the living room, out of the front door and to the car. The whole world had become her enemy, she felt.

* * *

The conversation with her parents had sucked strength from her. She gathered what strength she had left into a closed fist and tried to hold it there. She had to tell Denise, who had no patience when it came to men. Shawanda imagined her friend's response. Girl, are you crazy? Denise would probably ask.

When Denise visited Saturday morning, Shawanda was in her robe and slippers.

"Let's go to the club tonight," the trendily dressed visitor said after bouncing on the sofa.

"I might." She didn't know if Denise would want to go out with her after the news.

"If you're kicking me to the side to go out with Aaron, well, I guess I'll understand."

Shawanda sat in the chair. "We're getting married."

"We who? You and Aaron?"

"Yeah, Aaron. Who else?"

"The same Aaron that beat up Donte because he threw milk?" Denise crossed her legs.

"Even my father turned on me." Shawanda looked away.

Denise uncrossed her legs. She glided to the other end of the sofa, close to Shawanda, and said, "I wouldn't marry him after what he did. If he does it again, your life will be nasty. And he might do it again. But I understand how you feel. Admire you, really. I've been hurt so badly by men, I don't know if I can ever love a man again the way you love Aaron." Leaning toward Shawanda, she said, "Girl, I've got your back. Let's do this wedding thing. When is it?"

"Real soon."

"Okay, not much time. Where will it be?"

"Aaron says his parents' minister will marry us in his office."

"Now for the most important question." Denise smiled. "What are you gonna wear?"

"Haven't thought about that."

"I know of this store on Reisterstown Road. Let's go there first."

"Now?" Shawanda's face lit up.

"Yeah, now."

"I'll need new shoes, too. What should I do with my hair?" Shawanda rose and hurried upstairs to dress. She was happy for Denise's support. She dressed Donte, and the three of them soon hopped into Denise's car.

The afternoon was spent going from store to store and through racks of dresses. Shawanda enjoyed it. Finally they found the prettiest short, short white dress. Afterward they settled down long enough to eat pizza. Then they spend the early evening hunting the perfect pair of shoes to accompany the dress. They found them while Donte complained of the long hours spent shopping.

Late night, Shawanda left Donte with Kim and went to the club. When Shawanda had told her friend about the engagement, Kim had given her the warmest hug and congratulations.

* * *

Sunday Shawanda sat on the side of Donte's bed. She hugged and kissed him. "I love you." Tickling him, watching him laugh, she added, "Aaron loves you, too. He wants to take you to the circus. He won't hurt you. You just need to listen to him. Okay?"

Donte nodded. "Goin' to the circus, Ma?"

"Yeah, all three of us. Come on. Let's go downstairs. Aaron's waiting for us." Taking Donte's hand, she led him downstairs to Aaron, who stood in the middle of the living room.

"Hi, Donte," Aaron smiled.

The child grabbed his mother's dress.

Aaron kneeled in front of him. "I'm sorry about what happened. I lost it."

Aaron stood.

"Ready for the circus?" When Donte didn't respond, Aaron looked at Shawanda. "Why isn't he talking?"

"Because he's kinda of a quiet child. That's why." Shawanda took Donte's hand, and they went outside. Opening the rear door of Aaron's car, she waited until Donte climbed in, and then fastened his seat belt. Getting into the front seat, she turned to Donte. "Look how handsome Mama's little man is." During the ride, she turned several times to talk to her son.

Soon pulling into Mondawmin Mall, Aaron parked the car. The group headed toward the brightly colored tents of the traveling circus that were temporarily set up in the mall's parking lot. They stopped when running into a fenced-off area and ended up having to walk through the mall.

"Circus, Ma! Circus!"

"We're almost there."

Finally, reaching the entrance, they waited in a long, slow-moving line for tickets before going into the first tent, where food and souvenirs were sold. There they purchased a toy clown for Donte. Moving with the crowd into the big tent, they looked for their assigned seats. Finding them, Shawanda purposely sat Donte between her and Aaron. She began to engage the two in conversation.

"Like the circus, Aaron?" she asked.

"Yeah, Baby. You like the circus, too, don't you, Donte?"

Donte nodded and said in a high, little voice, "I like de circus."

"You like the clowns?" Aaron asked.

"Yeah, they jump up and down."

Aaron looked at Shawanda. "Up and down?"

She looked at her boyfriend. She knew he was trying to befriend Donte. Yet it was becoming obvious to even her that he wasn't naturally good with children. At least other people's children. For the first time she briefly wondered if her parents were right. Maybe it was unfair to Donte to expose him to Aaron. Stomping on the thought, she convinced herself Aaron simply needed more practice. Now stroking the top of Donte's head, she said to him, "Clowns are funny, aren't they, Baby?"

"Yeahhhhh!"

The performance started. Shawanda and Donte laughed and clapped their hands throughout.

During intermission Aaron turned to Shawanda. "I'm ready to go. Want to?"

"Not until the end. Really, I want to come back next weekend and see it all over again," she added seriously. Noting his expression of unhappiness, she said, "When you have kids, you do a lot of kids' things with them." Aaron seemed to relax. Shawanda's attention returned to the resuming performance. She was glad to have her two men together again. At the end of the circus, mother and son cheered.

* * *

The August day Shawanda married Aaron was so hot, Shawanda didn't want to get out of Aaron's air-conditioned car. But when his parents and siblings, Denise, and two more of her cousins gathered nearby on the sidewalk, Shawanda knew, despite the possibility of runny makeup, she had to.

"You look beautiful," Denise told Shawanda.

One of Aaron's sisters took photographs while Shawanda searched the street for her parents' car. It wouldn't surprise her if they didn't come, although she desperately wanted them there.

"Look this way," the sister with the camera said.

"You look beautiful," Aaron said.

"I need an air-conditioned room."

"Ma," Donte pointed. "Look Paw Paw."

Shawanda's heart jumped. She nearly clapped as she turned to see her parents' car. "Save some film. We have to take pictures of Mama and Daddy." Soon they were beside her. "You made it!" Tears moistened her eyes.

"We weren't letting you get married without us." Ernest kissed her cheek before graciously shaking Aaron's hand and speaking to the others.

Shawanda hugged Lena. "I'm glad you're here."

Aaron faced Shawanda's mother and uttered one word. "Lena."

Lena stared at him. "Yeah, that's still my name."

"What about a congratulations?" Aaron stared back.

"I haven't shot you yet. What more do you want?"

"Let's take a picture." Shawanda purposely interrupted. She quickly gathered Aaron, Donte, and both sets of parents around her. They all posed. When the photographs were over for the moment, the group went inside.

There, Shawanda introduced her parents to Reverend Douglas Hargrove, a tall, slender man with a pleasant smile and a comforting handshake. He showed them to his office. He told the couple where to stand. Their families encircled them. The couple held hands as they recited their vows. When Aaron put the ring on Shawanda's finger and kissed her, inside she shouted. Life had given her what she wanted.

When the ceremony was over, Shawanda and Aaron thanked Reverend Hargrove.

Everyone got back into their cars and they all headed to the harbor. There they walked along the promenade toward a popular seafood restaurant. The group stuck out. A woman approached and congratulated the newlyweds.

At the restaurant they were seated at a table with a harbor view. Shawanda sat at what seemed to be the center of the table and glanced out at the water and the boats. Someone had designed the most beautiful scenery just for her special day, she felt. Quickly the champagne arrived, the glasses were filled, and the toast was said by one of Aaron's brothers, Joshua.

"To the happy couple. It'll get rough sometimes, but you two stick it out."

The waitress came and laid the meal before them — fried shrimp and fish, crab cakes, and steaks. Shawanda had a sampling of it all. For dessert they shared the beautiful cake Aaron's mother, Gladys, had made. After dinner Shawanda opened the gifts and found towels, pans, platters, glasses, and two toasters. She thanked everyone for their gifts and for joining Aaron and her. She loved this day. She even wished she could live it all over again tomorrow. When the day was over, and night was spinning toward its close, Shawanda said goodbye to her guests in front of the Light Street Pavilion.

"The two of you should be alone tonight," Lena said. "I can take Precious Baby and bring him back tomorrow."

Shawanda slowly let go of Donte's hand and took Aaron's.

At home Aaron unloaded the car of wedding gifts while Shawanda changed. When he came into the room, Shawanda sat on the side of the bed. She spread the skirt of the short, red lace lingerie that she wore. It had been picked out during one of her and Denise's shopping trips. "Do you like it?"

He bounced on the bed, grabbed her, and kissed her lips, neck, and breasts. "I wouldn't wear it." He laughed and pushed her on the bed. He crawled on and hovered over her. "And neither should you." He pulled at the strap.

"Come on." She grabbed his hand. "Do you know how long it took me to find this?"

"Luv you," he said. "We're gonna be there for each other no matter what, right?"

"No matter what," she repeated.

She watched him turn off the lamp. In the quiet night they made love.

* * *

Monday Shawanda and Denise went house hunting in the suburban county. They started with a county real estate office. Five houses later, Shawanda couldn't afford anything she saw. Desperately wanting out of her drug-infested neighborhood, she searched daily until finding a lovely, small rowhouse on a quiet street. The previous owner had recently died. The house was priced to sell quickly. It was a two-story structure with a basement, small front yard, and a small grassy backyard for Donte to play in. Inside, it had newly painted cream-colored walls, gray carpet, and a recently remodeled kitchen. It had two bedrooms and one and a half baths.

"Do we have enough money for it?" she asked Aaron the day he first saw it.

"Didn't live with my parents all those years for nothing."

They made an offer. Shawanda didn't rest until hearing from the realtor. When informed the offer had been accepted, she screamed and leaped about the room. Donte came in.

"Why you doing that, Ma?"

"We're moving to a beautiful new house." She took his hands knowing he had no idea how his life had just improved. The two danced.

In the ensuing weeks, Shawanda quit her job at the mall. In between packing and tossing out worn items originally purchased secondhand, she would have talks with Kim.

Home inspections and paperwork on the new house also kept her busy, but not too busy to shop with Denise for a few cute household items.

The day came. Why had she doubted it would? Shawanda walked through the emptied deteriorating rowhouse. She could have stood in the center of the living room and remembered the pleasant and the awful times spent there. Or maybe have blown it a kiss goodbye, good riddance. Shawanda had no time for any of it. Closing the door, checking the lock for the last time, she spotted Kim and rushed over to her. "As soon as I get things together, you'll have to come over."

"I'd like that."

Shawanda hugged her dear friend. "Thanks for everything. I'll call you." Within two days, she had.

In the new house, lots of unpacking ensued. Finally clearing the kitchen, Shawanda decided to cook the first meal there. Stewed chicken, mashed potatoes, and green beans were on that Sunday's menu. Peeling potatoes, seasoning chicken, and cutting fresh green beans were not a burden. Pausing to check on Aaron and Donte, Shawanda went into the bedroom where the two played on the computer. She found them laughing and getting along well.

At dinner, a formal dining room set last on the list of furniture to purchase, the family gathered around the old kitchen table.

"Want mashed potatoes?" Aaron picked up the serving bowl and turned to Donte.

"Ah lit' bit," the brown-eyed child replied.

Aaron put one serving spoon of food on the plate.

"That's enough." Shawanda held up her hand. "He never eats a lot."

Aaron nodded. He filled his own plate and began eating. "Delicious, Baby. Mama can cook, can't she, Donte?"

"Yeahhhh!"

After a quiet, pleasant dinner, Shawanda washed the dishes while the males in her life watched television. Finishing, she went into the living room and spoke to Donte. "Ready for bed?"

"You ask a child if he wants to go to bed?" Aaron lay across the sofa.

"Want to stay up until this movie goes off?" Shawanda asked her son.

Donte nodded.

Shawanda looked at her new husband. "Think that's okay, Aaron?"

"Yeah. Okay."

Later, putting Donte to bed, she kissed his cheek and tucked him in. "Good night, Baby." Leaving Donte's room, Shawanda joined Aaron in their bedroom. She dressed for bed and slid in beside him. "I see how hard you're trying with Donte." She appreciated it.

"He's our son now." Aaron rested his head on the pillow.

She kissed his lips and concluded others had worried over nothing. It was her last thought before happily falling asleep in Aaron's arms.

12

On a Saturday afternoon in September, Margaret had a scheme. The object was Brittany, who had flown in from Los Angeles the evening before. Ashamed of her plot, as she purposely took a cab to Kathleen's home, Margaret planned to go through with it anyway. Paying the driver, and getting out of the cab, she walked toward the house.

The front door swung opened, and Brittany glided out into the sun, with her arms wide. "Sister Dear." Hurrying toward her, Brittany gave Margaret a big hug. "I'm glad to see you."

"How have you been?" Margaret smiled. It was good to see her again. Margaret mentally pinched herself for having had mixed feelings about this moment. Brittany was really a caring sister. "How are Russell and my three nephews?"

"Great. And you? Still single? No children yet?" She placed an arm around Margaret's shoulder and walked with her to the door. "Are you sure that womb of yours works? You should have it checked out. In fact, knowing you, you should have it all checked out." Brittany winked. "Be certain there's still life down there."

Margaret suddenly felt nauseated.

Inside they found Kathleen in the kitchen.

"Look, Mother Dear, my sweetheart of a sister is here," the thirty-four-year-old Brittany announced.

Margaret recalled Brittany's irritating overuse of words like *dear, love, darling, cutie, pretty, beautiful, sweetheart.*

"Hello, Margaret. Lunch's ready — chicken salad sandwiches."

"Mother Dear," Brittany exclaimed, "you made chicken salad just for me?"

"Of course. I know you like the way I make it. Sit down." Kathleen placed bread and a pitcher of iced tea on the table.

Margaret sat at the end of the table. Glancing at Brittany, she had to admit her sister looked good. Brittany had large, deep-set brown eyes and high cheekbones. In high school, boys had called her beautiful. She was shorter than Margaret and had managed to keep a slim figure after three pregnancies. Fashionably dressed in a pumpkin-colored skirt with a matching brown and pumpkin printed blouse, she had every strand of her long, thick brown hair lay perfectly in place.

"Like my necklace?" Brittany sat at the other end of the table.

"I noticed it outside. It's impressive."

"It's an I-love-you gift from Russell. Two carats. It wasn't my birthday or Christmas or anything."

"How nice of Russell." Margaret wiggled about the chair.

"Guess what! I have a maid two days a week."

"A maid!" Margaret echoed.

"Russell is one of the best and most successful doctors in Los Angeles."

"It's wonderful he's doing well," Kathleen said. Then to Margaret: "Brittany just remodeled her kitchen."

Brittany looked at Margaret. "Yes, Darling, when we brought our big, gorgeous house —."

"Four bedrooms, two and a half baths," Margaret recited, having heard it in every other telephone conversation with Brittany.

"I told the love of my life that one day I would have to change the kitchen. Of course, there was nothing wrong with it. It simply wasn't in any colors I would have picked. Anyway, with what I went through having the work done, not to mention the expense, we probably could have bought a little condo with the money, like the one you live in, Margaret."

"Margaret doesn't live in a condo." Kathleen poured tea.

"That's right. What was I thinking? Sorry."

Margaret forced a smile. If Brittany would stop talking about herself, Margaret could tell her where she lived. "How are the children?"

"Gerald is taking piano lessons. He's very talented. In one year, he's almost reached professional level. I simply couldn't believe it."

Margaret couldn't believe how much Brittany exaggerated her life. "Great for him."

"And Junior! I'm certain you'll be happy to know, Mother Dear, that your grandson is a straight A student in one of the best private schools in Los Angeles."

The aroma of the chicken salad was starting to make Margaret's stomach grind. Or was it the sound of Brittany's voice?

"Margaret's doing well, too." Kathleen sipped tea. "She has a good job with Social Services."

"How sweet." Brittany leaned back. "Little Margaret helps the poor of Baltimore."

Kathleen once told Margaret she thought Brittany was jealous of her because Margaret was many things that Brittany wasn't.

"You should have been a nun," Brittany persisted. "Wait a minute, you kind of are."

"I have a boyfriend."

"You mean that guy you were engaged to for ten years? Dear, someone should have told you. If you're engaged for more than two years . . . well . . . there's bad news."

"His name is Charles."

"He's a successful lawyer," Kathleen added. "He drives a Mercedes and lives in a custom built four bedroom house in White Marsh. On their first date, he took her to Julio's for lobster. And he gave her roses. On their second date, they went to Atlantic City."

"We talk almost every day," Margaret said. "He's easy to talk to."

Brittany turned to Kathleen. "Have you met this Charles?"

Kathleen shook her head no.

Brittany's glance rolled to Margaret, halted, and ran back to Kathleen. "I don't know. I remember hearing about . . . . Who was it? Pierre Champagne?" Looking at Margaret, "I believed you then. Although I should have realized something was up when you didn't tell mother about Pierre." Turning to Kathleen, she asked, "Do you think this one's real?"

"He's White," Kathleen whispered.

"White?" Brittany fell back in the chair and laughed. She glided forward, held her stomach with one hand, and laughed. Hit her thigh with the other and laughed. Rocked her head back and forward, laughing louder. "Margaret, I've never thought of you as having a sense of humor. Apparently, you've developed one. I was about to fall for that one again."

"So what he's White?" The laughter, naturally, annoyed Margaret.

"What was the name of that nerdy little guy you were engaged to all those years?" Brittany asked. "He was your type. Oops, but he didn't marry you."

"Stop it, Brittany," Kathleen shouted. "Why do you have to compete with your sister?"

"She's winning, Mother Dear. She's Baltimore's version of Mother Teresa."

"Charles and I are in love."

"Okay, Margaret." Brittany sat straight up. "I can play along. Are you having sex with this White man?"

"Have I ever asked you about your sex life?" Margaret snapped.

"Be nice to each other," Kathleen said.

"You're a virgin." Brittany spat the words at Margaret. "And you will probably die one."

"I am not a virgin!"

Kathleen put up her hands. "Stop it you two."

"Go confess your lies!" Brittany pointed at Margaret. "You know you're not dating any White man. As pure and holier than thou as everyone seems to think you are . . . well, just be proud of your virginity. Parade it around like it's a big sign of your purity. It's not, you know. It's only a sign you're too dysfunctional to get and keep a man!" Brittany turned away and folded her arms.

The doorbell rang. Kathleen got up. "Say nothing until I get back."

As soon as Kathleen left, Brittany unfolded her arms and looked at Margaret. "Why do you upset me so?"

"I didn't say anything to you."

"I guess I should apologize. My dearest Margaret, you were always the *good* sister. I was labeled the *bad* one." Her glance dropped. "When I was a teenager, because I dated a lot, people seemed to think I would spend my life going from one man to another. I haven't. I've stuck out my marriage through some hard times. I've only cheated on Russell three —."

"It's okay, Brittany. I know you didn't mean any of it." Just then, Margaret looked toward the entranceway and smiled.

"Who's this handsome, well dressed man, Mother Dearest?"

The man approached Brittany and extended his hand. "Good afternoon. I'm Charles Cooke."

Margaret watched Brittany's mouth fly open, and her eyes bulge. "Charles came to take me home." Right on schedule, and as planned, not that Margaret needed a ride. She could have driven.

"Have a seat, Mr. Cooke." Kathleen gestured toward the remaining chair.

Brittany's glance trailed Charles, Margaret noticed.

"How do you know my sister?" Brittany asked.

"We're dating." Charles looked at Margaret.

"You're a lawyer?"

"Yes."

"My husband's a doctor." Brittany lifted her head high. "I think he doesn't like lawyers because of all those frivolous malpractice suits that are filed every year."

"Doctors who don't malpractice have less to worry about."

Charles was quick, Margaret thought.

"I've heard lots about you," Kathleen said to Charles.

"I have, also, Darling," Brittany said. "But you must tell us more. How did you meet my sweetheart of a sister?"

Margaret relaxed. Looking at the chicken salad, she decided it was time to eat.

* * *

The next Sunday, Charles picked up Margaret and drove her to his home in White Marsh for a homemade dinner. Reaching his house, she stood in front of it and stared. "Wow!"

"Hope you like the interior as well." Charles unlocked the door.

Inside she surveyed the house — the foyer, with its white, black, and tan marvel floor, the square-shaped living room and adjacent formal dining room. Going into the huge family room, which almost looked like part of the kitchen because no wall separated them, Margaret proclaimed, "It's beautiful. Did you have it professionally decorated?"

"Only the living room, family room, and master bedroom. I can show you the rest of the house after dinner."

"Speaking of dinner, what's on the menu?" She reclined on the comfortable tan sofa.

"Seafood Newburg."

"Impressive."

"I have a few moves outside the courtroom."

She had noticed.

"Would you like a glass of wine?" he asked.

"Ice water, please."

He soon handed it to her. "Let me know if you need anything."

"Thanks." Margaret watched him return to the kitchen area. Looking around, Margaret said, "I like the way you can stand on the second floor and look down on the family room."

"The catwalk? So do I."

"Mother thinks you're intelligent and ambitious."

"That's good, right?"

"She's doesn't like the fact you're White. She probably never will. What would your family think of me?"

"My parents are deceased. Left are only my brother, an uncle, and a few cousins. My uncle would have a problem with the race thing. He once met my last girlfriend and hated her on sight. Later he asked me how could I date an Oriental. The proper term is Asian, I told him." Charles threw onions into a skillet. "His attitude didn't bother me. Generally, I don't like others enforcing their personal preference on my life."

"You're such a rebel. I like that in you." She watched him. "Why do we get along? I like to follow every rule. You like to challenge as many as possible."

"Because we each know a special person when we see one. Besides, you must secretly want to smash a rule or two, or else you'd stick to dating Black men."

Considering the theory for a minute, she concluded it was inaccurate. Margaret remained convinced that everything in her wanted to conform. "Brittany was very impressed with you."

"I sensed sibling rivalry."

"Mother thinks Brittany's in serious debt. Sometimes I think she hates me."

"I think if you needed her, she would be there for you."

"I'm positive you're right. I only wish she wasn't —."

"Such a bitch?"

"As self-centered and pretentious."

He went to the refrigerator. "I thought you were showing me off a little."

Margaret sipped the water. Why not? She thought. Men do it with women. "I confess I sometimes feel inferior around Brittany."

He returned to the stove. "There's nothing inferior about you."

"Did you like Mother?"

"She was gracious."

"I wish you could have met my father. He died three years ago. He still lives with me in spirit. When he was alive, we were very close. I told him about school and even more personal things like my shyness with boys. Many times he told me about his childhood and his struggles to become a doctor. I never tired of hearing it. It made me feel connected, like each generation before had left me something."

"Would he approve of your dating me?"

"I don't know. He endured lots of racism. But because he adored me, I think he would have respected my feelings. I believe he would have approved." She put the glass on the coffee table. "I want a man who will treat me as well as my father did."

"High standards, I'm sure."

Are you that man? Margaret wanted to ask. "When's dinner? I'm hungry."

* * *

Monday morning April came into Margaret's office to discuss work. After telling April about her first date with Charles, Margaret hadn't mentioned Charles again. April, friendly as ever, often had lunch with Margaret. She had quit offering to set up more blind dates and asking about Margaret's weekend.

"How was your weekend?" Margaret inquired after the work related discussion ended.

"We finished the house painting. Three rooms! I'm glad to be rid of that chore."

"I had a good weekend." Margaret got up and closed the door. She was eager to talk about Charles.

"With your rich White lover?"

"I never said he was rich." Margaret returned to the desk. "Yesterday I went to his place. He cooked a delicious dinner.

He's a better cook than I am. Afterwards, we listened to music. He likes classical music. I don't. But I listened to it with him. We had a glass of wine. Actually, I had two."

"Now you're a drinking woman? And on a Sunday."

"Then he put on a CD by an Italian pop singer named . . . Eros, who sings in Italian."

"Speaking Italian now?"

"Charles says the lyrics are the same nonsense that's usually sung in English. I didn't know there was such a thing as Italian pop. I enjoyed it, though. Eros has a magnificent voice. Anyway, we danced. He started kissing me — my neck, and my shoulders and . . . well. They were soft, warm kisses. Then he offered to show me the rest of the house. I guessed he meant the upstairs."

"The bedrooms?"

"Exactly. I told him I would stay downstairs. Turns out there's a guest suite on the first floor, with a Jacuzzi. He asked if I wanted to sit in it for a while. Absolutely not, I told him. He started kissing me again. I started to overheat, somehow. Maybe it was the wine? I pushed him away. But he kept advancing. Then he stopped and left the room. After a while, I wondered where he'd gone to and went looking for him. I found him in the guest area, in the bathroom, filling the tub. He poured something in the water, and I watched it bubble. He said, 'Why don't you get in? See how warm it is.' The bubbles *were* inviting. So I got in. Charles got in with me. In the Jacuzzi for the first time he told me he loved me."

"Sounds about right. Guys will say anything to get sex."

"And I believed him. Shouldn't I have? I do even now. We crawled out of the tub and onto the floor. He made love to me. He was very gentle. I had forgotten how wonderful sex was, and how addictive. After we . . . you know, I wanted to do it again. Instead, I got up and found a towel and wrapped it around myself. I walked into the den to look for the rest of that bottle of wine. I found it. But the bottle was empty. I turned around. Charles was behind me. I told him sadly that the bottle was empty. He took it from me and threw it on the couch. 'Cut off that music,' I said because it, something, was making me feel romantic. He came closer and started pressing against me. I backed away and fell onto the coffee table. For a minute I couldn't figure out what to do. So I just lay there. Then he started . . . . I won't get graphic. It's enough to say Tommy wasn't into that. And neither was I until last night. It was amazing.

"Afterwards, I rolled onto the floor. Charles lay beside me. I thought he would fall asleep quickly. After a few minutes passed, I got up and started to the stairs in search of a bathroom. I hoped to stay far away from the one with the Jacuzzi. Suddenly Charles was behind me." Glancing at April, Margaret said, "I'll spare you the details."

"You did it on the stairs?" April leaned forward.

"Afterwards, we lay there awhile before Charles suggested we go to the master bedroom."

"Not again?"

"I was exhausted. Upstairs I collapsed on the bed. Charles lay beside me. He pulled the covers over me. I fell asleep with my head on his chest. During the night we changed positions several times, but stayed attached. His alarm clock went off at six. He wanted to be certain I got to work on time. I didn't want to leave his side. I said good morning. He said good morning while stroking my hair. He got up and ran a bubble bath for me. He took a shower, got dressed, and went downstairs to fix breakfast for us. By the time I finished soaking, got dressed, and went down, Charles had breakfast on the table. There was a platter of scrambled eggs, also sausage, and biscuits out of a can, laid out on the dining room table. Knowing I wasn't a coffee drinker, he asked if I wanted tea. I said no and we ate. I wanted to tell him I loved him, although that fact makes no sense to me. We're such an odd looking couple. Yet I adore being with him."

"Maybe it's just sex?"

"It's not about sex at all."

"Not sex?" April sucked her teeth.

"Something about him clicked with something in me. It's spiritual. I can't explain it. It's as if nature created male/female attractions. Some things nature revealed about them. Other things she kept hidden."

"Spiritual? Never heard it called that before."

"I don't fit into his world. He doesn't fit into mine. He wants to have fun dating, probably indefinitely. I want a family right away."

"You're probably right. There's no hope you can ever marry this man."

"I'm convinced of it," Margaret said.

"Why waste your time on the playboys of this world? You're growing older. Your looks will fade, your waistline spread, and you'll never get a man to marry you."

"I believe you. But the attraction between Charles and me is like a tornado, brief, intense, and hard to fight off."

"Try to resist."

Margaret shook her head. "I'm too weak."

"Too weak for your imaginary affair?" April stood. "Well, Margaret, you got me with that one! What have you been reading or watching this time? Soft-core porn on cable? On the floor, the table, the stairs. Woman, please! The next time you find yourself having sex on a coffee table, wake up! And that stuff about, 'It's not sex. It's spiritual.'" April chuckled as she repeated the words. "Listen to me. I'm trying to help you. Stop daydreaming. Find yourself a husband and have a couple of kids before it's too late, and you regret the days you wasted." April marched to the door. Before leaving she turned to Margaret. "You're a good Catholic lady. You have a respectable position here. Stop making up stories. Lying doesn't become you." April swung open the door and left without bothering to close it.

Margaret looked out of the window. She could smell Charles's scent still on her and feel his hand stroking her skin. Knowing April wouldn't believe her had helped Margaret release some of last evening's intimate details. Now Margaret recalled the way she had felt when Charles entered her for the first time. The memory made her softly gasp.

13

During the month of October, Shawanda acted as if life would always be grand. On weekday mornings she fed and kissed Aaron before he left for work. She then got Donte dressed and fed and took him to pre-school, where he did well. Back home, cleaning, decorating, and cooking followed. Some days were filled with running errands. In the evenings at dinner, the family talked. Afterwards the three watched television or played games.

In November, Shawanda had Thanksgiving dinner with Aaron's family. It was a feast. She got to meet several relatives of Aaron's for the first time. And Donte made lots of new little friends.

By December, the new house organized, Shawanda went shopping. She found cute Christmas decorations to adorn the house. Aaron and Donte decorated the tree. Christmas Eve, Aaron helped wrap gifts. On the next day the three rose early. Shawanda and Aaron watched as Donte opened his presents. Then they exchanged gifts. He gave her a necklace and matching earrings, which she thought beautiful and adored. She gave him two sweaters that she thought would look good on him and he would like. He seemed to. Afterwards the three had breakfast. In the afternoon they went to Lena and Ernest's.

There, Shawanda greeted relatives she hadn't seen for a while and introduced them to Aaron. She took the macaroni and cheese dish she had made and placed it on the dining room table along side all of the other good things brought by the guests.

When Lena came out of the kitchen, Aaron said, "Hey."

Lena returned the greeting with, "Where's my Precious Baby?"

The two said only one other thing to each other during the gathering. When dinner was served, Lena asked Aaron to pass the salt shaker. The tension between them was obvious. Shawanda was happy there weren't any harsh words shared that day.

On New Year's Eve Donte stayed with Lena and Ernest and accompanied them to church. Shawanda, Aaron, Denise, and her new boyfriend went to the club.

On New Year's Day Shawanda invited Kim and her four boys over for dinner. Since Kim was without a car, Aaron picked her up while Shawanda finished cooking and setting the table. Kim arrived and immediately gave Shawanda a warm hug. Greeting the children, she was glad to see her old neighbor. She showed Kim the house.

"This is beautiful!" Kim said several times.

The children played before and after dinner while the adults talked. Shawanda enjoyed herself and the company of her friend.

January brought snow. February, the anniversary of Social Services' first visit, was unusually cold. On its first Friday, Shawanda and Aaron lay entwined on the couch. Stretched out on the floor, Donte watched the big screen television.

When the program was over, Shawanda asked, "Ready for bed, Donte?"

"I wanna watch TV, Ma."

She got up and put a children's video in the VCR before rejoining Aaron. An hour later, when the program finished, Donte asked, "Can I watch some more, Ma?"

She put in a second tape and went upstairs. In her bedroom, she changed into a nightgown.

Aaron came in. "Baby, it's eleven o'clock. Time for a five-year-old to be in bed."

"This is his treat."

"You gotta make kids go to bed every night at the same time. That's what Pops did with me."

"Let him be happy." She sat on the side of the bed.

"He ought to be happy. He's got everything. He don't have to do heavy construction work in the cold."

"What's the big deal?"

"Make a rule, stick to it. The boy knows you're not playing."

Why are you such an expert? She was tempted to ask. But instead Shawanda turned on the small screen television. She climbed into bed and pulled the blanket up to her neck. "Next Christmas, think I'll buy him a TV for his room," she announced.

"Three televisions in one house! I've got enough bills. Bad enough the money I had saved up is all gone."

"We'll catch up."

"I'm not griping, Baby." Aaron sat on the bed. "I want to take care of you."

"You do a good job of it."

"You can't tell that by Donte. He acts like his real father's taking care of him."

"He never saw him."

Aaron sat quietly staring at the television screen in between glances at her. Thirty minutes passed. Suddenly Aaron jumped up and left the room. Shawanda jumped out of bed, and ran behind him. When she reached the doorway, he was going down the stairs. She followed him. When she reached the first floor, Shawanda saw Donte sitting on the floor. Aaron hovered over him. Donte looked up at Aaron.

"Go to bed, Donte."

"Ma!" The child started crying.

"Move, Boy, right now."

Donte scurried across the floor to his mother. When he reached her, he grabbed her right leg and held on to it.

Shawanda looked down and saw the top of her son's head. She then looked up. "I got him, Aaron. You can go to bed if you want to."

"Oh, you can tell me to go to bed." He pushed the stop button on the VCR. "But you won't tell the five-year-old what to do." He clicked off the television. Strutting to the kitchen, Aaron turned off the light. Returning to the living room, he did the same. "Everybody's going to bed now, Donte."

"No, Ma! I wanna watch TV."

Shawanda had to do something quickly. "Donte, you listen to your new daddy. Go upstairs and put on your pajamas, right now."

The crying Donte went up the stairs.

"See?" Shawanda went behind Donte. "It's not that hard."

"All I saw was him listening to you and not me." Aaron followed.

In their room, she turned on the television.

"I can't stand this, Baby." Aaron came in.

"What?"

"He wouldn't even answer me."

"He's a child."

"Ma this. Ma that." Suddenly, he walked out of the room.

Again she pursued him, this time to Donte's room. There she saw her son sitting on the bed. Shawanda quickly got a pair of Donte's pajamas out of the drawer and put them on him. Aaron stood in the middle of the room, watching her. She pulled the blanket back and said, "Come on Donte, get into bed."

"I gotta go to the bathroom," he said in his high, little voice.

She dropped the blanket. "Well, go ahead, and hurry up."

Donte looked at Aaron, who moved over to the dresser and began tapping on top of it.

Donte, staying as far away from Aaron as possible, headed toward the doorway, his eyes steady on the adult.

After a couple of minutes, Aaron asked Shawanda, "What's he doing?"

"I guess he's in the bathroom."

Before the words fully left her mouth and cruised the air to Aaron's ears, before she could move, go out of the room and into the bathroom, before that, Aaron was gone.

"You had better get into bed!" Shawanda heard Aaron yell the words.

Donte ran back into the room and jumped into bed. Shawanda put the blanket over him as Aaron came in and stood next to her.

"Who do you think you're playing with, Boy?" Aaron yelled.

Shawanda saw Donte tremble. "It's all right, Aaron. He's in bed."

Aaron pointed his finger in Donte's face. "You ever give me trouble like this —."

"You're losing it again." Shawanda pushed his hand from Donte's face.

"I ought to whip his ass right now!" Aaron took one step closer to the bed.

Donte screamed, rolled across the bed, and off the other side.

"He's not in bed," Aaron said in a voice Shawanda didn't recognize.

"If he wants to sleep on the floor, let him." She only wanted this mess to end.

"You two ain't caught on yet." Aaron looked at her. "He can't have his way in my house!"

More frustrated with Aaron's behavior than Donte's, she went to the other side of the bed, and pulled Donte up from between the bed and the wall. "Give Mama a good night kiss, and we're all going to bed."

When she bent down to kiss him, Shawanda noticed Donte's eyes widen. Following his stare, she saw Aaron coming toward them. Suddenly Donte jerked away and bolted. Just as he ran past Aaron, Aaron's right hand went out and grabbed the back of the child's neck. Shawanda saw the hand tighten around her son's neck as if to hold him in place.

Donte struggled.

Shawanda rushed to them. Before she could speak or scream or do anything at all, she saw Aaron's other hand gripped the front of Donte's neck. Donte's mouth opened, and gargling sounds tried to escape from his throat.

"You're choking him!"

At the same time she uttered the words, she saw Aaron raise Donte into the air by the neck and fling him across the room and onto the bed.

Shawanda screamed. Again. Screamed. Again. She had not known, thought she had, but had not known pain until now.

Aaron fled the room.

Donte lay stomach up across the bed. He gasped for air.

"Baby, Baby," she called, wanting him to answer. Wanting him to say, 'I'm all right, Ma.'

There was something she should do now. She was Donte's shield. He was her responsibility. She should protect him. Scooping up her son, she held him close to her chest.

He began to cough. Saliva shot from his mouth.

Shawanda went into the hallway. She wandered into her room. She neither saw nor considered where Aaron was or what he was doing. The words, *he choked Donte*, stomped through her brain and stabbed at her heart. He could have killed him, she mumbled to herself. While those words sounded irrational, her eyes confirmed they were accurate.

Shawanda picked up the telephone. She pushed the nine, then the one twice. The night's events began to overwhelm her, and her brain shut down. Hearing the phone ring on the other end, her mind registered nothing.

By the time someone picked up, Shawanda had mentally disconnected. "He choked my son. He could have killed him."

"How old is your son?" The woman's voice floated about, it seemed.

"Five. He was four. He made five in July."

"Who choked him?"

"Aaron."

"Who's Aaron?" the voice asked.

"He was my boyfriend. Now he's my husband."

"Where's Aaron now?"

"He's around here somewhere."

"What's your address?"

Shawanda started to recite it, but the numbers got mixed up in her head. It took three tries.

"What's your name?"

"Shawanda Tia Matthews Washington. That's my whole name."

"I'll send out a car."

"A car?" Shawanda repeated, listening to and comprehending the words this time.

"It'll be there in a couple of minutes."

The phone slipped from Shawanda's hand. Her mind drifted to a peaceful place and lingered there awhile. A banging sound brought it back. Strange voices speckled the air. With the now sobbing Donte in her arms, she wandered to the top of the stairs and saw two policemen standing near the front door. She saw them in colors, blue uniforms, ruby faces, yellow crew cuts, black guns. A voice buzzed about her head, it seemed, and whispered into her ear, 'you shouldn't have called them.'

"Can you come down here, Miss, please?" the first officer, who was the shorter of the two, said.

Slowly sliding against the wall, she descended the stairs. At the foot of them, the first officer looked at Donte.

"He doesn't look good." He then surveyed his neck. "He's got bruising. He needs to go to the hospital. What happened, Miss?"

Aaron called to her, "Baby," as he stood near the door.

She looked at him. His eyes pled. She turned to the officer, and opened her mouth. No words got loose.

"What is he, your boyfriend?" the second officer smirked while taking out a pair of handcuffs.

"My husband."

"That figures." The second officer grabbed Aaron, pulled his arm to the back, rammed him against the nearby wall, and handcuffed him. Then he patted him down and checked his pockets.

Shawanda looked away.

"I'll call for back-up," the first officer said to Shawanda. "They'll take the child to the hospital."

"Aaron needs his coat," she blurted, turning to the officer. "It's freezing out there."

The second officer pulled Aaron toward the door. "He'll be good and warm. We're going to put him in a nice heated car and chauffeur him to the station." He went out of the door with Aaron, followed by the first officer.

Shawanda ran to the doorway. Outside, the night slept.

14

Another police car pulled up behind the first one. Two officers got out of the second car, one a tall, husky man with skin the color of molasses. The other a medium-height, red-haired woman. They walked up to the first car and conferred with their colleagues.

The first car pulled away with Aaron in the back of it. The remaining officers approached Shawanda. They introduced themselves as Ronald Hill and Sarah McKellen. Sarah helped to gather Donte. She put on his coat while Shawanda got her keys and purse.

"What happened?" Officer Hill asked Shawanda as the group prepared to leave.

But Shawanda was scared something awful would happen to Aaron, and their lives would even more horribly change. "I don't remember," she answered after locking the door.

In the back of the police car, while riding through her neighborhood, Shawanda felt like a foreigner in a hostile land.

At the hospital's emergency's ward, while Officer Hill spoke to the admitting clerk, Officer McKellan sat beside her.

"He's adorable," Sarah said. "I have three children, two boys and a girl. I worry about them the same way you must worry about Donte. It's awful your husband choked him."

Shawanda said nothing.

"You think, maybe, he didn't mean to do it?"

"He didn't." She thought the officer might understand, based on what she had just said.

"This whole thing must be terrible for you." Sarah leaned closer and asked, "How did it start?"

She was starting to feel comfortable with Sarah. After all, they were both mothers. "Donte wouldn't go to bed."

"Ahhh, children are like that sometimes. How did it turn violent?"

"Donte got out the bed and started to run out. Aaron grabbed him by the neck. Aaron was choking him. I don't think he meant to do it. He picked him up and slung him on the bed."

"He picked him up by the neck?"

Shawanda nodded, the salty taste of tears on her tongue.

"If it had been my son," Sarah said, "I don't know what I would have done. How long was it before you called the police?"

"Right when it happened."

"Has he ever done anything like this before?"

"One time." Shawanda told her about the milk, the beating, Lena, and Social Services.

Just then a female admitting clerk called Shawanda's name.

"Looks like the doctor's ready for you," Sarah said.

Shawanda got up and walked toward the clerk. She looked back at Sarah. Sarah was rapidly writing something in a notebook. Suddenly Shawanda realized the officer wasn't a sympathetic friend after all. But she was a police officer merely writing a report. Shawanda felt betrayed.

"Please follow me." The clerk got Shawanda's attention.

In the back, the polite Korean doctor asked Shawanda, "What happened?"

She hesitated.

"I need the information to treat your son," he explained.

"Don't tell the police." That he not inform them, somehow, at this moment, seemed of maximum importance.

"The emergency room is full of patients tonight. I don't have time for conversation with the police."

Shawanda considered Donte. She wanted to be certain he was all right. She told the doctor everything, including, "I should have never called 911. They came and took Aaron to jail."

"What did you think they would do?" the doctor asked.

"I don't know. I didn't think about it."

The doctor ordered x-rays. After the x-rays, Shawanda was given instructions on how to care for Donte over the next few days.

Hours after arriving, she went out and flagged a cab. The thought of seeing her pretty new house was unwelcome now. She gave the driver her parents' address.

Arriving there, she carried her son to the front door and rang the doorbell several times before Ernest finally responded.

"What are you doing here? Something's wrong."

"Let me put Donte in bed first." Taking him up to her old room, she tucked him in. Back downstairs in the living room, Lena had joined Ernest.

"What did that idiot do?" Lena almost yelled.

Shawanda gave them every detail.

"At least you called the police," Ernest said.

"I didn't want them to arrest him."

"He's right where he needs to be — in jail." Lena sucked her teeth. "That idiot was probably trying to kill my baby. I'm going up to see if Precious is okay."

"You must be tired," Ernest said to Shawanda after Lena left them.

She nodded. She was glad neither one of her parents had said I told you so. "Think I'll go to bed now."

Upstairs she found Lena coming out of her old room. "You did the right thing," Lena assured.

Shawanda went in and lay beside Donte. Within minutes sleep visited and stayed three hours. Awaking tired, she got up. At the top of the stairs, she could hear Lena's and Ernest's voices coming from the kitchen. She went down and joined them.

"All they're going to do is let him out of jail," Lena was saying when Shawanda entered.

"I'm sorry I called the police. I don't want Aaron in jail."

"Tell me you're never going back to that child abuser," Lena pleaded.

"I can't stand the way he treats Donte. I'm not going back to him."

Within the hour, Ernest took Shawanda home to get clothes and personal items.

Back home, in the late afternoon the telephone rang. Ernest answered and handed it to Shawanda, saying, "It's Peter."

She took the telephone and placed it to her ear.

"You put my son in jail!" Aaron's father said instead of hello. "Why did you call the police?"

"I wasn't thinking."

"If you had raised that boy of yours right . . . ."

"It's not Donte's fault Aaron acted like that."

"You had this boy out of wedlock. You don't know where the father is. You probably don't know who the father is. And my son ends up raising Donte."

"Your son don't have to raise Donte no more because I'm finished with Aaron."

"Finished with him? After all he did for you and that boy. He took good care of you."

"And choked my son."

"My son doesn't belong in jail. We're getting him out."
Peter hung up.

Shawanda's anger was so great that she felt nauseated.

The days passed. On Tuesday afternoon, Shawanda
answered the telephone's ring and was surprised to hear
Aaron's voice.

"Got out a couple of hours ago. I took a long shower. I
had to get the jail stink off me." After Shawanda said nothing,
he continued. "They've got me charged with assault and child
abuse. Can you believe that shit? The lawyer got my bail
down to twenty-thousand-dollars. Moms and Pops used their
house."

"Where are you?" Shawanda asked. She thought he might
have gone to his parents.

"Home. I was surprised you weren't here. I don't blame
you for calling the police. I'm sorry I hurt Donte. I lost it
again. Sorry I hurt you and messed up our lives. You've got
no reason to believe me. But I swear, it won't happen again."

"I'm leaving you."

"I'll go back to counseling."

"Too late," she said.

"You promised to stick by me."

"You don't care about me," she blurted.

"Take that lie back."

"I'm not taking anything back."

"Don't do this to me. Why don't you leave Donte with
your parents? Come home and let's talk about things."

"Leave Donte? That's my son. I'm not leaving him
anywhere. What do you mean, come home? You tore up our
home. And as for talking, we're talking now. And this is what
I've got to say: people thought I was crazy for staying with
you the first time, but now even I can't stick up for you
anymore. You act like a criminal. You ought to be in jail."

Anger guided her, told her to say things she didn't mean. "I don't believe they only gave you that little bail!"

"Don't talk to me that way."

"Don't you treat me and my son this way."

"I tried to be a father to Donte, Baby. It's hard raising somebody else's son and getting no respect."

"Respect this! I'm through with you. Goodbye."

"You better not hang up on me."

"Yeah?" She slammed the phone down.

* * *

In the following weeks Shawanda refused all calls from Aaron. She returned to the house to get more things while Aaron worked. At the end of February she found a job at a fast food restaurant.

At the beginning of March, Shawanda got a letter from the State's Attorney's Office giving her an appointment. By then her anger at Aaron had subsided. Shawanda had decided the state shouldn't pursue Aaron. He had been through enough. They all had. She would keep the appointment and tell the state's attorney to drop the charges.

On that day, Shawanda walked into the fairly new courthouse in Towson. She took the elevator, and then wandered about looking at numbers on the doors. She hated all courthouses, she decided, even the glossy and modern ones. They all scared her. Finally locating the correct room, Shawanda entered the prosecutor's office. Inside the plain room she stood at the receptionist's desk and waited for her to finish the business-related call.

"Good morning," the woman greeted. "May I help you?"

"I gotta see Miss Parker."

"Your name, please."

"Shawanda Washington."

"I'll let Ms. Parker know you're here." She picked up the telephone receiver and pushed three buttons. After speaking, she hung up. To Shawanda she said, "She'll be with you shortly. Please have a seat."

Shawanda obeyed. A uniformed police officer entered, spoke to the receptionist, and sat down.

Soon a woman emerged from a side doorway. "Mrs. Washington, I'm Tamika Parker." She extended her hand. "Glad to meet you. Please, come into my office."

Shawanda followed the woman with the braided hair. In the office, Tamika, who was dressed in a conservative navy blue suit, sat in the chair beside her. "This must be hard for you. It's one thing to have your son assaulted, but when it's done by your husband . . . ."

"It's really hard."

"I want to help keep your son safe. In my ten years as a prosecutor, I've devoted most of my time to physical and sexual abuse cases. No matter how many times I've seen it, and I've done about two thousand of these cases, each incident greatly disturbs me. Sometimes I can't sleep. Well, I'm sure you've had sleepless nights over this."

Shawanda nodded. She found herself liking Tamika.

"Please tell me about Aaron, your life together, your son, and the night of this horrible incident."

Shawanda gave her the details so Tamika would understand the case needed a dismissal.

"I spoke to your husband's attorney, Darrell Black. He's an attractive Black male who's about thirty. He has a pleasant personality. Personally, I like him. Juries tend to like him. I've spoken to him about your husband's case. I've offered him child abuse. I'll drop the assault charge. Darrell rejected it. He believes it's a family matter that doesn't belong in the system. He actually asked me to dismiss it. I told him his client was going to jail."

"No, don't send Aaron to jail!"

"We don't have to argue about this. Mr. Black has already rejected the offer. His client wants a jury trial. Can I count on your testimony?"

"Against Aaron?"

The prosecutor leaned closer. "For Donte. He's your son. You owe it to him."

"Am I your whole case?" If she was, Shawanda decided, Tamika was without a case.

"You aren't. At the trial, my first witness will be Donte. I don't expect to get a lot out of a five-year-old. But I want the jury to understand he's a real person, an innocent person. Whatever your son did that night, he didn't deserve what was done to him. My next witnesses would be the police officers. I don't need all four of them, although I'll use them. The more uniformed officers, the more the jury will appreciate the seriousness of it all. I'll start with Sarah McKellan, the one who took the statement. At some point, I'll introduce the 911 tape. It shows you were clearly in shock and groping to remember your own address. Do you recall the second words out of your mouth?"

Shawanda shook her head no.

"You were there. You saw everything. The second thing you said was, 'He could have killed him.' Think I'll play the tape twice in court for greater effect. Once when one of the officers is on the stand, and again during closing arguments. Maybe I could end with the tape? Anyway, I also have the medical reports. I'll bring in the doctor. He made note of the bruising. His findings substantiate your statements. As for whether or not I can make the case without you, I don't get to that question. I plan to call you to the stand."

"I don't think I can do it."

"Tell me this. When you were at home with Aaron and the police, you refused to make a statement. At the hospital, without Aaron, you told the police and the doctor what happened. Why? Are you afraid of Aaron? Has he hit you?"

Shawanda remembered the day he raised his fist to her. "Never! He wouldn't do that!"

"When you're on the stand, if you don't testify or you do poorly, I'll have to wonder if Aaron's presence in the courtroom intimidates you. I'll have to ask the jury to make that decision."

"My life is turning bad. I can't go through this no more. Please just drop the charges."

"No way. Donte's a citizen. The state will protect him."

"Please, don't do this. Putting Donte on the stand will hurt him more. He's shy."

"All I can do if your husband takes the plea is to offer him probation." Tamika rose from the chair and walked to her desk.

"What happens if he doesn't plea?" Shawanda asked.

Tamika sat in the swivel chair behind her desk. "Jury trials are lots of work. And lots of stress. Yet I enjoy them. They get the adrenaline going. I'll admit I'm competitive. I must always win. But I've learned I must keep other things in mind, too. Like, this job isn't about me. An adult choked a child. My job is to protect the victim. If your husband wants a trial, the state will gladly give him one. I can't imagine a jury will appreciate his charge. If he loses the jury trial, it's my job to see he gets as much jail time as possible." Tamika twirled in the chair. "Don't worry. It's his first charge. He wouldn't get a lot of time. Maybe two or three years."

Shawanda jumped up. "Two or three years!" She couldn't believe what she had done to Aaron.

15

In the month of March, Margaret went to the Canton area. It was an area she seldom visited. The occasion was the opening of a new bookstore. Pulling into the parking lot, Margaret admired the prettiness of her surroundings. There were new, fairly expensive looking townhouses and luxury apartment buildings. Margaret knew that nearby was a marina. Entering the large bookstore, she looked around. Margaret decided to began by browsing through the books in the front of the store.

Someone called to her. Turning, she saw the man approach.

"Margaret," the man said when he stood in front of her.

"Tommy." Margaret swallowed.

"Good to run into you." Thomas Green hugged her.

Her body stiffened.

"It's been a long time." He looked at her and smiled.

"Almost three years."

"How have you been?" he inquired.

She considered various ways to answer the question. She could say, 'After the break up, I was alone and bitter. I prayed to God that He would comfort me. There was no one else strong enough to do it. Thankfully, God answers prayers.'

But she had shared enough with Tommy during their six-year engagement, Margaret now decided. She wasn't unlocking herself and letting him in. On the other hand, Margaret could tell him about Charles. The only point in doing so would be to make Tommy jealous. To let him know she hadn't recently thought of him or their dead and rightfully-put-to-rest relationship. But something in her didn't care to share Charles with him, didn't care what Tommy thought.

Now not wanting to start a conversation with him, afraid to, Margaret groped for any reason to get away. "Actually, I was on my way —."

"Would you like to get a cup of coffee? I have things to tell you."

Margaret had a few angry, accusing chunks of information to aim at him. Yet being the polite Catholic she was, Margaret resisted. "I don't have a lot of time."

"Please, fifteen minutes?"

If she talked to him for five minutes, anger might run up from her heart, kick against the walls of her mouth, and try to burst out and act up. She started to decline when curiosity whispered, let's hear what he has to say. Maybe it would be something rewarding like, 'I was an idiot. I never deserved you.' That would certainly be worth hearing. "Sure, for a couple of minutes."

They walked to the bookstore's coffee bar, and up to the counter. Tommy ordered coffee. She got a hot tea with no sugar or cream. They sat at a small table near the window.

As he stirred cream into his coffee, Margaret glanced at him. She noted that Tommy, who was slightly taller and slightly darker-skinned than she, had physically changed little. Dressed in brown pants and a white shirt, he looked younger than his thirty-three years. He was thin and muscular with dull black hair. He wore glasses.

"How's your mother?" he asked. "I always liked her."

"She always liked you. She's dating a retired train conductor."

"Great. And your sister?"

"Well. She was here six months ago."

"Still with Social Services?" he asked.

"Do you care?" she answered.

"Yes."

"That's something new."

"I always cared."

"You kept it a secret."

"When we started dating, what, ten years ago?"

She didn't bother to answer him.

"I was young and idealistic," he continued. "Remember we were going to change the world almost all by ourselves? I went to medical school because I wanted to help people. But I lost my purpose there. I became obsessed with my career and forgot everything and everyone else."

"Right, you did."

"By the time I started practicing medicine, I had become the center of my world. Being a doctor was about me, my skills, my talents, and my potential to make lots of money. I had a good woman by my side, but I was too busy to notice."

"That sounds almost like an apology." His words made Margaret consider her own revelations since their break-up. "When you weren't acting like I wanted you to, I became disappointed and frustrated. You said I was suffocating you. I don't blame you. Those were stupid times. You were the only woman I've ever wanted to spend my life with. Yet when things got really bad, I let go."

"We let go." Searching his eyes to gauge his sincerity, Margaret liked what she saw and heard. Her anger took a deep breath and relaxed.

"These past three years I've had some bad relationships. The last one was the worst." He paused. "She used sex and affection as weapons to get what she wanted."

"I'm in love with Charles."

"I'm happy for you. I'm doing well. For a while there, I lost my way. Now I'm finding it. I work full-time in the clinic on Greenmount Street. Most of our patients see a doctor only when they're really sick. They have low incomes and no insurance. They don't get regular checkups. Also, two days a month I volunteer with the Homeless Project. We go into homeless shelters and even on the streets to aid people who aren't together enough to make it to a clinic."

"Sounds like you're living out the goals you had before medical school." She was impressed.

"I'm happy with my career. Before, working so hard in school, I thought I deserved things — luxury cars, boats. Now I know there's time for that. Right now I'm searching for something, like, maybe, a family. You know, the plans we had when I proposed to you." He gulped the coffee. "After we broke up, I was bitter. I'm sure you were, too. Maybe if we talked every once in a while, it would help us both?"

"No. There's nothing to talk about."

"What would it hurt?"

"I'm concentrating on the relationship I'm in now."

"A few innocent conversations . . . that's all I'm asking."

She considered his proposal. A couple of innocent talks might help her to understand the past and not repeat her mistakes. "Okay, we can talk." She gave him her home telephone number before excusing herself and heading toward the bookshelves for new reading material. Maybe running into Tommy was a good thing, she conceded. Talking to him, seeing how he had changed his life made her dislike him less. If she could release all of the old bitterness left from their relationship, certainly she would be a happier person.

* * *

Within days she saw Charles. He dropped in late one night on his way home from work. They sat on the sofa. He told her about his day, which had been tiring. She sympathized and offered food. With his acceptance she made a sandwich, brought it to him and watched him devour it.

"Ran into my ex-boyfriend," she said.

"Were the two of you civil?"

"He apologized —."

"Wimp."

"Almost apologized. I kinda did, too."

"Did the two of you decide to date again?"

"Don't be ridiculous."

"Should I keep an eye on you, lest you start whoring around?"

Margaret considered her image changing from plain and dull to slut. She chuckled. "Tommy was like his old self."

"Ah! My competition has a name."

"He's not competition."

"Are you still in love with him?" Charles sat back.

She considered the question. "You mean am I excited, even high, and almost out of my head with feelings for him?"

"That wasn't exactly the question." He smiled.

"You make me feel that way. With Tommy, it was about having a future and getting the things I wanted in life. He was stable and practical. I think in a lot of ways he's like me. You, on the other hand, are an attraction I can't explain. I don't know the side of me that loves you."

"That doesn't sound positive."

"You're the great romance of my life. If only I could combine you and Tommy."

"You're talking nonsense." He got up.

"My parents were married for thirty-five years," she continued. "There was love and affection and support between them."

"My parents divorced when I was four." He stood near the sofa. "My mother left my brother and me with our father. I never knew why. My brother thinks it may have been about money. Father had it. She didn't. Mother and I were never close after that. We would engage in polite conversation, but never anything of importance. I was twenty-one when she died of cancer. But I think I lost her before then, maybe when I was four."

"I'm sorry."

"I can't tell you how I felt about any of it because it's all still mixed up in my head."

"Although you came from a broken home —."

"And fighting parents who used us."

"You can have a happy marriage," she said.

"I have no desire to marry anyone anytime in the near future. I have a bad image of marriage. It's all work and few rewards. How can two people sustain a relationship all of their lives, anyway? Wouldn't you get tired of looking at each other? And what if it doesn't work? Even worse than the horror of divorce is two unhappy people staying together for the sake of the children."

"Want children?"

"I may make the worst father."

"I want children." She moved to the edge of the couch. "Right away."

"I can't give you those things, at least not now."

"Then where are we going?"

He slid next to her. "Let's take it slowly, enjoy each other's company, have fun, see what develops."

"I need goals," she said.

"Caring about each other, that's our goal."

"I'm thirty-three. I had that long engagement that went nowhere. I need more."

He stroked her hair. "Since I've started dating you, I haven't gone out with anyone else."

"Were you supposed to?" she asked.

"It was my habit. This is the longest romantic relationship I've ever had. Nine months!" He looked at her and grinned. "You don't know what effort it's taken."

She tried not to smile, but failed.

Charles leaned toward her and brought his face in close to her face.

She put her hand up. "Don't try to kiss me."

"Mad?"

"And wanting to stay that way. You kiss me, and I might forget the fact we're two different people who travel in different social circles and are going in opposite directions."

"I want you," he said.

Her resistance suddenly fell. "I want you, too."

"See." He stayed close. "Same goal, same direction." Then he kissed her.

* * *

During the rest of March, Tommy called every other day. They talked sometimes for as long as an hour. They talked about their work and their families. About the past, and their future aspirations. They laughed together again.

On the first Saturday in April, they went to the bagel shop across the street from Margaret's house for breakfast. On their next outing, the two went jogging.

"We should do this at least two or three times a week," he said as they jogged down the sidewalk. "You know, for the exercise."

She agreed exercise was needed and managed to get it regularly with him. They were old friends, she concluded, nothing more. When he asked her to a movie, Margaret declined. She dated only Charles. In mid-April, Tommy invited her to a barbecue at his parent's, who were both doctors.

"Mother just wants to see you. Remember how well the two of you got along?"

She told Charles about the barbecue. That weekend, Charles would have to work because of an upcoming trial. His response: Margaret spent too much time with Tommy. She insisted it was only jogging and an innocent visit to his mother's.

Seeing Tommy's mother again was great. Margaret had forgotten what a lively and humorous woman she was. Spending the afternoon with his family, many of whom were in medicine and other professions, was comforting. They all welcomed her.

At the end of April, Tommy appeared at her apartment. He had an announcement to make.

"When I ran into you at the bookstore, I knew it wasn't just luck. Destiny brought us back together."

"I don't believe in destiny," she said. Her second thought was: Charles had warned her. Still, she hoped Charles was wrong.

"Calling you, jogging with you, taking you to see my family were all about deciding if we should try this relationship thing again." They stood in the center of the living room.

"I'm dating Charles."

"After my last girlfriend, I didn't know how I was going to make it in another relationship. With you, I don't have to wonder. We know each other. We did the groundwork years ago. The only thing left was how we would click now. And we do."

"I have Charles."

"We're steady. We know how to work together."

"I think I know how. But I can't work with you. The romantic relationship between us is gone."

"We never had bells and music, right, Margaret?"

"Friendship, love, and commitment. We talked about it." Margaret remembered.

"Two people with both feet on the ground," he said. "None of this head in the clouds stuff for us. Two people working each day to keep the relationship alive is as good as it gets."

She had once thought that.

"Marry me," Tommy said.

"What? No!" What was Tommy's problem? Didn't he understand that Charles was in her head and heart?

"I don't mean to repeat the last time, waiting six years. Let's forget about everything else and get married soon, like next month."

"Why don't you understand? I'm dating Charles."

"He doesn't sound like the marrying type."

"Not your business." She backed away from Tommy.

"Let's have children, at least three, right away. Remember we talked about it years ago? You love children and there's no reason for us to wait."

She twirled around. Her eyes searched the room for refuge. Her body almost fled to the kitchen. "This is happening too fast."

"No, things are moving too slowly. Think about it. A year from now, we could have a house and a newborn. What do you want? A boy? A girl?"

"Either. Both."

"Or a year from now," he moved toward her, "you could still date Charles."

She covered her ears.

"You don't have to say yes today. I can wait." He approached her and tried to take her hand. She pulled away. "Margaret, I never stopped loving you."

"Why did you come back into my life? Was it to ruin it again? Get out!" She watched him stand there. When he didn't move, she did. Margaret turned and ran to her bedroom. There she closed the door and stood against it. Her breathing hard. Her life too complicated.

* * *

Monday morning in the office, Margaret sat behind her desk with lunch. April sat in front of it. Margaret gave her friend the latest details on Tommy. "He asked me to marry him."

April screamed, "Wonderful!" She bounced up and down in the chair and clapped her hands once. "No more made-up lovers for you, Margaret." Then, "I must tell you something now that you have a real boyfriend again. When I found out you made up Pierre, I thought you were pretty pathetic. I couldn't imagine being that lonely and desperate. And I really wanted to help you."

"I told Tommy no."

"Come again? Get out of dreamland and back to reality. This is what you've been waiting for."

Margaret frowned at the thought of not having Charles.

"What is wrong with you?" April put her hands on her hips.

"I'm in love, but not with Tommy."

"In love?" April dropped her arms. "You mean you have a strong, physical attraction to someone? If that's all you have, when the feelings pass, and they will, you're left with nothing."

"I don't think that's all we have."

"Take advice from a married woman. You need dependable companionship, someone you can count on in your old age."

Margaret considered April's point of view for a minute. "You don't even believe Charles exists."

"You have to admit he sounds only slightly more real than Pierre. You don't need a fantasy. You need something real."

Margaret started to tell April to take her advice and get out. Instead she looked at her watch and said, "Time for me to get back to work."

The following day, Margaret told Kathleen about Tommy's proposal. They sat on the sofa in Kathleen's antique filled living room.

"It's about time. Thank God you ran into Tommy."

"What about Charles?"

"Is he still White?"

"In this day and age, who cares?"

"You mean besides me?"

"I want to marry Charles."

"Fine. Dump Tommy again. When you're fifty and still unmarried, I'll remind you why. You waited for something that was unlikely to ever happen."

"What's the big deal about marriage anyway? If Charles wants to date indefinitely, maybe I'll do just that."

"Dating by definition is temporary."

"Don't confuse me more."

"You dated Tommy all those years and got an engagement ring out of it. With Charles, you'll get absolutely nothing."

"I'll try it Charles's way."

"You're not twenty anymore," Kathleen warned.

"Please, Mother, enough."

"Brittany has three children."

Margaret's head jerked toward Kathleen. "You've always encouraged competition between us."

"Oh, blame me because you want to waste your life on Charles."

"Try to understand the way I feel."

"I am trying. But I can't see it. All I know is you were once a stable person."

"I'm not now?" Margaret sat up.

"You're involved with two men."

"I am not!" Suddenly Margaret considered it. "Wait a minute. Maybe I am." Her head fell into her cupped hands.

"Your life's a mess." Kathleen beat her with the words. "Straighten it out." Kathleen threw up her hands. "Tommy? Charles? Just pick one."

Margaret lifted her head. Yeah, she nodded. Choose. Good idea.

Kathleen moved closer. "Remember how much your father liked Tommy? Think about it. If Carl was still alive. And you were married to Tommy. And you and Tommy had children." She clasped her hands. "Your father would be so proud of you. And so would I."

16

On a sun-speckled day, Shawanda, Lena, and Donte went to the Towson courthouse in the county for Aaron's hearing.

Lena grumbled as they headed toward Tamika Parker's office. There Lena informed the receptionist, "I want to see the state's attorney on Aaron's case."

"You're too loud," Shawanda told Lena.

"What do you mean I'm loud? I want to know how much time the idiot's getting!"

"Do you know the prosecutor's name, Miss?" the petite receptionist asked.

"What's the name?" Lena turned to Shawanda.

"Miss Parker." Shawanda took Donte and sat in a nearby chair.

"I'll tell her you're here." The receptionist picked up the phone.

When the woman began speaking into the phone, Lena went over and sat next to Shawanda. "That's right. Get her out here so I can find out what's going on."

Shawanda wanted to tell Lena she was embarrassing her. Knowing better, she only said, "Please Mama, they're getting her."

Soon Tamika came out and introduced herself to Lena.

"I'm the victim," Lena told her.

"You ain't the victim," Shawanda snapped.

"When he hurt Precious Baby, he hurt our whole family."

Shawanda's eyes rolled upwards. "Will you please stop?"

"Ladies, can both of you come into my office?" Tamika asked.

Lena took Donte's hand, stepped in front of Shawanda, and marched behind Tamika down the hall.

In the office Tamika gestured toward three chairs. Shawanda sat on one end, Donte in the middle, Lena on the other side of him.

Tamika sat behind the desk. "I've spoken to Darrell Black —."

"Who?" Lena leaned forward.

"That's Aaron's lawyer, Mama."

"What respectable person would defend him?" Lena insisted.

"They're lawyers, Mama. That's their job!"

"Instead of taking an attitude with me, you ought to —."

"Ladies," Tamika interrupted.

"Why couldn't you stay home?" Shawanda looked at Lena.

"Because I want to see them drag his crazy butt to jail!"

"You're making things worse." Shawanda had a headache.

"Ladies!"

Lena and Shawanda turned to Tamika.

"Because the dockets are enormous today," Tamika began, "I had to make some tough decisions. I offered Aaron probation."

Lena jumped up. "The next thing you're going to do is give him a hug and a kiss."

"If he violates probation, he'll do two years," Tamika added.

"Why can't he do two years now?" Lena put her hands on her hips.

"His lawyer is talking to him. He's hasn't taken the offer yet."

"Well, what's he waiting for?" Lena's head rocked right to left. "A congratulations?"

"Mr. Black's in a bad position. He probably doesn't want his client to plea. On the other hand, it'll be hard for Mr. Black to find a sympathetic judge or jury. My guess is that he's hoping the case will fall apart, that is, you won't testify. I told him my case was solid. And if he doesn't believe me, well, he can gamble with his client's freedom in front of a jury."

"Give him a trial." Lena sat back down. "Put me on that jury."

"Mama, you can't be on the jury!"

"I think I know that, Daughter! But I want to be."

"Ladies, I must wait for Mr. Black to get back to me. I'll take you to the witnesses' waiting room." Tamika got up. "You can have coffee and donuts and relax until the case is called."

"We had breakfast." Lena got up and took Donte's hand.

"She doesn't want to know all that." Shawanda followed Lena and Tamika.

Lena stopped and turned to Shawanda. "Will you let me say what I want?" She returned to following Tamika. When they reached the waiting area, Tamika left them. "I can't believe they're talking about giving that clown probation."

"Can you at least call him by his name?" Shawanda whispered in the small, people filled room.

"Child abuser," Lena said loudly. "That's a good name for him." She went over and got a cup of coffee.

Shawanda waited for her to rejoin them before saying, "Please watch Donte. I'm going to the bathroom." She didn't need to go, but had to get away from Lena for a while. Wandering the halls, she noticed Aaron and a man, presumably Mr. Black, at the other end of it. They were standing and calmly talking. She slumped onto a nearby bench and watched them.

Aaron looked in her direction. He returned his attention to Darrell Black, while periodically glancing at Shawanda. Soon Aaron left the lawyer and headed toward her.

She kept her eyes on Aaron. When he stopped in front of her, she said the first thing that popped into her head. "I asked Miss Parker to drop the charges. She said no. I don't want you to plead guilty and people think you're a criminal. I know you're not a bad person."

"Want me to have a jury trial?" he asked.

"I won't talk against you. I wouldn't say bad things about you to strangers."

"Only to my face, huh?" He didn't wait for a response. "Don't matter. I'm not gonna put you and Donte through that."

"You gonna plea'?"

"Yeah. Then will you come back home?"

His eyes seemed to beg, she thought. "What do you want from me?" She folded her arms. "That night, all that stuff didn't have to happen. I told you I could handle it."

"I made a big mistake."

"That's what you said last time. This time, you can tell it to your lawyer 'cause I don't want to hear it."

"Why you treating me like this, Baby?"

"You're pissing on my life. Look what you've done to us."

"You oughta stick by me, mistakes or not," he said.

"I tried."

"Come back home."

She looked toward the floor. After a while, Shawanda saw his feet move. She looked up to see his back as he walked away. She was angry, scared, depressed, and blaming him. Getting up, Shawanda returned to the waiting area.

Soon Tamika came and took the three of them to the courtroom. The modern, functional room was plain and crowded. Shawanda noticed Peter, Gladys, and three of Aaron's siblings sitting together on the first row. Lena spotted a bench near the back that had some vacant space on it. She went over and urged everyone on it to move closer. They did. Lena, Shawanda and Donte squeezed onto the hard bench.

Sitting, Shawanda wished it would all end quickly. She watched as a set of lawyers completed a case. She looked at the judge. He was a gray-haired, ruby-faced man. The nameplate on top of the bench read, Judge Harry Knowles. Shawanda thought he looked mean. When Tamika stood, Shawanda's glance followed her. Tamika went to the trial table.

Immediately Tamika announced, "Calling the case of the State vs. Aaron Washington. Your Honor, the state and defense have reached an agreement." She then proceeded to give him all of the details. She ended with, "The usual conditions of probation, see a probation officer, don't pick up any new charges, don't leave the city without permission, and so forth, shall apply. The conditions specific to this case are: the defendant shall attend counseling until discharged, and shall not use any type of corporal punishment on the victim. Your Honor, the state wants to be certain the defendant, who's married to the victim's mother, understands that if anything else happens, he's going to jail."

"Is that the agreement?" Judge Knowles turned to Darrell Black.

"Yes, Your Honor." Darrell stood at the trial table on the other side of the room. Darrell gestured to Aaron, who was next to him, to stand. Then he asked him questions. "Can you read and write? Has anyone forced you to plea? Do you know you have a constitutional right to a jury trial? And that you're giving up that right?"

Aaron answered all of the questions. Afterwards, the prosecutor read the police report to the judge.

As Tamika read, Shawanda recalled that hideous night, and shivered.

When Tamika finished, the judge looked coldly at her and said, "I understand. You want me to give probation to someone who grabbed a child by the neck and threw him onto a bed. But shouldn't a grown man know better?"

"Yes, Your Honor," Tamika softly replied.

The Judge's glance glided toward Aaron, then Darrell. "Counsel, what's your client's problem?"

"The child refused to go to bed."

"Children are known to do that."

"Mr. Washington lost it."

"Doesn't take much for him to lose his temper, does it?"

"He knows it was wrong. He regrets it."

"Your client figured out it was wrong *after* he did it?"

"It was an isolated incident."

"I'm glad to hear it." The judge sat back in the big leather chair. "After all, how much choking can any child take?"

The defense attorney began to tell Judge Knowles about Aaron, his lack of a criminal record, his work history, and stability in the community.

"How long was he in jail before making bail?"

Mr. Black conferred with Aaron before giving the judge the answer. "Almost a week."

"Not very long." The judge sat motionless. "We talked about this case in chambers, and I said I would give him probation. And I will. If he violates one condition, once, he'll do every day of his time?"

"Yes, Your Honor,"

"Mr. Black, I'm going to do something different in this case. I believe one thing is most effective in these inappropriate discipline cases — jail time."

"You promised —."

"And he'll get probation, Mr. Black. Just not today. Madam Clerk, please give them a date for sentencing." After the clerk gave a date that was three weeks away, Judge Knowles continued. "Mr. Black, do you have anything to say about your client's bail status pending the next hearing?"

"Mr. Washington works and —."

"The defendant's bail is revoked," the judge announced.

"But, Judge," Mr. Black began, "all that does is endanger his job. He won't be able to support his family —."

"Didn't his family include this child?"

"The child's all right," Mr. Black said.

"The victim was grabbed by the neck and tossed on a bed by someone who was supposed to look after his best interest and set good examples. The victim is not all right."

"Mr. Washington hasn't had any other arrests since making bail. He's appeared promptly for court." Darrell spoke fast. "I believe he's entitled to stay in the community until the next hearing."

"No one's entitled to anything in my courtroom. Now say good-bye to your client because the sheriff needs to take him away."

Shawanda stiffened as the sheriff approached Aaron. The sheriff pulled Aaron's arms behind his back and handcuffed him. Shawanda wrung her hands as they led Aaron through a side door. She was thankful for one thing: Aaron took it calmly.

"That judge has a lot of sense," Lena blurted.

Shawanda got up and pushed passed Donte and Lena. She went into the aisle, rushing down it and out of the door. Outside, confused about what had happened, she paced the halls.

Minutes later, Tamika emerged from the courtroom. "I was surprised the judge did that, although this wasn't an unusual thing for him." Putting a hand on Shawanda's shoulder, Tamika said, "You don't look so good. Why don't you go home and lie down?"

"I'm okay." Shawanda lied. She felt guilty.

Tamika said goodbye just as Lena and Donte came out into the hall.

Donte looked at Shawanda. "Ma, they put those things on his hand."

"That's right," Lena interjected. "He's going to jail."

Suddenly angry, Shawanda took Donte's hand and started quickly down the hall. She remembered they had all come in Lena's car and regretted that decision.

Lena caught up with her.

"I don't believe that judge did that to Aaron." Shawanda kept walking fast. Abruptly stopping in the middle of the hallway, she cried, "Aaron messed up, but he shouldn't go to jail."

"What are you whining about? The judge said he'll give him probation next time."

"You always put Aaron down for his faults, Mama. But you don't lift him up for the good he does."

"You might be better off with no man than with Aaron."

"Are you kidding?" Shawanda twisted her head, and looked at Lena out the corners of her eyes. "You've been married for a long time. You don't know how hard it is out there. Soon as most men found out I had a kid, they took off. But not Aaron. He stayed and tried to help me with Donte." Shawanda shook her head and started walking again. Finding the exit, she quickly left.

Outside, the pale day looked as if it wanted to cry. At least Shawanda perceived it that way. Hurrying to the car, Lena matched Shawanda's every step. Donte pushed to keep up. Shawanda was aware of Lena's mumbling.

"That judge acted like he didn't want to give Aaron probation," Lena said as they neared the car. Inside the car Lena added, "He showed Aaron he wasn't playing."

By the time the group reached home, Shawanda was listening only to her own pain.

* * *

Twenty-four hours later, Shawanda went to her and Aaron's home to get more clothes. It was a mess. Clothes, shoes, cans, food wrappers, trays from microwaveable frozen dinners littered the furniture and floors. Dirty glasses and silverware filled the sink, while the smell of decayed food and dirt scented the air. She couldn't leave her once beautiful home like this. Picking up the clothes, she threw them in the washer. Picking up the trash, she took it out, came in, and washed the dishes. No time to thoroughly clean the entire house, she promised herself to return and get it done before Aaron got out.

The next day Shawanda kept a doctor's appointment. She sat in the waiting area of the doctor's office almost daring life to get any harder. Picking up a magazine, she scanned the pages. The pictures of the colorful kitchens and bathrooms reminded her of the home she once shared with Aaron. She had lost almost everything, she felt.

The nurse called her back to the examining room. There, Shawanda looked at the magazine while waiting for the doctor. She was thankful for the insurance Aaron had through his job.

Soon the black and gray haired Doctor Beverly Greenberg came in. She greeted Shawanda with a quickly fleeing smile, as if she was in a rush. "What problems are you having?"

"I missed my period. Might be because I'm stressed out."

Doctor Greenberg asked her to lie on the table. She began the examination. Afterwards she gave Shawanda the diagnosis.

17

Margaret sped to White Marsh that Sunday afternoon. She parked in front of Charles's home. Jumping out of the car, she ran up the walkway to the front door. Pushing the buzzer, she kept pressing it. When Charles opened the door, she stepped back. One look at him and every well-ordered thought in her head got confused.

"Margaret, come in." Charles opened the door wide.

She didn't move. "I have to tell you some —."

"Tell me inside."

You won't welcome me for long, she wanted to say. Instead, entering the dwelling, she stood near the door. "It's about Tommy."

"Let's go into the den. Would you like a glass of wine?"

She followed him. Stopping in the middle of the room, she watched him pour the red liquid into a wine glass. Her eyes stayed on him as he walked back across the floor and handed her the glass. She took it. Drinking, the wine tasted bitter. Yet she began to gulp it until it was half gone. Charles gently removed the glass from her mouth. He took it over to the counter that separated the kitchen from the den and placed it there.

"What's on your mind?" Charles sat on one of the stools in front of the counter.

"I have to tell you about Tommy. We met during our freshman year of college. We had a class together. I didn't pay any attention to him at first. But we had friends in common. Then one day a bunch of us were in the cafeteria talking. Tommy was there. He started telling us about a book he had just finished reading. It was about political history, World War II. How it got —."

"Why do I need to know any of this?"

"Because I had read the same book," she replied. "Over time, we talked. We had a lot in common. Not just things like hating the same foods. Like me, he's not a big bread eater. And he doesn't eat a lot of sweets."

"Should I care?"

"That we have things in common? Yes. They're important things. We think the same way. When we were young, we wanted to help the poor. We thought we should take our piece of the world and make it better. You understand, don't you?"

"I have no idea what you're talking about."

"I'm telling you we both have this liberal view of the world. We're both Democrats. Both of our fathers struggled to become doctors in a racist society."

"I understand that. And I sympathize."

"Right. You look on and you sympathize. But Tommy and I lived it. When we started dating, it wasn't like we heard bells ringing. We were best friends. We could talk about everything. But as the years passed, we began to not appreciate each other. He started to wonder if something better was out there." She noticed Charles stared curiously at her. But because of her nervousness, she couldn't stop talking. "Now he thinks there isn't anything better than what we had. Tommy thinks that maybe just knowing someone will always be there for you is enough." It was the way she had felt, too.

Margaret continued, "We both liked bookstores and libraries. When I saw him again at the bookstore, I realized I almost hated him. I blamed him for leaving me. Although he didn't, you know. We left each other. I only talked to him at the bookstore because I was curious about what he was up to now. He surprised me. His life had changed back to his old goals. I was impressed with that."

"Fascinating story, I'm sure." Charles leaned against the counter.

"When my old friend Tommy —."

"You mean your former fiancé," Charles interrupted.

"When he invited me to go jogging, I didn't think anything —."

"Except we talked about the fact the two of you were spending a lot of time together."

"No, not a lot. It was occasional jogging. Tommy thought it meant more. I knew better."

"But you were wrong?"

"I was right. When he asked me to marry —."

"You're getting married?" He quickly sat up.

"I told him no. I want to get married and have children. Maybe not with Tommy because we tried that before and went —."

"You were dating two men at once?" He shifted on the stool.

"No, never, except Mother said I was. When I thought about —."

"Did you sleep with him?"

"I didn't. Only you."

He stood up and walked across the room. Standing in front of her, he said, "I forgive you."

"What did I do?"

"You must have done something. You got a marriage proposal."

"I only went jogging."

"Stick to that story."

Her head fell against his chest.

"No more jogging with Tommy," he whispered.

She repeated it. "No more jogging with Tommy."

"Don't talk to him. Don't see him again."

"No, not again." She put her arms around his waist and laid her head on his chest. She felt guilty. If was as if Margaret had been unfaithful to Charles. And she hadn't realized it.

"Stay with me," he said.

"Yes, I want to."

They stood in the middle of the room. The silence between them was relaxed and comfortable.

After a while, he asked. "Hungry?"

"Yes. I haven't eaten today." She clung to him. "Would you like me to cook for you?"

"*Can* you cook?" he asked.

"Southern Black women have a reputation for being good cooks."

"Oh?"

"I can steam vegetables in the microwave, and I do all types of chicken very well."

"So you don't cook?"

"What do you have in the frig?" She was glad for the change of subject.

"Spaghetti, maybe."

"I don't like spaghetti very much," she said.

"I never knew that."

Tommy did. She quickly shoved the unfair thought from her head.

"I'm finding out all sorts of things about you today," Charles said.

"Do you have any kind of fish?" She didn't want to leave his embrace.

"No, steaks maybe. Margaret, I care a lot about you."

"I care about you."

"But I'm disappointed in you," he added.

"I didn't realize Tommy thought we could pick up where we left off until he said it."

"Promise me this is the end of it."

She lifted her head from his chest and looked into his eyes. "I promise."

He softly pecked her lips. Then he moved away and headed toward the kitchen.

Margaret went over to the stereo and put on a CD she had purchased on an outing with Charles. She had purposely left it at his home because she enjoyed listening to it with him.

Soon Nina Simone sang about out-of-control passion. Margaret understood the lyrics. Loving Charles, the feeling so intense, it sometimes nauseated her.

Shortly they sat at the dining room table, with plates of steaks in front of them.

"Please pour me another glass of wine?" she asked.

"No more wine for you," he replied.

"Why?"

"Not after the way you guzzled the first glass like a wino."

"I was nervous." She cut into the steak.

"As you should have been."

"The steak's delicious." She popped another chunk into her mouth.

"Thank you."

"I go to court tomorrow." She started telling him about her current cases.

After dinner, they did the dishes together.

"I've gained four pounds since I've been dating you," Margaret announced.

"Is that good or bad?"

When the dishes were finished, he turned out the lights. They went upstairs. In the bedroom they changed for bed. She put on a gown left in the drawer he had set aside for her. In bed they cuddled while watching television. They watched a war movie, which Margaret also enjoyed. When the movie ended, Charles turned off the lights. His head fell against the pillow.

Margaret moved close and laid her head on his chest. She could hear him breathing. It was only minutes before they began to physically express their passion for each other. When they made love, Charles found quiet spots and spaces inside of her and excited them.

The succeeding weeks, time still generous to them, brought them laughter and good times. On a Saturday night, Charles picked up Margaret. The couple rode to the Inner Harbor. They were going sailing. Walking along the crowded promenade, they held hands. Reaching the big commercial sailboat, Margaret admired its beauty. The sails were high and impressive. Margaret figured the boat could easily hold a hundred people.

Charles purchased tickets, and the couple got on the noisy, crowded boat. They went past the reggae band that lay in wait. They squeezed by standing and sitting people. At the bar Charles purchased a beer. "Did she want anything?" he asked. She gestured no with her hands and head to avoid yelling over the loud chatter. Soon they carved out a spot for themselves along the left side of the vessel. There they watched as the boat pulled out of dock. The band began to play. Margaret moved to the beat of the music as the warm breeze stroked her face. As they sailed through the light dotted night past odd-shaped buildings and smaller boats, Margaret felt good.

Charles turned to her. "It's too noisy here. Let's find someplace quiet." He took her hand and they went up a few steps to where the captain steered. A dog lay at the captain's feet. The couple sat nearby.

"Are you cold?" he asked.

"No." She rested her head on his shoulder. "I like the boat." Looking out, she said, "Tell me about us five years from now."

"I don't think about it."

"You have no vision for us?" she asked.

"Forget five years from now. Let's live in the present. Besides, couldn't we date indefinitely?"

"I did that once before. I need goals in life."

"We can date three years and see what happens next. What do you think?"

"Three years? Our time is short."

"It wouldn't end in three years. Maybe we'll do the . . . uh, *m* word."

"Anyone who refers to it as the *m* word probably shouldn't ever get married."

"What if he doesn't have a choice?"

"You have a choice."

"You think so?"

She wanted to change the subject. The conversation was starting to depress her. Noting the music that emerged from downstairs, she said, "Sounds like people are doing the limbo."

"Want to join them?" he asked.

"Only to watch."

They went downstairs and cheered on the limbo players. They stayed there for the rest of the sail. An hour later the boat returned to dock. The couple returned to the car and had a quiet drive home.

Outside Margaret's apartment, Charles accompanied her to the front door, as was his habit when they returned late. She invited him in.

"For a little while," he said. Inside, they sat in the kitchen. Margaret made tea for herself. Charles declined anything.

Wanting to say something to him, she searched for the proper words. Deciding they didn't exist, she settled for the ones she grabbed first. Opening her mouth, she released them, however they might sound. "You can date casually. I can't. Not for three years, not for two. I need goals, marriage and children. I love you, but I won't wait for you to change into the man who will give me those things. The wait would be a waste, anyway."

"What are you saying?"

Margaret gathered the hardest sentence ever brought to the tip of her tongue, and forced it out. "Let me go."

"Go where? Certainly not to marry some other guy?"

"You can't give me marriage. Let someone else do it."

"Do you love him?" Charles asked.

"I loved him once before, I think."

"Why go to someone you aren't in love with? Do you want marriage that badly?"

"I'll learn to love him again. And why not? I have a biological clock. My only hope is to grab what I can while I can. This time next year, I could be a mother."

"I don't believe we're having this conversation."

"You know I'm in love with you and too weak to let go. You be the strong one. Tell me to go."

"You're being silly. "

"You can date fifty women after me."

"I don't want to date fifty women."

Margaret took a deep breath. He was right. The request was strange, she decided. "I'm sorry. I shouldn't have asked you such a stupid question."

He got up. He walked over to her and kissed her on the forehead. "It's late. I should go. Good night."

Watching him walk out of the kitchen, she listened to his footsteps against the living room's hardwood floor until she heard the door close. Then she got up and went into the living to check the door. Afterwards Margaret went to bed. She felt her life was out of her control and despised the feeling.

Time strolled by. It never had to stop and acknowledge anyone's problems.

The next Saturday after work, Charles stopped by Margaret's apartment. They decided to go for a walk. Outside the sky and the clouds were getting together and discussing whether they should act out and rain. Charles and Margaret decided to walk anyway. They headed toward Johns Hopkins University. Margaret wondered if Charles was trying to replace the jogs Margaret had with Tommy. She had not seen or spoken to Tommy since the marriage proposal.

As they walked through the campus, Margaret pointed out the buildings she once had classes in. Since the conversation at the kitchen table, things had been tense between them.

Walking back toward Charles Street, Margaret asked, "Would you like to go to mass with me tomorrow?" She understood they were casually dating; yet Margaret naturally wanted to get closer.

"Not Catholic. Don't do mass. I'm Lutheran."

"The next thing you're going to tell me is that you're a Republican." It was a joke.

"Yes, I am."

She hadn't known that. She stopped and faced him. "You've never met any of my friends. Not even April. She sort of believes I made you up. It's my fault, really. Would you like to meet her? I can make dinner and invite April and her husband over."

"I don't know."

"You haven't met most of my family. My mother's relatives are in Louisiana. But my father has quite a few of them here. There's Joe, my favorite uncle. He has a big sense of humor. He has two daughters my age and four cute grandchildren. Would you like to meet them?"

"Meeting your mother and sister was enough."

"I've never met any of your relatives or friends," she said.

"There's only my brother —."

"Have you told him about me?"

"I don't tell him much about the women I date. He has a conservative life, a wife, and two children."

"I've never seen your office or met any of your coworkers. What have you told them about me?"

"They know I'm dating."

"We stay in our own narrow world. We almost never let anyone one else in."

They crossed the street.

"Once we were happy in our own world," he told her.

"I feel desperately in love," she said.

"Desperately?"

"Tragically, I guess, is a better word."

"Why tragically?" he asked as they walked down Thirty-third Street.

She opened and closed her mouth, knowing what she meant, but was unable to politely express it. Something in her, the part that wanted what Charles could probably never give her, didn't care to love him anymore.

They walked back to the apartment with an unfamiliar silence.

There he sat on the sofa. Margaret sat in a nearby chair.

"I'm losing you," he said.

"No, you're not. While I thought about ending our relationship, about reaching for something more, I decided not to." Margaret tried to reassure him.

"You decided to stay tragically in love?"

"It was a joke."

He sat back. "Doesn't it mean you don't want to date me?"

"It was just something I said."

"I don't believe you." His eyes focused on her. "You feel obligated to stay with me."

"It doesn't matter. I'm here."

"Your body's here. But your mind is slowly leaving."

"You're wrong," she said.

"I've been in this apartment many times. I've never seen you sit in that chair. You've always been on the sofa. You've always been next to me."

"I'm having a hard time. It'll pass."

"You're starting to resent me. I can tell. I've become someone who not only won't give you what you want, but in your head I'm now an obstacle."

"Let's not argue." She moved to the sofa to convince him he was wrong.

"When you promised to stay away from Tommy, I declared myself the winner. I prefer to win," he said. "But something has snatched victory from me."

"Nothing has."

"Yes. Seeing you unhappy has."

"I'm happy." In a miserable sort of way, her mind added.

"For the first time in my life, I've considered marriage," he said. "I don't know if I can. I'm happy single. I love life as it is now. I have the freedom to do whatever and go wherever I want, without consulting anyone. If the relationship I'm in has soured, we can quickly call it quits. You can't do that when you're married. You're stuck then holding onto something that's long gone. And maybe hating each other. I don't want to ever hate you."

"Let's do what you said before. Let's not talk about the future."

"I've come to realize that we don't have to marry for you to hate me. Your resentment of me will soon turn to hatred."

"I've never seen you like this before." She tried to explain this mood of his to herself. "It's natural for a person with a fear of commitment to bail out when things get a little rough."

"I've already lost pieces of you," he almost whispered. "I hate losing."

"Don't say anything else," she cautioned.

"You asked me to let you go."

"What do they say in the law? I withdraw the question."

"You have to do that before the answer is given."

Wanting to immediately end the direction of this conversation, Margaret changed the subject. "I'll fix lunch for us."

He shook his head no. "I've been thinking."

"Thinking's no good." It's what they felt that mattered.

"About being a good loser."

She pushed near. "Please stop."

"We could hang on," he persisted. "But what's the point?"

"Don't you care about me?" she asked.

"Yes. But you want to marry Tommy."

"No. I want to stay with you." She wrapped her arm around his.

"I sense you blaming me and emotionally pulling away. I don't know if I can ever marry any woman. Knowing this about myself, I don't want to be selfish or cruel to you."

"You're not cruel. I'm okay. Whatever you're seeing in me will pass. We can be as happy as we were in the beginning. Remember?"

"I remember. But we've lost something. I think . . . if you feel you must . . . you should go. Go and marry Tommy."

She jerked away. "Don't be stupid!"

"I'm being a good sport."

"This isn't a game!" she yelled.

"Say it, say you will never hate me for standing in the way of what you most want — marriage."

She kept staring at him. His words jumped, somersaulted, and rolled in her head, mocking and daring her to speak.

"If you could only have answered that question." He got up. "Go to Tommy. Be happy. Have what you want in life." He turned his back to her and walked to the door.

When he opened it, she screamed, "No! You can't do this!" She ran to him, grabbed his arm, and exclaimed, "What's the future, anyway?" She recited his philosophy. "It's just something that may never exist." She tasted her tears. "Let's not care about it. Just hold onto now."

He went out of the door.

She started to run behind him. Started to scream and cry, no Charles. Don't leave me. But she didn't want to be that pathetic woman. Slamming the door shut, she pressed her back against it. Her glance jogged around the room, seeing all, yet registering nothing.

She told herself it was just one bad day. Tomorrow, this strange mood of his would pass, and Charles would return to her.

18

Three days after Aaron's confinement, one day after the visit to Doctor Greenberg, Shawanda went to see Aaron. It took her awhile to find the visitor's entrance. Inside she waited in a long line before having her handbag inspected and her person subjected to a metal detector. Walking into the barren visiting area, she waited on a metal stool until Aaron came to a window carved into a metal wall. She peered at him through the hostile bars. Seeing his eyes reveal the sadness within him, she felt sorry for him.

"Hey, Baby," he said.

"Hey, yourself." Pushing depression back and forcing a smile, Shawanda searched for positive comments. "You don't have too long to be here, three weeks."

"Five minutes in here seems more like a year. Ma and Pops came to see me."

"Bet they didn't have anything good to say about me," she said.

"Don't worry about them."

"Got something to tell you." She revealed the recently learned information: "I'm pregnant."

"Pregnant!" He grabbed the bars. His face lit up. "I'm going to be a pop!"

"What are you so happy about? Look at us. How we gonna have a baby?"

"Stupid question," he said.

"I don't know how I'm gonna make it," she told him.

"We gotta make it, Baby."

"You really want this baby?" Under the circumstances, she had to ask the question.

"Don't talk shit."

"It's so hard raising Donte. I couldn't do it by myself. If it wasn't for Mama and Daddy . . . . "

"You don't have to raise our baby alone. I'm getting out of here and taking care of my business."

"Daddies who don't live with their kids sometimes forget —."

"Not me, Baby."

"What we gonna do?" she asked.

"Be together with our baby. You've got to come back home now."

"Everything's all messed up."

"We'll get it straightened out," he told her.

"I'm mixed up."

"We gonna have this baby together, right?"

She nodded, letting his reassurances convinced her.

Just then the guard informed them visiting time was over. Aaron got up. "Glad you came."

Looking through the bars, she waved to him. After he was out of sight, wiping her moist eyes, she went home.

* * *

Next day at her parents' home, Shawanda stretched out on a blanket on the floor. Denise lay on the bed.

"You're thinking about going back to Aaron!" Denise repeated.

"You should have seen how sad he looked peeking through those bars."

"After what he did to Donte, that wouldn't have bothered me."

"He's a good man," Shawanda said.

Denise sat up.

Shawanda continued. "He goes to work every day, always brings home his check, and pays the bills. He doesn't hang on the street corners. He stays with me. We can watch TV and have a good time. Most times when he goes out, I'm with him. And I never worry about him cheating."

"He beat up your son. You had to deal with Social Services. You ended up in court and almost lost custody of Donte."

"We have a house in the county. It's hard paying the mortgage every month, but we've got it."

"Well, he's in jail now." Denise slipped to the floor. Now she and Shawanda were eye to eye.

"I promised to stick by him no matter what," Shawanda told her.

"You're hopeless," Denise said.

"You've never been in love like this."

"And never want to be." Denise got up. "You go back to Aaron. When something else happens, well, you asked for it."

"Act like a friend."

"Okay." Denise went to the door. "Here's some friendly words. Get rid of Aaron. And if I were you, I would forget even his name." She turned and left.

Shawanda balled both hands into fists and counted to seven. The conversation with Denise had been disappointing. She took a deep breath and counted to twenty. Her parents were next.

* * *

That night at the dinner table, between bites of fried chicken and potato salad, Shawanda nervously tapped her feet. While her parents ate a dessert of bread pudding, she watched Donte play in the potato salad. "Had enough, Sweetie?"

"I'm full."

"Want to go upstairs and watch TV?" Shawanda asked.

Donte nodded, climbed out of the chair and left the room.

Sticking a fork into the bread pudding, Shawanda blurted, "I'm pregnant."

"Lord, have mercy!" Lena slapped the table. "Will it ever get better?"

"It's a baby, not a tumor, Mama. What about a congratulations or something?" Shawanda desperately needed the support.

"Congratulations," Ernest said.

"Thanks, Daddy."

"What are you going to do?" Lena looked at Shawanda.

"Raise Donte and the new baby."

"Have you told Aaron?" Ernest asked.

"He wants me to come back to him."

Lena pushed her plate away. Shaking her head, she said, "I know you're not going back to him!"

"He should be with his baby."

"Are you seriously thinking about this?" Ernest moved forward.

"It's hard raising kids without a daddy in the house."

"I don't believe this!" Lena hit the table, this time with her fist. "When will you learn?"

"He doesn't have a problem with all kids." Shawanda swallowed. "I'm going back to him."

Lena jumped up. She folded her arms. "What about Precious Baby?" Her head moved from side to side.

"He can live with me and Aaron. Ain't nothing gonna to happen to him again."

"You heard that state's attorney. If he gets probation, and anything else happens —."

"When he loses his temper again," Ernest joined in, "he won't think about being on probation."

"There's no reason to talk about this." Lena unfolded her arms. "You want to go back to that clown?" Lena pointed at Shawanda. "You go. But Donte's staying with us."

"He's my son. He's staying with me."

"You aren't thinking straight," Lena yelled. "You can't look out for Donte. You take him out of this house and I'm calling Social Services —."

"No, Mama." Shawanda jumped up.

"Let's see what they think about all this!" Lena added.

"You know all the trouble I had with them. Daddy, please tell her."

"It's not about you," Ernest responded. "We've gotta think about Donte." Ernest got up.

"Are you against me, too?" Even the thought hurt.

"I'm not against you. Somebody's gotta think straight. I was against calling Social Services last time. But now, if you take Donte out of this house, there's nothing else we can do. We have to call them. He turned his back and walked out of the kitchen. Lena stomped out behind him.

Alone, Shawanda was sad enough to cry, yet didn't have time for it. She had to decide what to do next.

The days walked past. Shawanda went regularly to jail to visit Aaron.

On the day of the hearing, Judge Knowles growled the word, "probation." He warned that if there were any violations, Aaron would serve two years.

Outside of the courtroom Shawanda and Aaron hugged. She was relieved he was out of jail.

"Things gonna get better," he told her as they bounced down the steps of the suburban courthouse.

"I'm coming back home," she announced at the foot of the steps. He gently grabbed her body and held it against his own. She felt strength in his arms. When he released her, they said goodbye for now and parted in front of the courthouse.

Shawanda hurried to work, then back to her parents' where she discreetly packed. There wouldn't be any more discussions with Lena and Ernest, Shawanda had decided.

Time seemed vague, reality made-up, on the night Shawanda waited for her parents to fall asleep. When assured they had, she quietly took previously packed suitcases from the closet and tiptoed down the dimly lit stairs. At the front door, there was only light from the stairwell to see the lock. Afraid that even the sound of unlocking and opening the door would alert Lena and Ernest, she did both slowly and carefully. When the door was opened, she took the suitcases outside and stood on the porch.

It was after midnight. Looking around, she saw no one on the corner or on a porch. All windows appeared vacant of prying eyes. Stepping off the porch, a suitcase in each hand, she hoped the night would be a lookout and guard her moves. Placing the bags in the trunk, she went back into the house and into Donte's room. Wrapping the blanket around him, she picked up the slumbering child. Hoping for his continued sleep, she felt her way back downstairs. She closed and locked the door behind her. At the car she lay Donte on the back seat. Climbing into the driver's side, she started the car and headed toward the county, finding the streets deserted. At her destination she quickly got Donte into the house and into bed. Going into the master bedroom, she noted Aaron had slept through her arrival.

"Aaron," she called, "It's me." She turned on the light.

He sat up and blinked his eyes. "What are you doing here in the middle of the night?"

She bounced onto the bed, slipped off her shoes, and got under the top sheet. "Aren't you glad I'm back?"

"Yeah." His head dropped to the pillow. Within minutes, he was snoring again.

In the early morning, Aaron rose for work. Shawanda glided out of bed and into the bathroom to shower with him. Afterwards he dressed. She dressed. Downstairs in the kitchen she fixed breakfast.

He came down and sat at the table. Smiling at her, he said, "Look at you, Baby. You're back home!"

She smiled, too, and put a plate of sausage, scrambled eggs, and toast in front of him. She sat beside him. "Yeah. I feel good about it," she said.

From upstairs came a flushing sound.

"What's that?" Aaron looked toward the ceiling.

"It's the toilet."

"The toilet flushed by itself?"

"Naw, Donte must have used it."

"Donte! What's he doing here?"

"Where else would he be?"

"Baby, I'm on probation. Anything goes wrong, I'll get time. Wouldn't Lena keep him?"

"Yeah, you know she would." She pushed the plate closer to him, knowing he needed to eat and go to work.

Well?" He ignored the food.

"Your food's gonna get cold."

"Listen, Baby, take Donte back to Lena's."

She stared at him.

Shaking his head, Aaron said, "I can't take any chances. He's gotta go."

19

During May, after Charles told Margaret to go to Tommy, Margaret became depressed. She had to force herself to the office. The work she once enjoyed was now a burden. She left at quitting time, unusual for her, and went straight home. There she did little. Often she would find herself sitting and staring, or pacing, or tossing in bed.

Sometimes Margaret hated Charles. At other times she wished he would call. On four, five, six occasions, she grabbed the telephone to contact him. But pride snatched the receiver. Charles had broken up with her. Let him call first, she told herself.

Eventually, as time stumbled past her, she began to claim responsibility for her participation in the breakup. Wanting to marry right away, she had asked out of the relationship. Charles had ultimately complied. By mid-June Margaret had accepted the fate she helped bring about. Meanwhile Tommy had been waiting for her. Finally she turned her attention to him.

Tommy invited her to his apartment in the county. She was surprised it had a doorman and a receptionist. The woman buzzed Tommy to inform him of Margaret's arrival. Margaret took the elevator to the sixteenth floor. Getting off of it, she admired the beautifully decorated hallway with its dark blue carpet, blue and white wallpaper, and antique table with a large silk floral arrangement.

Tommy appeared at the end of the hallway and greeted her. "Right this way." He led her to his apartment. Inside he offered to show her around the modern apartment that had two bedrooms and one bath.

Margaret stood at the living room window and admired the awesome view of the county. Liking Tommy's place, she nevertheless couldn't imagine herself living here.

She sat on the sofa. Tommy sat next to her. He went into his pocket and pulled out a small jewelry box. He opened it and showed Margaret the diamond ring. She held out her hand, and he placed the ring on her finger. They embraced.

"If we invited only a few close family and friends, we can get married next month," he said.

"I want everybody I know at my wedding," she began. "I've always wanted a big wedding at the basilica. And at night. I'll have on a beautiful flowing formal wedding gown. And we must have limousines, black and white ones. The reception hall will be decorated in black and white. We'll have long, beautifully laid out tables with all sorts of tasty things to snack on. Our guests can walk around and talk to each other." She described the event the way she had often daydreamed it. "No sit-down dinners where everyone's confined to a table. And we must have a band. Everyone must dance. And pictures. Got to have a good photographer. And a honeymoon in Bermuda."

"Sounds expensive. Not only that, it would take at least a year to pull all of that together."

"I can plan it in six months," she said. She also needed time to emotionally put the last relationship behind her, and to make new memories with Tommy.

"Why were we engaged for six years?" he asked.

"Strange question." She considered the answer. "I guess we waited for the perfect time. We were in school and starting careers. At one point my father was sick. Then there was his death. And the money issue. We never had enough time or money to do all the things we wanted."

"You wanted," he said.

"But now we're settled. We must have enough money for the wedding of my dreams."

"Not if you're planning to invite everyone you know."

"I suppose I could be happy with a smaller wedding," she decided.

"Let's keep the guest list down to thirty," he suggested.

"Only thirty!" she said. "I can't promise you anything."

"I guess I can wait six months. But no longer than that. Let's not repeat the six-year thing."

"Promise you'll be more attentive than last time. Make sure you spend time with me. Don't put your career before me."

"Told you, I'm a changed man."

"Where will we live?" she asked.

"You can move in here."

"I prefer a house in the city. Some place we both pick out."

"When we start a family, you can quit work."

"Quit work? Never. I like my job. I can't quit it for good."

"You're going to send our children to daycare while you work?"

"Maybe I'll stop working for three months after the baby's born. Let's have four children."

"Four!" he moved away. "Let's start with two. I'll have to pay tuition for them."

"I can help. I work."

"You can buy clothes and get your hair and nails done with your income."

"Are you confusing me with someone else? I'm an equal partner in this relationship."

"You're taking my last name, of course."

"I'm keeping my maiden name."

He got quiet. Then, sliding closer, he said, "It will all work out."

Margaret nodded. Having given up Charles to pursue something long-term and stable, her sentiments were, "We can't fail." She attempted to convince herself of it. "It's gotta work this time."

"No sense in us being alone when we can be together," he said.

He took her hand and held on while Margaret wondered if she could go through with the marriage.

* * *

Weeks skipped by. April came into Margaret's office with two bridal magazines and lunch. Taking the usual chair, April unwrapped her sandwich and began flipping the pages of the magazine.

"What do you think of this wedding dress?"

Margaret looked at the picture of the flowing white dress. "Dull."

April again turned the pages. "I like this one. What do you think?"

"Ugly."

More flipping. "This one's gorgeous." April again displayed the magazine.

"I don't like it."

April slapped the magazine closed. Taking both publications, she handed them to Margaret.

Margaret pushed away the dry tuna. She surveyed the first magazine and then the second one. "I hate all of these."

"As always! It was the same thing with the invitations, the cake, the caterers, and the hall. Nothing makes you happy. You must be the strangest bride-to-be ever."

"I have bad anxiety. Sometimes I feel sick."

"Know what I think?" April put down the sandwich.

"I'm sure you're going to tell me."

"Cold feet. You were in love with Tommy. You two fell out of love and broke up. Now he's back. You're remembering the way you used to feel about him. It's not enough. You need to have new experiences together. You know, bond all over again."

"Stop analyzing my life." Margaret pushed the magazines toward April.

"Keep them. I brought them for you."

"Thanks." She put them in the drawer.

"What? Don't want to look at any white dresses now?" April picked up the bottle of soda.

"I'm saturated. I can't think about wedding plans anymore."

"Don't commit to someone you don't love just for the sake of being married," April warned.

"I love him."

"You don't act like it! Instead of being excited, you're feeling sick."

"I've made a decision. I'm sticking with it."

"Think about the time right before you and Tommy broke up. You must have been unhappy. Imagine feeling that way for the rest of your life because you're stuck in a bad marriage."

"I thought you were all for me being with Tommy." Margaret twisted in the chair.

"You're better off single than with someone you aren't interested in."

Margaret was growing intolerant of April's constant friendly guidance. She jerked opened the desk drawer, snatched out one of the magazines, and quickly went through it. "I like this one. The bride's maids will wear black. They can pick any long black dress they want."

"They *won't* match."

"Don't have to." Margaret took a booklet from another drawer. Thumbing through it, she said, "I think I'll get invitations like this." She showed April. "And I've decided on which hall I want. I'll run it all by Tommy tonight."

"Terrific." April finished lunch and tossed the brown paper bag into the wastebasket. "What are you going to do about the fact you aren't exactly in love with Tommy?"

"Love will grow." Margaret recited the cliché.

"Maybe you two should think about this some more."

"No. We're shooting for early November."

"I hope you're making the right decision." April stood.

"I am. I can't be flaky about this. I told Tommy I would marry him, and I must."

"Must?"

"I want to."

"You want to be married." April said. "The question is, do you want to spend your life with Tommy?"

Margaret opened her mouth. Then she closed it. Her heart couldn't address the question now. "I have to get back to work."

"Sure." April started toward the door. Stopping at the door, she said, "Let me give you some advice."

"Can I stop you?"

"Face your feelings before you ruin your life and Tommy's."

"Just think if I had to pay for all the advice you've given me over the years."

"Pay?" April smiled. "How could you? My insights are priceless."

Margaret smiled, too. She liked April, even now when Margaret was happy to see her go. Alone, Margaret returned to her favorite distraction — her work.

* * *

By September the wedding plans were still stumbling along. Margaret often had a queasy stomach. She finally realized it wasn't pre-wedding plans and nervousness. Her queasiness came from missing Charles. Finally, on a warm Sunday night, Margaret was no longer willing to ignore her feelings. She dialed Charles's number. The phone rang ten times before she hung up. An hour later, the scenario was repeated. At midnight, she was usually in bed at this time, Margaret dialed again. Three rings and he picked up.

"Charles, it's —."

"Margaret," he said. "Good to hear from you."

"Sorry for calling so —."

"Don't be ridiculous. I thought about contacting you many times, but I didn't want to interfere with your wedding plans."

"It's in two months."

"Did you call to rub it in?" he asked.

"No, of course not. I wanted to tell you. . . ." She grabbed the words before they left her mouth. The words were, I want to be with you more than with Tommy. I told myself it was a feeling destined to soon pass. But it hasn't.

"I've been working even longer hours than usual," he began when she stopped.

"Have you been dating?" she asked.

"I've had one or two."

"Different women?"

He didn't answer.

"Promiscuous," she accused. Once she thought she had changed him, had made him monogamous. Or was she lying to herself?

"I am not promiscuous. I simply enjoy the company of women."

"One day soon you'll be an old man. Maybe it's time you settled down." After saying it, she realized she was still angry with him for letting her go and was acting out her anger. "I take it back."

"You mean you think it's *not* time I settled down?"

"Stop confusing me."

"Did you call to rehash the past?" he asked.

Why had she called, Margaret now questioned herself. The answer came quickly. She wanted to hear him say it. Say, Margaret don't marry Tommy. Silly her. Margaret immediately chastised herself for falling in love with a man who was happy dating indefinitely. And then refusing to wait for him to change. "Sometimes I tell myself you never cared about me," she said.

"That's a lie."

"If we really adored each other, we should have stayed together."

"I wanted to. You didn't," he told her.

"I did. I just needed some things."

"You had to have something I couldn't give you right now."

"You're a coward."

"Do you mean that?" he asked.

"How can you let me marry someone else?"

"Why are you blaming me?"

"I'm not. I blame myself. I wasn't strong enough to stay with you. I took the easy way out. But if you had said, please stay, I would have."

"I know. But part of you would have resented the wait, and regretted not getting out when you were offered marriage. I couldn't have tolerated your resentment."

"I don't know if I can marry Tommy. Can I come over tonight — to talk?"

"I would love to see you. But then what? What happens tomorrow and the day after?" he asked.

"Say it!" she blurted.

"Say what?"

Margaret considered the question. And mentally answered it. Say, please marry me, Margaret. She opened her mouth, and listened to her own words. "Nothing. Forget it." She started to cry. "I'm sorry for hurting you."

"I forgive you. Forgive me for not being different."

"I like you the way you are," she said.

"I was always very impressed by the person you are." He added, "You were right, you know, from the beginning. We're headed in different directions."

"What should we do?"

"We made that decision months ago. Remember?"

"I've missed you."

"Don't tell your soon-to-be husband that." He cleared his throat. "I've missed you, too."

Margaret didn't want to be some poor woman tormented by desire. Yet she in fact was that woman. "I'm a little unhappy." She felt stuck with her decisions. "But I'm okay. Are you okay?"

"My anger at you is starting to subside, if that's what you mean. I'm sorry it didn't work out between us."

"Don't apologize." She paused. "I hope life will always be good to you."

"You're an extraordinary woman."

She closed her eyes and searched her mind for anything else she had to say to him. Quickly she realized they were so emotionally familiar with each other that words were unnecessary between them. They had more than words. They could feel life dancing inside each other. She let the silence dwell between them, comfortable in this place. "Sleep well." She whispered the words, as she had done many times before when they dated and had late night phone talks.

"Margaret. . . . ." His voice cut off, and the silence started talking for him.

She held the receiver, aware of her own breathing. When nothing else came, her pain, pulling and punching, Margaret decided she could live with it now. "Good night," she said.

"Good night, Margaret."

Hanging up, tears moistened her face. She assured herself that all decisions made had been the proper ones. Margaret was unable to further disrupt the lives of three people, Charles, Tommy, and her own. Knowing all of this, Margaret acknowledged one last thing. She was still in love with Charles.

* * *

After the September conversation with Charles, Margaret argued with herself late nights when she couldn't sleep. She concluded Tommy was everything she wanted in a man. He was offering to make her dreams come true. Of course she could learn to love him again.

She made a point of speaking daily with Tommy. They went out often and slowly bonded all over again. They talked constantly of their upcoming wedding. Together they planned for it.

On a cool Saturday evening in early November, Margaret saw the day she had long dreamed of. It was her wedding day. After dressing in the gorgeous white gown, Brittany announced there was never a bride who looked more beautiful. Soon getting out of the white limousine and entering the basilica, Margaret walked down the aisle.

Before sixty people she vowed to love Tommy, to stick with him on days when she didn't feel like it, to stick with him when it was easier to walk away. She meant it. It was her decision, the one made months earlier. And after all, maybe that's what love was, a decision. When Tommy kissed her, as they stood at the altar, Margaret knew the two of them could have a good marriage if they worked hard at it. That's what marriage was about, she thought. Two people working at it. It wasn't about bells or floating on clouds or feeling almost high, she told herself. But about friendship and two people looking after each other's interest. Convinced of that, it was easy for Margaret to marry Tommy.

The reception was held in a hall decorated in black and white. The food, which Margaret was too excited to eat, was a variety of finger snacks that were pleasing to the eye. By the time the local band started to play, Margaret was floating, it seemed. She and Tommy danced alone in the center of the room to music composed just for them. Or did it only appear that way to her?

At the end of the night, Margaret was exhausted. The bride and groom said good night to their guests and took off to the newest downtown hotel. It faced the harbor. Their room had a view of the water. Margaret got to wear her new black lingerie with red trim, an outfit that was so unlike her. Tommy told her she looked beautiful. The next week, too cold for a cruise to Bermuda, the couple flew to Miami. There they went sightseeing and lay on the beach.

Thanksgiving was spent with Tommy's family. Kathleen joined them for dinner. She planned to spend Christmas with her fiancé, Milton.

In late January Tommy and Margaret moved into their three bedroom, two-bath house in the city. Margaret sang as she shopped for and decorated it. Now going into the office seemed an intrusion.

Life had given Margaret her greatest desire — marriage, children to come along soon, and a man she had known and cared about for years. She was happy.

20

After Aaron told Shawanda that Donte had to go, he left for work. Shawanda got Donte dressed and took him to preschool. Returning home, she washed the dishes and cleaned two rooms. Later she got Donte. They went to the supermarket. Back home she cooked, chopping carrots and potatoes while Donte played. Feeding him, Shawanda next took the child upstairs to play. She left him in his room and closed his bedroom door.

Two thoughts went pop, pop in her head. She had made a decision to stick with Aaron. And her son was staying with her.

When Aaron came in, he kissed her. "Glad you're back."

"Want to get out of those dirty clothes? I'll put some water in the tub for you." She went upstairs to the bathroom. She soon took his cement-laced khaki shirt and pants and put them downstairs in the washer. Shawanda then warmed dinner. When Aaron came down, they sat at the kitchen table. They ate and talked.

"Like the beef stew?" she asked.

"I was sick of frozen foods and stuff out the can. Every once in a while I went over to my parents." He chuckled. "Did they talk about you? I had to tell them, 'That's my wife.

Cut it out.' Well, it's all over now. We're back together. And Donte's with Lena."

Letting his words lie in the air, Shawanda ignored them and kept eating.

"That was good," Aaron said after gobbling the meal.

"Donte's upstairs." Shawanda surrendered the fact knowing she couldn't keep it hidden indefinitely.

"What do you mean?"

"I'm not taking him anywhere."

"What!"

"If you keep yourself together, nothing will happen. You won't break probation, and my son can be with me."

"You've lost your mind."

"My mind is all right," she said.

"Woman, I'm looking at jail. I'm not taking any chances."

"Social Services might come." While he was worrying, she might as well tell him all there was to worry about.

"Social Services!"

"Mama said if I took Donte out the house, she was calling them again."

"Naw, Baby. I can't deal with probation people and them, too."

Shawanda stood up. "Don't worry. I'm not letting Social Services take Donte." She noticed Aaron gave her an unfamiliar look. Forget him, she said to herself. Picking up her plate, she put it in the sink and walked out of the kitchen.

Upstairs she went to their bedroom, closed the door, pounced on the bed, and turned on the television with the remote. A program was starting, a comedy. She turned her attention to it, happy for the mindless distraction. Twice she wondered what Donte and Aaron were doing, but quickly returned to the program. As it was ending, Shawanda heard the doorbell ring. Her body stiffened as she imagined the worst. Maybe it was a social worker, not the nice one, Danielle, who was last on the case, or the quiet lady, Margaret, who let her keep Donte. But it was Vanessa Graves, the mean one. If she tried to take Donte out of the house, Shawanda would fight her.

Jumping from bed, an urge to check on Donte overtaking her, she dashed to the door just as someone on the other side knocked. Halting, she listened for any indication of the intruder's identity.

"Shawanda, open up."

Recognizing Lena's voice, she opened the unlocked door. "What are you doing here?"

Lena came in and closed the door behind her. "Aaron called. I don't believe you ran out in the middle of the night. That was uncalled for."

"I told you I was going."

"But you didn't say when. Didn't say you were gonna sneak out at night. Your father's very upset with you."

"You too, right?"

"Upset doesn't even describe it." Lena sat in the only chair in the room. "Your father and I talked. We decided not to call Social Services. We didn't want to do that to you or Donte, and it didn't seem like it would solve anything. We're hoping you'll come to your senses and see that what you're doing isn't good for Donte. Aaron goes off. Even the court threatening him with jail may not be enough to stop him. I don't want Precious Baby here. And neither does Aaron. Can you blame him?"

"He knew I had a kid when he first got with me."

"I think he will be a good father to the child you're carrying. But not to Donte. Aaron called and told us that if we don't come and get Donte right away, he'll call his parents."

"Gladys and Peter ain't taking Donte nowhere!"

"Try to understand Aaron's point. I'm beginning to. Maybe he is a good man trying to do his best. It just isn't working."

Shawanda's ears delighted in her mother's concession.

"Your father and I will raise Donte," Lena continued. "He's the son I always wanted. You can see him whenever you want. You can take him out for as long as you want. And maybe, one day after the two of you go to counseling and this probation thing is over, you can have all your children in the house with you."

"You're not taking him!" Shawanda ran out of the room, hurried down the hall to where she had left Donte. She found the door open and the room empty. Turning, she got a glimpse of Lena rushing toward the steps. Shawanda followed her. Heading down the stairs, Shawanda missed a step, and almost fell. But she managed to grabbed the banister, steady herself, and continue. Nearing the foot of the stairs, she saw Ernest holding Donte. Lena was beside him now. Aaron was on the sofa.

"No, Daddy!" She rushed toward him, grabbing Donte around the waist and attempting to pull him away from Ernest. Then suddenly Lena and Aaron were upon her. Aaron grabbed one arm, Lena the other. Together they pulled her away. Ernest fled with Donte. "Bring my baby back here!" she screamed. Lena let go of her and ran out. Shawanda struggled to get to the door. But Aaron held her back. He managed to kick the door shut with his foot. "Leave me alone!" she yelled.

"Let them go, Baby." He released her.

She hurried outside, reaching the porch just in time to see the car pull away. She cursed under her breath. Turning around, Shawanda went back into the house. "Why did you do that?"

"I had to, Baby." He closed the front door and locked it.

"I'm going to get Donte and bring him home."

"This is my house, too. I say right now he can't live here. I say," he held up two fingers, "you've got two choices: Me or Donte. Remember, that's what Social Services told you. To keep Donte, you had to send me away. And you did. You won in court. And we got to be together again. But Baby, Donte don't want me to be his stepfather. He's used to his grandfather and those boyfriends you had before me that didn't stick around."

Shawanda considered his words. Aaron knew Tavon, one of her former boyfriends from the neighborhood. He was also an acquaintance of Denise. Shawanda, feeling confident about their relationship, had told then three-year-old Donte that Tavon would be his father. Donte was excited. But when the union with Tavon abruptly ended, she said nothing to Donte. She couldn't explain to him that Mama needed a man in her life. That Mama had thought Tavon was the one. But sometimes boyfriends, husbands, fathers don't stay.

"I don't feel like his father yet," Aaron was saying.

"You two gotta live in the same house and get used to each other."

"It's not working. I'm sick of trying to make it work."

"Don't give up."

"Baby, you can't play. Donte can't stay here no more. Who do you want to live with? Him or me? Pick one."

"What? I know it ain't come down to that."

"Yeah, Baby. That's exactly where it's at." He held up one finger. "You pick one." Slowly dropping his hand, he said, "I hope you stay with me."

21

On a windy Thursday in February, Margaret went to court on a case in which a father had sexually molested his daughter. Iris won it on behalf of Social Services. Margaret was relieved the child was in foster care. It was possibly the only safe place for her now.

Leaving the courtroom, Margaret walked down the halls of the old, dimly lit Clarence Mitchell Courthouse, and left the building through the front entrance. She started down the steps. People were behind, to the side, and in front of her. Halfway down she noticed Charles approaching the building. She had not seen him since the breakup. She stopped. The urge to turn and run into the courthouse tried to overtake her.

When he happened to glance in her direction, she smiled in an attempt to cover her nervousness. Continuing down the steps, Margaret stood at the bottom of them. Now letting go of her anxiety, Margaret admitted to herself she wanted to talk to him. Taking on calmness and allowing fate to have its way, she welcomed her former lover. When he stopped in front of her, she looked into his familiar eyes. And Margaret remembered Julio's, Atlantic City, the sailboat ride, daily phone talks, and nights spent in his arms. In the mornings he had made breakfast.

"How have you been?" he asked.

His voice sang a romantic melody in her ears. Margaret smiled. She had forgotten the warmth and deepness of his voice.

His words repeated in her head. How have I been? She could answer this way: the wedding was all I imagined. Married life comforting and peaceful. The loneliness is gone. Tommy is an attentive companion. We talk and spend lots of time together. On weekends we go the athletic club. He's teaching me how to play racquetball. On Sundays we go to mass. But deciding against telling him any of it, Margaret simply said, "I've been okay. And you?"

"Did you get married?"

"Yes, in November."

"Still living in Charles Village?"

"No, we bought a house in the city."

"Yes, I remember your devotion to the city."

"We're near Mother."

"How is your mother?"

"She's getting married."

"I think she always disliked me."

"She wasn't dating you."

"I want to talk to you, briefly," he said. "But not now. I have a case to do. Can you come to my office one day after work? Monday, maybe?"

She realized her affection for him was still breathing and beating. Inside of Margaret was the space he had vacated. She had become accustomed to its emptiness. "No, Charles, I can't."

"Monday. I'm in the office all day, and probably until about ten at night. See you then."

"I work until four-thirty, sometimes later. After work, I have to rush —."

He turned his back to her and went up the steps. That hurt. She hurried down the sidewalk telling herself she was a happily married woman. Tommy was a perfect husband. He had promised to stay with her for the rest of her life.

Later, at home, Margaret quickly changed into comfortable clothes. She went into the kitchen with its green and white plaid wallpaper, green tile floor and modern white appliances. Margaret started to prepare dinner. She put chicken pieces into a pan and was sticking them into the oven when she heard Tommy come in.

Reaching the kitchen, he approached and kissed her on the cheek. "Hi, Sweets."

"Hi. How was your day?"

"A homeless guy walked into the clinic. We treated him for several ailments. But as long as he's living on the street . . . . Don't tell me we're having chicken again?"

"Sorry. We can order out — pizza, maybe."

"You hate pizza, Sweets. Besides, chicken is okay. I'm sure I'll enjoy it." He walked out of the kitchen.

Margaret made a mental note to find different things to cook.

Soon she and Tommy had dinner. Afterwards they did the dishes together. After cleaning the kitchen, they went into the living room and watched television. A comedy came on. Tommy laughed throughout it. His easy and heartily laughter made Margaret join him. When they had finished watching the program, the couple went to bed. In the bedroom, sliding in between the dark red and brown comforter and red sheets, Margaret lay in her husband's arms.

She thought of no one but him.

"Good night, Sweets." He reached toward the nightstand and clicked off the light.

"Good night, Love."

The next day, Margaret went to work. At lunch April came in. Margaret noticed, now that she was married, April talked more about her own family. Margaret talked about Tommy. She was proud of him, the man he was and the work he did.

In the late afternoon Margaret left work and drove to the supermarket nearest her home. There she purchased a variety of items including steaks, pork, and shrimp. On the way to the checkout counter, she thought of Charles and immediately kicked his image from her head.

On Saturday Margaret called Kathleen and got some recipes from her. At noon Margaret and Tommy played racquetball. In the late afternoon they went to the mall. There they first stopped at the food court and got Chinese food. Next the couple visited a department store, where they bought household items. Afterwards they went to the movies. When Margaret saw the selection of films, she concluded that only one interested her. It was a love story. Tommy frowned when she told him.

But he said, "If you really what to see it, okay."

She loved that about him, the fact he always thought of her. While watching the film, she laid her head on his shoulder. For once she didn't envy the man and woman in the movie. She had had Charles and now Tommy. Love had found her, too.

Later at home Tommy made love to her.

On Sunday they went to mass. Afterwards they joined Kathleen and Milton for brunch.

On Monday Margaret went to work. In the afternoon she had a meeting. It ended at three. Margaret returned to her desk. Looking at her list of tasks to complete, she remembered Charles. He wasn't on the list. She had no intention of seeing him. She decided that the polite thing to do was to call and tell him not to expect her. Picking up the telephone, she dialed his office; surprised she still remembered the number.

"Law Offices of Charles Cooke. Nina Rossini speaking."

"Hello. I'm Margaret Green. I mean Holmes. May I speak to Mr. Cooke, please?"

"Just a minute."

While on hold, Margaret rehearsed what she would say: I would like to talk to you but something's come up. Maybe some other time, she would lie.

"Miss," the voice on the other end said.

"Yes," Margaret responded.

"I'm sorry, but he can't come to the phone."

"He's busy?"

"I don't know. May I take a message?"

"Yes, I had an appointment with him."

"You do? When?"

Margaret paused. "Please tell him I can't make it."

"Yes, I'll give him the message."

Margaret said goodbye and hung up the telephone. She twirled around in the chair and looked out of the window. Recalling her brief talk with Charles outside of the courthouse, she wondered how he would react to the message. He would probably get mad at her. She didn't want that. When he recalled their relationship, she wanted the memories to be of the pleasant times.

Margaret looked at her watch. Three-thirty. She had a memo to write. Turning to the computer, she prepared to write it. Pushing the keys, she peeped at her watch and thought of Charles. If she didn't go, he would hate her, Margaret feared. Unable to concentrate on the memo, she made a decision. She would go to see Charles, briefly. After all, one conversation couldn't hurt.

She made plans: quickly get downtown in rush hour, find parking, get to Charles's office, stay no more than fifteen minutes, hurry home and start dinner before Tommy arrives. He was usually home by six-thirty. Tapping her feet, she realized there wasn't enough time for all of it. But if Margaret left now, maybe she could get it all done by six.

It was three-fifty when she grabbed her handbag and walked to the elevator. Margaret had never before left work early. Downstairs she passed employees who were usually gone before her. Outside the full parking lot reminded her of the early hour. Getting into her car, Margaret felt like a bum.

Downtown was minutes away in traffic. Arriving there she easily found parking in a garage. Quickly getting to Charles's office, she stood outside and pushed the intercom button.

"May I help you?"

Margaret recognized Nina's voice and replied, "I'm here to see Mr. Cooke."

"Your name, please."

"Margaret."

After a minute, Nina buzzed her in. Inside Nina greeted her. "Please go right in."

Margaret went to Charles's office and pushed back the door. She saw him sitting behind the desk. Walking in, Margaret closed the door behind her. "Why didn't you take my call?"

"I knew it was bad news," he said. "I'm surprised to see you."

"Why?" Margaret sat in the chair in front of the desk. "You asked me to come." What was she saying? She was surprised to have made it.

He got up and moved to the chair next to Margaret. "I'm glad you came."

Just then there was a knock on the door. "Come in," Charles said.

Nina stood in the doorway. "See you tomorrow."

"Yes. Remember I have the district court case in D.C. in the morning. I won't come here first."

"Okay."

After Nina left, Margaret said, "I've never seen your office."

"Would you like a tour?"

"Sure."

They got up.

She followed him.

"The building was originally a house," he began when they reached the next room. "This would have been one of the sitting rooms. As you can see by the table and chairs, I've converted it into a conference room." They went out of a side door and into the hallway. "I inherited the building from my father, who had his law practice here. The second floor has been rented to an accounting firm for years." Then he pointed to a small space off of the rear hallway and said, "Back here, as you can see by all of the cabinets, is our file room." He gestured toward the door across from it. "That's the bathroom. The last room is the kitchen and lunch area. It's much larger than is needed in an office be —."

"Because it was originally the kitchen in someone's home."

"Yes, that's right."

"Your office is beautiful."

"Thank you. I didn't decorate it. Would you like anything to eat or drink?"

A gallon of wine was her honest answer. "No, thank you," she said.

"Would you like to return to the office?" he asked.

They headed back that way. Pausing in the conference room, she looked at the oblong, black table with aqua trim, which had six matching chairs. "Nicely decorated," she commented. "I wish Social Services could afford such elegance."

"Margaret, I was afraid." Charles stood behind her.

Margaret turned around and looked at him. She suddenly felt a need to embrace Charles, to let her warmth engulf him, to forbid life from dragging him down into its cold spaces. "Charles." She moved closer.

"Life's ironic," he said. "I have no problems speaking to judges and juries. But now I can't seem to organize my words."

She took a deep breath, waiting for him to continue.

"When I realized the only way I could keep you was . . . . I thought I would make a bad husband. And you would hate me. But I wanted to keep you. Then when I lost you, I hated myself. When you called in September I wanted to date you all over again. I had to keep telling myself you were engaged. I've dated one woman since you. We went out three times. It wasn't working. Now, for you and me, it's too late. I was proud and stubborn. I told myself I could live without you, without anyone. Forgive me, please Margaret, because I can't forgive myself."

She put her arms around his waist. Suddenly she heard footsteps. "Who's that?"

"The accountants. They all leave every day at the same time. We're the only ones left in the building now. Maybe you should go."

She nodded. "What time is it?"

"The accountants leave at five."

"Okay. I'm going." Clinging to him — it was now a good-bye embrace — her head laid against his chest. She could hear his heart beat. It was familiar and comfortable here.

"I don't think I've ever said this to any other woman." He put his arms around her. "I love you, Margaret."

She lifted her head and looked at him. Time, distance, marriage to someone else had not killed her affection for him. "I love you, too."

He stroked her face and neck. Then he kissed her.

All she could think about was how much she cared about him.

Charles kept kissing her. He unzipped his pants. His left hand went under her dress and stroked her thighs. Soon they were on top of the black-with-aqua trim conference table. With moans and gasps, they rediscovered each other. Their passion, once pushed into a corner, now easily came forward, excited to be released.

Their desire peaked. And they rested.

Charles got up.

Margaret did too.

They fixed their clothes.

Running into the bathroom, Margaret was there only a minute. Coming out, she returned to the conference room. Charles was gone. She went into his office and found him sitting behind the desk. Grabbing her handbag, she said, "I have to go." Heading toward the door, Margaret stopped when Charles spoke, but didn't turn around.

"Come back to see me again, please," he said.

Margaret went straight out of the door. Outside, retrieving her car and leaving the parking lot, she remembered something. "Oh no," she yelled. They hadn't used a condom. Wanting to have children with Tommy, she didn't have any need for birth control. She couldn't think about the possibility of being pregnant by Charles. Life couldn't go that wrong, she convinced herself.

Looking at her watch, she noted it was six o'clock. The traffic moved too slowly, it seemed. Margaret changed lanes often. Now a yellow light meant drive faster. For her, it had never meant that before.

At home, she spotted Tommy's car parked in front of the house. Jumping out of her car, she took a deep breath and walked slowly toward the front door. Charles's scent filling her nostrils, she tried to think of excuses for her lateness. As soon as Margaret entered her home, Tommy emerged from the kitchen.

"Sweets! There you are!"

He was approaching her as if he wanted to hug or kiss her, something he usually did.

"Sorry. Have to go." She ran up the stairs into the bathroom and closed the door. Standing behind it, she continued to panic. Margaret had to jump into the shower. So she did. Quickly washing, she wrapped a towel around her body, picked up all of her clothes from the floor and dumped them into the hamper, even the dry-cleaned dress. She went into the bedroom and grabbed the first outfit she got her hands on. It was a red jogging suit. Back in the bathroom, she brushed her teeth, rinsed her mouth, and combed her hair. Taking a deep breath, she slowly walked back downstairs.

She found Tommy in the kitchen.

"Would you like to eat out tonight?" He stood against the counter.

"No. I'll fix something."

"How was your day?" he asked.

"Busy. I had a long meeting."

"Worked a little later than usual?" He folded his arms.

"Yes." She went to the refrigerator. Looking inside of it, she was happy to spot the package of steaks. It was something she could cook quickly.

"Why were you showering?"

"Showering?" She repeated the word to buy time.

"I heard the water running."

She closed the refrigerator door. "I . . . ." She looked Tommy straight in the eye. "This is embarrassing. I had to go to the bathroom before I left work. But I . . . rushed out and . . . the traffic was bad. And before I could get inside and to the bathroom, I had a little accident."

"Ah, Sweets." He came over and hugged her. "Poor, Baby."

"I'm okay, really. After I showered and changed, I felt better." What an awful lie, she thought settling into her husband's embrace.

She hadn't realized such evil was inside of her. Now Margaret almost prayed that God would withhold from her the mercy he displayed to everyone all of the time. That God and her husband would give her what she deserved. The floor would slide back. The ground would open. And some force beneath it would suck her down into the earth. And straight into hell.

22

After Aaron told Shawanda to choose, she was too mad to spend the night in the same house with him. She got her purse and car keys and left. She decided against going to her parents'. There wasn't any point in fighting with them anymore. That left only one other place. She drove to Denise's apartment. Getting out of the car, Shawanda noticed an empty can lying on the sidewalk. She kicked it hard, and watched it cruised through the air. Soon Shawanda knocked on Denise's front door.

"Wassup?" Denise opened the door while straightening her blouse and short skirt.

"Mama and Daddy got Donte." Shawanda noticed the living room was dark. She wondered if coming here had been a mistake. "I've got no place to go."

Denise pulled the door back. "Come on in." She flipped on the nearby light switch.

Inside Shawanda saw a man in an oversized jogging suit sitting on the sofa.

"Jamal," Denise began, "this is my friend Shawanda."

"Hey," Jamal said.

"Shawanda's sleeping on the couch."

Jamal got up and moved to the chair.

"I'll get some sheets and pillows." Denise left the room. Soon she came back with floral sheets and two pillows. "Want something to eat?" she asked Shawanda.

"I ate already. Thanks."

"Let me know if you need anything." Denise said goodnight, and she and Jamal left the room.

Shawanda lay on the sofa. It was awhile before she fell asleep.

In the morning Shawanda was awakened by voices. Denise and Jamal were in the kitchen talking. Soon Jamal left. She turned over and said to Denise, "He looks good."

"I really like him. Think I'll give him a chance." Denise sat in a nearby chair. "What went on with you last night?"

Shawanda sat up and told her.

"Can't blame him, can you?" Denise asked after Shawanda finished. "He's looking at jail."

"I shouldn't have to pick."

"You don't have to. You can get an apartment and a job. Maybe Kim will keep Donte and the new baby while you work."

"I tried that with one child," Shawanda said. "I don't want to think about doing it with two."

"You can move back with Lena and Ernest. They'll help you with the kids."

"I'm too old to live with Mama and Daddy."

"You can go back to Aaron and leave Donte with your parents."

"With all I went through to keep Donte!"

Denise threw up her hands "Then what are you going to do?"

Shawanda thought about it. She felt defeated. "There's only one thing to do." She shook her head slowly, knowing she was out of options. "Leave Donte with Mama and Daddy." Hopelessness spoke for her. "Maybe I can go over to see him everyday, get him from school and take him to Mama's. It wouldn't be like leaving him, really." Shawanda tired to convinced herself.

"You couldn't do that everyday."

"I don't want to be alone."

"You mean without a man?" Denise asked.

"Without Aaron."

"You're going to put a man over your son?"

"I put up a fight for Donte. But now what else can I do? I don't want Aaron to go back to jail, or Donte to get hurt anymore. Besides, I'm pregnant. I've gotta stay with Aaron."

Denise sighed. "Well, do what you gotta do."

* * *

After the conversation with Denise, Shawanda got dressed. She had breakfast and lingered awhile before heading to her parents.

There, Lena blocked the front doorway.

Shawanda stood on the porch. "Hey."

"Don't come in here starting nothing." Lena stood in the doorway.

"I'm not, Mama. Let me in."

"And don't try to take Donte out of this house!"

"I won't."

Lena stared.

"You ain't letting your own daughter in?"

Lena looked a few more seconds before slowly moving away.

Shawanda went inside.

"Where's Donte?"

"I'm warning you."

"I'm gonna stick with Aaron."

"That figures." Lena turned and walked toward the dining room.

"I want him to be with his baby." Shawanda followed her. "You should see how happy he is when he talks about the baby."

In the kitchen, Lena got a pan from the cabinet. "Don't worry about Precious Baby. I'll take good care of him."

"I'll come over and help. After the baby's born, maybe I can get a part-time job and give you money for Donte."

"Stay home with your baby. Donte will have what he needs." Lena walked to the refrigerator, took out a package of pork chops and laid them on the counter.

"Stewing them?" Shawanda asked, knowing that Lena usually stuck the chops in a gravy.

"Yeah," Lena answered.

"I want to tell you something," Shawanda said, mentally searching for all of the words that would describe her feelings. Unable to pull them together, she managed to only say, "Thanks."

Lena looked at her.

Shawanda walked over and hugged her mother. While the two had conflicts, Shawanda always felt fortunate to have a caring mother who looked out for her.

"You're welcome, Daughter," Lena nearly whispered.

Minutes later, Ernest came home. Shawanda heard him in the living room and rushed to greet him. Running up to Ernest, she wrapped her arms around him.

"How's my only daughter?" he asked.

"I'm gonna let Donte stay here if that's all right with you."

"We'll look after him. You concentrate on the new baby and take good care of yourself."

"I want to have a home with Aaron."

Ernest nodded. "If you ever need anything, we're here for you."

Shawanda smiled. She had always adored her father. Nothing could ever change that.

The two talked for a while.

Afterwards, Shawanda went upstairs. She found Donte in his room, playing with toy helicopters and trucks.

"Ma!" He ran to her. "Where you been?"

She picked him up and went over to the bed. Sitting down, she placed him in her lap. "Want to live with Grandma and Paw Paw?"

"See the 'copter? Paw Paw gave it to me."

"I'm going to live with Mr. Aaron, your new daddy."

"Why?" the child asked.

"Because Mommies and Daddies are suppose to live together. I'll come over almost everyday and see you." She kissed him on the forehead. "I love you."

"La ya, Ma."

She played with him for a while. The thought that he hated her popped into her head. Finally she acknowledged it wasn't him. Her guilt made her dislike herself.

After a long time, she said goodbye to her son and parents and drove home. Reaching the house, she unlocked the door and went inside. She could hear the water running in the bathroom and knew Aaron was in the shower. She went upstairs. There she found Aaron getting out of the shower and reaching for a towel.

"You came back!" He looked at her. "Sorry about the mess last night. Guess I wasn't thinking about how you would feel when Lena and Ernest took Donte like that."

"I'm staying with you," she said.

He smiled. "I'm glad, Baby."

She turned and went downstairs with the intent of going into the kitchen and preparing dinner. Getting as far as the living room, she stood in the middle of the floor. She felt life had slapped her in the face. She punched back. It was a nasty fight. In the end, it was easy to determine the winner. Life won. Although Donte was just with Lena, Shawanda knew she had lost something. She had lost the right to be a full-time mother to her son. Now bitterness, anger, defeat, and hopelessness all joined together. And she cried. But her gushing tears were not enough to wash away the guilt. *She chose a man over her son.* Her actions convicted her. Her sentence was to live with the pain for life. But her short life already seemed long.

23

On Wednesday Charles phoned Margaret. "Do you mind my calling you at work?" he asked.

They talked for a while before saying good-bye.

On Friday when Margaret got into the office, she thought of Charles. At eight-thirty she called his office. The telephone rang. At nine she tried again and got Nina. Margaret left a message. At nine-thirty Charles called her back.

"What are your plans for today?" she asked, wanting to know every detail of his life.

"I have court this afternoon." Changing the subject, he said, "I would like to see you."

"We shouldn't."

"I haven't been to Julio's lately. Would you like to join me?"

"When?"

"Sometime next week. How about Wednesday at noon? I'll meet you there."

"I only have an hour for lunch."

"Okay, Margaret. If you can't . . . ."

"Wednesday?" She flipped the pages of her desk calendar. There was nothing pressing scheduled, and she wanted to see him. "Noon? I'll meet you inside of the restaurant."

"Are you certain?"

"I'll be there." After hanging up, Margaret rose from the chair. Leaving her office and going to the elevator, she pushed the up button. Reaching the third floor, she walked to her supervisor's office. There, Margaret greeted Karen Hudson.

"Come on in," the forty-three-year-old woman with off-black straightened hair said.

"I have to attend to some personal business next Wednesday," Margaret told Karen. "I need about three hours of leave, from eleven-thirty to two-thirty."

Her request shamed her. In all of her years at Social Services, she had strived for excellence. No one had a greater work ethic than she, Margaret had always thought.

"Of course you can," Karen responded. "After all, you rarely take leave."

Margaret thanked her and headed back to the second floor to fill out the leave slip. She remembered the last time she filled one out. It was for her wedding and honeymoon. For the rest of the day Margaret was bothered by her decision.

On Wednesday when Margaret walked into Julio's, she immediately spotted Charles at the bar.

"I thought you wouldn't come," he said.

She was disappointed at his lack of faith in her. "I said I would." Not even a happy marriage could keep her away.

They got a table.

Charles ordered a small pitcher of red sangria. "Do you like sangria?" he asked.

"I've never had it before. What's in it?"

"Wine, brandy, fruit, sugar. Would you like to try it?"

She nodded. When the waiter returned with the pitcher and filled both of their glasses, Margaret took a sip.

"Good," she said. After taking another sip and putting the glass down, Margaret asked, "What are you doing for the rest of the day?"

"I have a lot of paperwork to complete — motions, contracts. I'll finish up late and head for home. And you?"

She didn't want to remind Charles or herself of the marriage. "When I get back to the office, I have letters to write and calls to make. At home I'll watch a little television and go to bed early."

Charles moved to a new subject. "My brother and his wife just had their third child — a girl."

"They must be very happy. Are you ever having children?"

"Recently I've started to imagine myself with them."

"You're making progress." She took another sip of the sangria. Talking to Charles again was easy. It was almost as if they had never left each other. Emotionally they never had, Margaret was convinced. "Mother's busy planning for her wedding. Brittany's flying in for it. She's staying a week, and coming alone. Mother thinks Brittany's in so much debt that she can't afford plane fare for her sons."

"You won't be happy to see her, will you?"

"Of course I will. We're sisters. We have bitter fights, but we love each other."

"I guess I don't have to understand that."

"Really, I'm looking forward to seeing Brittany. I have a lot to tell her."

* * *

The day of Brittany's arrival, Margaret didn't wait for her sister to settle in. It was a cool Wednesday in late April when Margaret drove to Kathleen's.

"Where's Brittany?" Margaret asked Kathleen.

"Upstairs unpacking."

"I'm going up to say hello to her."

Climbing the stairs, Margaret acknowledged that Brittany was possibly the only person she knew who would understand her affair with Charles. Since Margaret's wedding, and during their telephone conversations, Brittany had gradually released details of her own marital indiscretions.

Knocking on the door of Brittany's old room, Margaret entered after hearing, "Come in."

"Sister Dear," Brittany dropped the blouse she was unpacking on the bed and hurried toward Margaret with wide-open arms. The two women hugged. "I'm so happy to see you. Isn't it exciting? Our mother's remarrying."

Margaret took one look at her smartly dressed, color coordinated sister and decided Brittany looked as beautiful as ever.

"I need to talk to you about something," Margaret said, closing the door. She went to the side of the bed and sat down. Brittany sat next to her. "You can't tell Mother or anyone else."

"Darling, please, no secrets. You know I have a big mouth."

"Promise!"

Brittany sucked her teeth. "I'll try. I just hope it's forgettable. That way I won't have to worry about ever telling it."

Margaret understood what her sister was saying. But she had to tell someone. "I'm still in love with Charles. I did things too fast. I wanted to get married so badly that I ran to Tommy. I love Tommy. We have a lot in common. We're about building a future together. But Charles is like . . . cocaine for me. I can get high off of him. He's even addictive. I don't want to love him because I think doing so is crazy. But I can't help myself. Something in me naturally loves him. I can't ignore that fact. Ignoring it wouldn't make it go away, anyway. You know what I mean, don't you, Brittany? You've been in love with two men at once."

Her sister frowned. "Really, Dearest, I've never done that! It sounds dumb. Why would you risk your happy marriage by going back to your old boyfriend?"

"You've told me about the other men in your life!"

"Yes, yes, there have been others. But I was never in love with any of them. They were harmless flirtations with attractive, well-built men who turned me on. They were exciting diversions from my routine life. You know how it is when you're having an affair. The sneaking around. When and where will I meet him? The planning and plotting. The secrecy. It all makes life interesting. Twice I almost got caught. Hon, did I panic! I had to think quickly."

Margaret recalled the lie she had told Tommy when coming home late and showering early.

Brittany continued. "What I do doesn't hurt anyone. It's just sex and fun. After two or three times in bed, I'll cut off the relationship because I don't want to get involved and jeopardize my marriage. But you, my beloved Sister, are screwing around with fire. You're going to get burnt. You know who ends up getting divorced? It's not the ones who are just having a little sex on the side. It's the pathetic ones who fall in love with someone else."

"What should I do?"

"You married well. Get rid of Charles. You could have chosen him in the first place. You didn't. You must have had a good reason not to."

"I can't just leave him again. Leaving the first time was a mistake. We both admit that now."

"You've already hurt him by making him the other man. And we both know how devastated Tommy would be if he found out. Listen, Charles could have married you in the first place. He didn't. You can't keep both of them. Maybe if it was only occasional sex it might work. But being in love with two men!" Brittany threw up her hands. "I can't imagine it."

"Why are you better than me because you don't love the men you cheat with?"

"I'm not better. As always, Darling, you've won. You are the nobler one. Marriage to me is an arrangement. It's about how far it will get me. And with Russell, I've gone far. But you fall in love. If you want Charles, divorce Tommy."

"I don't want to be a divorced woman!" Margaret cried.

"What do you want?"

"A happy marriage, Charles, and not to hurt Tommy."

"A happy marriage to whom?" Brittany sighed. "My poor sister. You went from being the Mother Teresa of Baltimore to cheating on your husband. We never had much in common, did we? At least not until now."

* * *

Two days later on the Friday before Kathleen's wedding, Kathleen called Margaret at the office and demanded she come over immediately after work.

When Margaret arrived at her mother's home, Kathleen said, "Brittany is visiting an old friend. She should be back soon."

Margaret cleared a spot on the sofa and sat down. The house seemed even more cluttered than usual.

"Your sister swore me to secrecy. I don't want you to tell her that I told you."

Margaret slowly shook her head. It had been stupid to tell a secret to someone who admitted to being unable to keep one.

"I'm so disappointed in you, Margaret." Kathleen stood in the middle of the floor. "I would have expected this from Brittany, but not from you."

"It just happened, Mother. It was like something came up behind me and attacked me. I didn't see or expect it. I didn't want it to happen. Even after it did, something in me couldn't believe it."

"I'm glad your father isn't here to see this. I can't imagine his reaction."

Margaret lowered her head. The shame was almost unbearable.

"And poor Tommy. He's a decent man. The last time I talked to him he told me how happy the two of you were. How could you do this to him?"

Margaret couldn't lift her head. And she couldn't begin to answer that question.

"When I first saw you with Charles, I noticed the way he looked at you. And the way you looked at him," Kathleen said.

"Something in me was dead," Margaret mumbled. "He touched it and made it live again. Made it dance and sing again."

"Yeah, yeah, yeah," Kathleen responded. "I know. I felt that way when I first met your father." Kathleen moved to a nearby chair. Instead of sitting in it, she stood to the side of it. "I like Charles. But not as a son-in-law. I thought he wouldn't fit into our family. I still believe that." Kathleen paused. "What are you doing with your life?"

Margaret looked at the stack of magazines that sat on the floor against the opposite wall. "With Charles I feel like a little girl who's gotten everything she wanted for her birthday."

"But with Tommy you have to grow up." Kathleen gripped the back of the chair. "What are you going to do about Charles?"

"I don't know. Maybe I'm too weak to do anything."

"I will not let you treat Tommy like this!" Kathleen yelled.

Margaret looked at her mother. A spirit of rebellion suddenly possessed Margaret. "Mind your business."

Kathleen gasped. "I don't care how old you are! You are never to talk to me like that again!" Kathleen put her hand on her hips. "You think it's not my business? I'll show you. You have choices. You want Charles, fine. I can't stop you. Tell Tommy you're cheating on him. Divorce him. Date Charles. Marry Charles. Do whatever it is the two of you do. Or do the decent thing. Don't break your husband's heart! You made a vow to Tommy. Keep your promise."

"I can't leave either one of them."

"Well, you are going to have to do something soon."

"Please, Mother. My life is bad enough. I'm begging you. Stay out of it."

"I won't stay out of it! If you keep cheating on Tommy, I'll tell him about your affair."

"How can you even say that?"

"I'll do more than say it. Decide what you want. I won't wait long to tell him."

"Please, don't tell Tommy anything!" Margaret began to cry.

"I used to be proud of you," Kathleen said with sadness in her voice. "Choose quickly."

* * *

The next day was Kathleen and Milton's wedding. It was well attended and went as planned. Margaret attended with Tommy. The reception was nearly perfect. The hall beautifully decorated. The food exceptionally good.

Margaret had quickly pushed Kathleen's threat from her mind. Margaret believed Kathleen couldn't and wouldn't tell Tommy. Her mother was incapable of hurting her so deeply, Margaret had convinced herself.

Before Brittany's return to California, Margaret enlisted her in a scheme. Margaret wanted to spend more time with Charles. Pieces of time here and there were increasingly becoming insufficient.

Her scheme: she would tell Tommy that Brittany invited her to California. She hadn't seen her nephews in years. With the debt Brittany was in, she couldn't afford to bring them on her two past visits. Margaret could fly to California on a Friday and return the following Monday. With Tommy's job, it was unlikely he would offer to accompany her for such a short visit. Margaret would give him an emergency number at which to reach her. It would be Brittany's cell phone. Also Margaret would call Tommy often. That way he wouldn't need to call her as much. When he called, Brittany would make an excuse such as, she's in the bathroom. When she comes out, I'll tell her to call you. Then Brittany would contact Margaret, and Margaret would call immediately.

Of course Margaret would be with Charles in Baltimore the entire time.

In May Margaret and Charles drove to Rehoboth, Delaware. Charles knew of a hotel that was right on the ocean. Their hotel room had a balcony that overlooked the water. Arriving in the afternoon, they unpacked and went for a walk along the beach. Margaret liked walking barefoot in the sand. She held on to Charles's hand. And watched the waves slammed against the shore with a crashing sound.

After a while they went in, dressed for dinner and soon departed for a nearby restaurant. Afterwards they returned to the beach. Margaret liked the ocean at night.

Back at the hotel, when Margaret got into the room, she went into the bathroom. She turned on the shower, and started to peel off her clothes.

Charles came in. "I was about to take a shower," he told her.

"Wait your turn." She joked.

He undressed. She didn't pay any attention to him. But instead pulled a bar of gardenia scented soap from her bag. Charles came up behind her and started kissing her shoulders and back. He forced her to the wall. And they expressed their passion. When they were completely satisfied, they caught their breaths and relaxed. Gliding into the shower, she washed him. And he washed her. Afterwards, as the warm water trickled down their bodies, she kissed his chest.

Back in the bedroom, they lay in bed with their arms around each other.

"Do you ever consider Tommy?" she asked.

"I saw you first."

She lifted her body up. "How long can we go on like this?" she whispered.

* * *

On a Wednesday in mid-June, Margaret and Tommy talked on the telephone during lunch time. They ended the conversation with an agreement to see each other at the house at the usual hour.

Quitting time, Margaret left work and headed home. There she changed into comfortable clothes before beginning dinner. On the menu were baked salmon, roasted potatoes and steamed broccoli.

When Tommy had not gotten home by seven, Margaret called his office. A colleague answered and said that everyone else had left. She dialed Tommy's cell phone. He didn't pick up.

At eight o'clock Margaret ate small portions of the dinner and put the rest of it in the refrigerator. At nine, uncertain what to do, Margaret had to share her anxiety with someone.

Using the telephone in the kitchen, she dialed Kathleen's number.

"Tommy hasn't come home yet," Margaret told her mother. "I don't know where he is." Margaret heard Kathleen clear her throat.

"I called Tommy at work late this afternoon," Kathleen finally said. "I asked him to come over before he went home. He did. Milton was in the living room. So I took Tommy into the kitchen. I told him you were sleeping with Charles."

"What!" Margaret screamed.

"The only reason I didn't tell him sooner was because I was busy with my new marriage."

"How could you ruin our lives?"

"You ruined his life!" Kathleen hung up.

Margaret held the telephone. She could hear herself breathing. What to do next? Margaret pondered. She dialed Brittany's number. Her sister answered. "Tommy hasn't come home yet. I don't know where he is. Mother told him I was having an affair."

"I don't believe Mother Dear! Thank goodness I live in California! The distance keeps her out of my business."

"What am I going to do?"

"Let me think. Tommy knows only what he heard from Mother Dear. You could deny it. It's her word against yours."

"Deny it! How can I?"

"Oh, try this. You ran into your old boyfriend. You saw him a couple of times. All the two of you did was talk. Realizing Charles was getting the wrong impression from your purely innocent conversations, you stopped talking to him weeks ago. You know, right after Mother Dear married Milton."

"That didn't happen," Margaret said.

"Do you have any better suggestions, Darling?"

"I'll tell him the truth."

"You can't do that! What if he gets angry and . . . ."

"No more lies! I can't tell another one."

"Dearest, please listen to me. You don't know where Tommy is. Or how mad he is. Maybe you should get out of the house. Go to a hotel."

"No, I won't run."

"But Margaret, Darling . . . ."

"I'll talk to you tomorrow." Margaret hung up.

Clicking off the kitchen light, Margaret went upstairs to their bedroom to wait for Tommy.

24

Being pregnant made Shawanda feel special. She wouldn't lose this child. Overcompensating, she slept too much and overate to ensure a healthy baby. The stretch marks on her belly didn't bother Shawanda. She would do anything for her baby.

She enjoyed browsing stores for infant clothing. There wasn't money to purchase much; the house in the suburbs was all the debt they could handle.

Denise gave her a baby shower. Relatives came, some of the cousins and Lena. Lots of friends were there, too. The women ate fried chicken and potato salad. They talked and laughed. Shawanda opened her gifts: blankets, tee shirts, booties, baby bottles, diapers, and pretty little outfits. She needed each one.

Just before her due date, Shawanda went into labor during the night. Aaron hopped out of bed and got her bag for the hospital stay. He put his arms around her waist and gently led her to the stairs.

"I can walk."

"The pain might get too much for you. Hold on to me."

Outside the street was deserted. The night was a friend, it seemed.

At the hospital Shawanda sat nearby while Aaron gave information to the admitting clerk. He appeared impatient with the woman's attitude, Shawanda concluded, as if he thought the clerk should get excited about the baby. Soon Aaron rolled a wheelchair toward her.

"Get in, Baby."

"I don't need —."

"Come on!"

She got up and into the wheelchair.

The rest of the night was spent in the delivery room. At 7:43 in the morning, their baby was born. She weighed seven pounds and three ounces. They named her Charmise Dionne Washington.

When Shawanda was taken to her room, Aaron was beside her. He grinned, squeezed her hand and said, "I've got me a little girl!"

Two sets of grandparents, Denise, and Aaron's brothers and sisters came to visit. Shawanda was exhausted, but happy. Within days mother and baby were headed home.

At home Aaron helped a lot. He fixed baby bottles and watched Shawanda change diapers. It was two weeks before he was comfortable enough to change them, too.

He went out and got dinner: fried chicken and Chinese food. When Lena discovered their fast food diet, she brought over homemade dishes: baked fish, collard greens, and fruit salad.

Donte came with Lena. He looked at his sister and said, "Let me hold the baby, Ma."

"When you get older," Shawanda responded.

That night Shawanda walked into their bedroom and found Aaron sitting and holding Charmise in his arms.

"She's all that," he said. "Now I understand how you feel about Donte."

* * *

When Charmise was six weeks old, Shawanda returned to counseling with Aaron. Gladys baby-sat.

After ten months in counseling, one Saturday morning the couple greeted Frank Boyd in his office.

He was tall, thirty-seven, and had cinnamon-tinted skin. He always had a pack of cigarettes nearby and was a heavy smoker.

"After all of these months, I think we're finally making progress," said Frank, who had a master's degree in social work and counseling. "Let's start by going over the points we've talked about."

Aaron went first. "Me and Baby got to talk about how to raise Donte before we go to him."

"Right," Frank said. "Your father was strict, but . . . ."

"He and Mama didn't fight over what to do in front of us."

"If Donte sees we don't agree," Shawanda joined in, "he'll run to the one that's on his side. Me and Aaron will get pitted against each other."

"Very good. Now if Donte was in the house with the two of you, what time would he go to bed?" Frank asked the couple.

"The same time every night." Shawanda adopted Aaron's viewpoint.

"No, we'll talk about it each time," Aaron offered.

"We can't talk about every little thing all the time," Shawanda told her husband.

"Okay, he goes to bed at the same time, except on weekends," Aaron said. "He can stay up later then. It'll be his treat."

"How late is later?" Frank inquired.

"Ten." Aaron looked at his wife. "Okay?"

Shawanda nodded.

"Good," Frank said. "Aaron, I know being in counseling has been difficult for you. But you've worked hard over these past months. You've done well."

"You should see him with Charmise." Shawanda smiled.

Frank's glance rolled from Shawanda to Aaron. "If you stay in counseling, you'll become a good stepparent, too."

25

Margaret heard the front door slam and shivered. She held her breath while waiting to hear Tommy climb the stairs. When he didn't, Margaret exhaled, listening to the downstairs noises — his footsteps against the hardwood floor, the clicking on and off of the radio, the opening and closing of a cabinet — the everyday sounds now seemed threatening. Nevertheless, Margaret got out of bed and headed downstairs. It was not courage that pushed her, but a sense of hopelessness. She halted in the living room when hearing glass break. Margaret prayed Tommy wasn't hurt as she rushed toward the kitchen. She found him standing at the counter and staring at the floor.

He looked up. "I dropped a glass, Sweets."

"I'll clean it up." She hurried to the adjacent laundry room and returned with a broom and dustpan.

"I'm a little late getting home tonight," he said.

She swept up the glass.

"I talked to Kathleen." Tommy watched Margaret. "She told me you went back to your old boyfriend."

Margaret dumped the broken pieces into the nearby trash can. "I'm sorry." She forced herself to look him in the eye. "I shouldn't have let it happen."

"I couldn't imagine you doing it. Not the scared, proper little Margaret I've known for years. But you've changed. You seem more willing to take risks. It's like you don't care as much about what other people think."

"I hadn't noticed that. I made a mistake."

"When you went back to him? Or when you left him in the first place to marry me?"

"I didn't mean to hurt you."

"Did you think about me at all?"

"I did. I care about you. Our marriage wasn't all a lie. I want to keep our home together. We can still have children. Please forgive me."

"Now that's the Margaret I know, always has to do the right thing. We always had that in common — wanting to be respectable. I know I saw myself with all of the social trappings — a wife, a house, kids."

"Please don't send me away."

He moved closer. "Remember the bookstore? I ran into you and got comfortable again with you right away. I knew we could have a good marriage. You told me about Charles. I ignored the fact that he was around. He didn't want what you wanted. I knew if I waited patiently, I could take you from him. Now it seems I was wrong."

"You were right. I'm here with you."

"We love each other, don't we, Margaret?"

"Yes."

"But we're not in love," he said.

"I don't think that matters," she insisted. "We respect each other. We work well together."

"When I asked you to marry me, that was my viewpoint, too. I'm not sure anymore."

"Our love for each other will grow," she told him.

"Will it?"

"We can make this marriage work. I won't see Charles again."

Tommy sighed and sat at the kitchen table. Margaret joined him.

"Before Christmas," he began, "I met Sara. We had sex a couple of times —."

"You cheated on me!"

"Marriage to you wasn't enough," he said. "I met Lisa in February —."

"Lisa! So many women!"

"We started dating a couple of weeks later. She's a wild woman, the kind you don't take home to your parents. My being married has kept her at a good distance."

"How could we do this to each other?" Margaret wrung her hands.

"It was like being married only made me want to date more." Tommy leaned forward. "I think, maybe, I wanted to be married more than I wanted you. I hope that's not insulting."

"Actually, I understand."

"There's this side of me that wants to be the perfect son, doctor, husband. You know what I mean, Sweets. We have that in common. But the other side wants to break all of the rules."

"We have to stop this!" She slowly shook her head. "We'll drop the others and recommit to each other." Margaret started to cry. "I won't cheat on you ever again. You don't cheat on me, either."

"I can't promise you anything. Listen, I'm surprised you were as unhappy as —."

"I was happy!"

"Something was missing for you, too. Look, I forgive you."

"I forgive you, too, Tommy."

"Let's not do this to each other anymore."

"Okay, we'll forget about the others."

He leaned back. "Not what I mean. This marriage isn't working."

"It can work."

"I don't want the pretense anymore," he said. "Let's separate, at least for a while. Let's not become bitter over this. I'm sorry about everything. Would you mind moving out? I want the house."

His words rioted in her head. She couldn't hold them down long enough to address them. Margaret got up and left the kitchen.

Tommy moved into the extra bedroom that night. Over the next week, whenever the couple passed in the hallway, they were polite.

Margaret couldn't believe the marriage was over. She hoped Tommy would change his mind.

But she was shoved by reality the day Tommy asked, "Would you like me to leave?"

"No, I'll go."

Margaret got the newspaper and started looking for an apartment. She signed a six-month lease on the first one she saw. It was a small, reasonably priced studio in a converted Charles Village rowhouse two blocks from her old place. She purchased a sofa bed and a small table that seated two. Margaret cleaned her new living space and began to move in.

Tommy helped her. After all of the boxes were stacked into the small room, he stood at the door. Margaret went over and hugged him. Then he turned around and walked away. She closed the door and sat among the boxes.

Margaret had thought of her life as boring. Now it was a disaster.

Too confused for a romantic relationship with anyone anymore anytime in the near future, Margaret started to screen her calls at the office. When the receptionist told her Charles Cooke was on the line, Margaret would say, "Please take a message."

On the first day of August, Margaret paid rent on the apartment for the second time. The act emphasized the fact her marriage was over. Finally, Margaret began to unpack.

She went to mass the following Sunday. Afterward Margaret stood outside and waited for Milton and Kathleen to come out. She had not spoken to Kathleen since June. When she walked up to the newlyweds, the tall, distinguished Milton warmly greeted her.

"It's good to see you," he said with a gracious smile. "We've missed your coming over to the house."

"How have you been, Dear?" Kathleen asked.

"Not well."

"I'm sorry for what I did." Kathleen looked her daughter in the eye. "I didn't think it would end your marriage. I was only trying to force you away from Charles."

"You and I disappointed each other," Margaret said.

"Milton and I are going for brunch. Will you join us, dear, please?"

"Yes," Milton added. "You two need to start talking again."

He reminded her of her father. "I would love to come to brunch."

They walked to a restaurant on nearby Charles Street. Settling in, they immediately began to talk about Kathleen's striving garden and her getting rid of some of the clutter in the house — for Milton's sake.

"Of course you know about Tommy," Kathleen said.

"Know what?"

"I spoke to him a couple of times after the two of you split. I wanted to understand what happened. Anyway, that woman moved into the house last week."

"Lisa?" Margaret put down the fork.

"Her moving in is a secret he keeps from his family. Tommy said he wasn't in love with her. How did he put it? He's enchanted. Milton thinks he's enchanted with the sex."

"How could Tommy do this to me? We're still married!"

Kathleen glanced at her husband. "You were just two single people with a marriage license. What you had was a convenient arrangement."

"That's not true. I cared about Tommy."

"The two of you looked good together and had a lot in common. But did you ever have an argument?"

"Of course not. We had nothing to argue about."

"After eight months of marriage!" Kathleen again looked at Milton.

"How did you do it?" Milton shook his head. "Your mother and I started fighting after the first week. What was the first one about? Let's see. The magazines! Why would anyone need seven-year-old magazines?"

"I remember the bedroom door slamming," Kathleen said. "I won't say who slammed it."

"She did," Milton volunteered. "At least I was thrown a pillow and a sheet to make the sofa comfortable."

"We fought over whether my beautiful oyster-colored lamp with the hand-painted flowers was an antique or just old," Kathleen added.

The three laughed.

After the laughter settled, Kathleen offered, "Tommy said the whole time the two of you were in the house, he walked on eggshells."

"Of course we were always kind and polite to each other."

"As if it would be a crime to even slightly upset the other. How can two people live like that?" Kathleen took a sip from the glass of iced tea. "How is Charles?"

"I don't know. The last time I spoke to him was in June. I need to get things straight with Tommy."

"I guess Charles isn't a bad person," Kathleen said. "He could grow on me. I suppose you can't choose who you fall in love with. Some things just happen."

"Mother, you understand!"

The next day, Margaret called Tommy at work during lunch time. He confirmed that Lisa had moved in. They were clicking, was the only other thing he had to say on the subject.

Margaret was getting over her anger at him for wanting the cover of marriage while he played around, and for giving up on them so quickly. But she understood. Margaret had to admit that there were places inside of her that she could not let him into, and that he had similar spots.

She had failed at marriage. Her desperation had been the problem, she now understood. Forget marriage for its own sake. Margaret needed to want a man so intensely that she would gladly pledge her life to him. Charles wasn't that man. He never committed to her. But what if that man never came, she asked herself. Margaret froze. The thought terrorized her.

26

The day Shawanda went to Lena's to get Dontc and take him home would always stick out in her mind. After her hair had turned gray and she was tired of coloring it odd colors, even then, Shawanda would remember this day. When her children had had children and could therefore understand her troubles and triumphs, she would share with them this day. When her last hour was here, life withering like the grass and fleeing like the evening shade, and every dream born in her head had hopefully been seen by her eyes, then too, she would recall this day. Her heart would leap; her hands would fly into the air and dance. Praise would fill her mouth.

This joyous day made her wonder about her mother's God. Maybe he really *was* there, looking down on her and caring. Maybe her pain was not an indication of his coldness.

That day, when Shawanda woke, it was raining. Aaron suggested that they leave when the weather cleared. She said no and got out an umbrella, only one, because she knew Aaron wouldn't carry one. They went to her parents' home. There she jumped out of the car, opened the umbrella, and walked through the rain. She knocked on her parents' front door. Shifting her weight from leg to leg, she shouted, "Come on, open up."

She had been anxious and excited since Frank Boyd had okayed Donte's return.

Aaron, still on probation, had consented with the words, "Yeah, it's time Donte came home."

What she had always most liked about Aaron was his strength and his nobility.

Ernest opened the door.

"Hey, Daddy." She kissed him on the cheek. "Where's Donte?"

"In the kitchen eating breakfast."

She hurried through the living room. Having waited a year, she was unable to wait any longer. Her son was coming home to the mother who thought that out of all the children in the world, certainly he was the most handsome, the brightest, and the most special.

As she reached the kitchen, her joy overtook her. She rushed up to Donte and hugged him.

"We packed last night." Lena put a breakfast dish into the sink.

"I got ten toys in the bag, Ma. I have to take them home."

"He was more concerned about his toys than his clothes," Lena added.

"I'm gonna sleep in the same room with Charmise?"

Shawanda exhaled. The part of her that had stayed tense since Donte went to live with Lena and Ernest began to relax. "Yeah, you're going to sleep in the room right next to me."

Soon Shawanda took Donte home.

The family continued in counseling.

Each day she saw Aaron work at being a good stepfather. Finally, she had her family together.

* * *

Two weeks later, Margaret woke early with an urge to see and hear Charles — the same as always —, but didn't fight it this time. She went into the closet and pulled out the pink dress worn on their first date. It suited the mood she was in. Putting up her hair, doing her makeup, taking one last look in the mirror, Margaret grabbed her handbag and went out of the door.

Outside the mid-August day was sun-dipped and hot. Jumping into her car, she headed to White Marsh. It was eight-thirty on a Sunday morning when Margaret parked across the street from Charles's house. His Mercedes sat in front.

In his driveway was a burgundy-colored sedan. It was something Margaret couldn't imagine Charles driving. He must have an overnight guest, Margaret surmised, wishing herself wrong. She hoped there was some other explanation. Convincing herself of it, getting out of the car, she summoned courage. Actually, it was more like a shameless nerve born of a disgust with her life.

At his front door, she stared at the sedan. What was the worst that could happen? Margaret asked herself. Unforgettable embarrassment was the answer. Yet she forced herself to knock on the door and wait. Soon hearing the click of the lock on the other side, Margaret watched the door open and saw the woman.

"Hi," the tall, longhaired blonde greeted. She wore a short, white terry cloth robe.

"I'm sorry," Margaret backed away. "I have the wrong house." She turned around, and rushed down the walk way and then across the street.

"Margaret!"

She turned to see Charles rushing toward her. He was dressed in khaki pants and a pale green shirt.

One look at him and Margaret knew the attraction was as intense as ever. It was as if winter with its snow and cold nights had fled. Spring followed with brightly colored flowers, purple, blue, and yellow. Summer arrived with singing. That's the way the mere sight of Charles made her feel.

"I thought you had deserted me," he told her. "I gave up on you."

"Tommy and I broke up. He's living with another woman."

"I'm sorry. Was it because of us?"

"I told Brittany because I had to talk to someone. Brittany told mother. Mother told Tommy." Nervousness made her talkative.

"That wasn't nice of your sister and mother."

"I'm past that now. Tommy was sort of unhappy. He was cheating on me."

"Really? Bad situation! I myself didn't care for being the third party in a marriage."

"I didn't mean to make you that. Tommy and I cared about each other. But there wasn't enough there to keep us together."

"I assumed there was a problem the day you came to my office."

"Remember this dress?"

He looked at it. "No."

"I wore it the first night we went out."

"Sure. It doesn't look any better on you now."

"What's wrong with it?"

"It doesn't say anything about the woman I fell in love with it."

"Yeah?" She felt awkward. "I have to go now."

"Where are you going?" he asked.

"You have to go, too, back to your lady friend."

"Would you like to come in and meet her?"

"No!" Margaret grabbed the handle of the car door. "I'm too old-fashioned for that."

Charles gently removed her hand and held it. "She's an intelligent lady who has a sense of humor." He began to lead Margaret across the street. "Lynn's married to my brother. They're visiting. The children are with them. I told him about you."

"What did you tell him?"

"That you're making me crazy."

Margaret halted and looked at Charles. "What are we going to do?"

His eyes rolled upward. "Why do you always ask that question? I guess get married. I suppose it won't kill me."

"No! You don't want marriage. You're one of those eternal bachelors. We could just talk; see what we have in common. Well, we already know we have nothing in common. But we could be friends."

"Enough! We're getting married as soon as your divorce is final. That's the end of it!"

His words glided into her ears. But she was stabbed and bleeding from the last failed relationship, and afraid to take any more risks.

"Listen," he said, "we have as much a chance of making it as any other couple."

She nodded, too weakened by love to protest. Drunk, really, by a feeling more intoxicating than ten glasses of a sweet red wine.

He stroked her hair and smiled.

When he smiled, she saw fireworks burst red and orange and green into the sky — saw them in her mind. And there, too, she heard invisible fingers stroke an invisible guitar. It all made her lightheaded.

Charles took her hand and led her toward the front door.

Walking with him made Margaret think. Was it really possible they would last?